What Hope Wrought
A novel by Jason Dias

Also by Jason Dias

The Girlfriend Project
For Love of Their Children
The Worst of Us
Shooting Blanks
Half-Lives

Acknowledgements and Dedications

Parts of this story were helped along by my critique group, Colorado Springs Fiction Writers' Group. Some friends also looked through the manuscript: RED, Bret Wright, Harmony Earls and, as always, Kim Hsin.
This one is for everyone who fights and reasons why.

One

I punched the guy in the face.

What he thought of getting punched in the face by a woman in a summer dress he never really got the chance to say. It wasn't a hard punch. I didn't think so, anyway. But the man fell backwards, smacked his head on a barstool, flopped on the wooden planks that passed for a floor.

I shook out my hand. I was glad I hadn't hit a tooth, cut my hand.

"Drink," I said, and the man behind the bar made another weak Cosmopolitan. The bartender was a small man with eyes like a rat and a nose that had been broken too many times to be attractive. He brought it out to the wicker-topped table as I perched back on the stool. A breeze kicked up and it should have been cool, coming in off the Black Sea. But it wasn't. It was hot, smelled of flint and booze. Everything was hot now, everywhere. Africa had been insanely, brain-cookingly hot and here it was just in the forties centigrade but I still didn't like it.

At least the Cosmopolitan was cold.

I sipped. Behind me, the man I had smacked started to get up. He had on a dingy Hawaiian shirt, brown with yellow picnic baskets all over it. I wanted to hit him again just for that. I glanced back, saw he had a nice bloody nose but his eyes were clear and focused. He got to his feet with no obvious dizziness or unsteadiness. Well, that was good. At least when the authorities caught up to me I'd go down for simple desertion and not for grievous bodily harm, too.

My table faced the water. The sea level had come up, and about twenty meters from shore one could still see a pair of rooves poking up out. The top of a tree, denuded and bone white, a relic of a former life. Most of Odessa was down there. Behind me, the city was mostly new. New Odessa, they called it, thought it was nothing at all like old Odessa. Mostly concrete.

"You hit me," the guy said.

"Want I should hit you again?" I offered, not turning around this time.

He was silent. I took that for a "no."

The bartender heard it first. There were six little tables around his cabana, a faux wooden roof over us, and no walls. Views all around, the way I like it. When he heard the helicopter, he turned and scanned the horizon between the sea and the ceiling. The noise seemed to come from everywhere. There were other people, an elderly couple wearing matching T-Shirts, a young woman with a backpack and shoes suitable for walking, a brownish man with board shorts and no shirt. They each heard a moment later and mimicked the bartender.

The helicopter emerged into view from nearly overhead, ducking down below ceiling height little by little. It was flat black, clean but well-used, with narrow skids and heavy armaments. Big rotating machine guns hung from the sides. Not subtle. The civilians gawked. Wind from the rotors blew fake sand into the cabana where it scoured my bare shins.

"What the fuck?" said the guy in the Hawaiian shirt.

"They're here for me," I said.

The bartender somehow heard that comment over all the noise. "You pay now," he said.

Seems my credit has dried up.

The helicopter was fully settled in now. Brown crud flew everywhere and the hatch opened, one door up and one door down, the lower making a crude ramp. People started to climb out into the haze. A man of Indian origin, two women, a tall white guy with hair so blond it was almost platinum. They were armed as heavily as the helicopter. Black shirts, black canvas pants, black boots. Black guns, rifles over shoulders and pistols on hips and shins. Black knives strapped to thighs. Black web belts with all sorts of exotic killing things attached.

Shirt man stepped out in front of me as they came into the cabana. He got between them and me. "You can't come in here," he said.

"Best get out of their way," I told him. "Summary justice is the penalty for interfering with a One World Government operation." That was bluster. They wouldn't shoot him just for a misguided macho act. Probably. "Hello, Raskin. Nice day for a visit to the beach."

"You know these people?" shirt man said, blood still dripping from his face.

"Yeah. I used to work for them." I took a sip of my drink, reached in my purse for a bill to lay on the table.

"Want to come along peacefully?" Raskin said. His accent was British even though he used the same operational lingo as the rest of us.

"Alternatives?" I said.

Williams stepped up. She was a smallish black woman from the former United States of America. Captain, company lawyer. She consulted a document on her wrist device. "June Anne Blankenship," she said. "You are under arrest for desertion from One World Army military service in a time of engagement. The penalty..."

"No need for that," Raskin said. "Right, Blanks?"

That's what they called me. Blanks. Major Blankenship. "You going to shoot me, Williams? Garcia?" Garcia was the other woman. "Thompkins?" He was the tall guy. Finnish, tall and strong, uncomfortably fair in a world given over to summer.

"Don't make this hard," Raskin said.

"Not so hard," I said. "You only brought four people. I'm almost insulted. Anyway, I filed the appropriate paperwork."

"Guess we lost it," Raskin said. He stepped forward and shirt guy decided not to get involved, after all. He moved to one side.

I put up my hands. "OK, fine, you win. Coming quietly." And I did. Other options were not really feasible, anyway. I could fight them, but they were my friends. Someone would get hurt or killed. I could dive into the water and try to swim for it or run into the concrete maze behind us, into New Odessa, hoping to disappear. In the end, though, even if I could outrun these people, I had the same device as they did implanted in my wrist – a black, flexible screen that stretched from the wrist bones to halfway up the forearm. It enabled communications, accessed databases, had some other tools I'd never even fully explored. Handy, sometimes, except that I could be tracked and found anywhere in the world. So I grabbed my purse and stood up.

"Beach was boring anyway," I said.

"Purse?" Garcia said. She'd never seen me in anything but a uniform.

"Hard to conceal a forty-cal and a carton of frag grenades in a sundress," I said, actually blushing. Thompkins laughed at me. I'd missed him.

Shirt-guy said, "I'm sorry I called you sweetie."

Then we walked to the Truck. That's what we called the helicopter because that was the job it did. "Hey, why was that guy bleeding?" Thompkins said. He had just a trace of an accent, a way of putting y's behind h's where they didn't really go, of saying his o's as though he really meant them.

"I might have popped him in the face a little bit," I said.

"You smacked him in the nose for calling you sweetie?" Williams said. "That's a little much even for you."

"Well, he was touching my ass at the time," I said.

Thompkins laughed again, but his eyes narrowed and he looked back at the cabana. His knuckles were white.

We climbed into the Truck, a dark interior compartment with seats around the outside and gear storage in the middle. I strapped in, welcoming the air conditioning that blew around my ankles, over my bare legs.

"Sorry to interrupt your vacation, Major," Raskin said, once I was patched in. "But we have a situation. Search and destroy mission, your kind of thing. We need you for this one." His voice came through the cabin wireless system directly into my auditory implant. I hadn't missed that.

"I'm not in your army anymore, Colonel," I said. "Dropped off all my army-issues at the front desk in Liverpool, you remember?"

"And just how in the hell you got to Liverpool from Zaire is a question of some interest at the higher levels. The Wizard would really like to know. Seems like you forgot to sign some paperwork, though," he said. "Desertion is a serious charge. You can't have been that serious since you waited someplace we'd almost certainly turn up eventually. We'll call it AWOL, an administrative error, forget about the whole thing."

"If."

"That's right, if."

"How do you know I won't just split again the next time we make landfall?"

He tapped his nose. "You aren't going to want to."

"You know, you guys all seem to know what I want and don't want lately."

"Lewinski," he said.

I smiled, settled into the creaky leather chair as best I could, crossed my ankles in front of me. There was nothing else to talk about.

The doors sealed. Inertia pushed me down. We were airborne, bound for Liverpool, England, and I was back in the army.

***

Headquarters was on a small rise, under an old hospital on reclaimed land. It was surrounded by salt flats. Most of Liverpool had, like Odessa, sunk below salty water. A newer, concrete version rose in the distance a few miles further inland.

We were in the main conference room. Three floors underground. It was dark, just a few LED lights in the corner where the wall met the floor. A big table dominated the room, an oval thing three meters by one at the ends and two meters through the middle. I was at one end, across from Franks. He was a short, stocky man who seriously overflowed his chair. Williams sat by my side, Thompkins next to Franks. Raskin had a middle seat and Garcia was near him. She was about my height with similar brown skin, brown eyes and hair. Another fifteen people were packed into the room.

"Come to order," Raskin said, and the low murmur stopped. We knew how to pay attention. I looked down the table at Raskin and most everyone else did, too. Except Franks. Franks glared at me from under heavy lids. "First order of business: Blanks is back and we're to consider her righteous. In fact, Blanks, you're to lead an op."

There was some grumbling. I heard Franks mutter but he did it in German, and I didn't have much German. "Target?" I said.

"Bolivia. Smuggling op."

"You didn't drag me back from vacation to break up black marketing."

Franks said, "You weren't on vacation."

"She's righteous," Raskin said. "I told you."

"Yes, sir," Franks said, staring hate at me.

"Franks, you got a problem?" I said. "Maybe with the manner of my departure, or the manner of my return?"

He stood up, shoving his chair backwards with his legs. Maybe he hoped it would fall over or at least make a dramatic noise but it was flimsy plastic, a ridiculous thing that seemed even more absurd next to him. Like a kindergarten chair on parents' night. "You ran out on us back there."

Back there meant Africa. Zaire. "The op was over," I said.

"There were still bullets in the air when you split," Franks said.

"Well, it was over for me." I stayed seated although I wanted to get up and smack him. "I was in recovery from a bullet wound. A wound I got saving all your asses, is the way I remember it. I charged that barricade, got close and personal with some armed resistance."

Franks looked momentarily abashed. "I guess. Thompkins was wounded too, though. And Davids."

"Yeah."

Raskin spoke. "Blankenship, it seems like unit cohesion might be an issue here. You got something you want to say?"

I had some things I wanted to say, sure. But I kept most of them to myself. "I won't be a party to executing civilians," I said.

"They were armed insurgents," Franks said, sitting down again. The chair wobbled a little under him as he pulled it forward.

"They were hungry people. They could have torn me to pieces but they sent me on."

"They kept your gun and your body armor."

That was true. "They were pacifists," I said. "Their elder, a half-starved old woman, she said, 'Thou shalt not kill.' I think she meant it: she said it twice. You want the moral high ground here, but you shot at the people we were supposed to be defending."

Franks looked angry. I thought he was going to stand up again. But it was Raskin who spoke. "Orders from as high up as they came, I don't think we get to just ignore."

"I didn't ignore them," I said. "I gave them their due attention. And then I found them to be immoral and illegal and took the appropriate measures."

Williams raised her hand as though this were elementary school. Raskin said her name. "The ability to refuse an illegal order and to resign one's commission are central to our mandate," she said.

"I thought German was bad," I said. "You want to say that in English?" Even Spanish or Portuguese would have done.

She did. "You don't trust us because you think we fired on civilians."

Think? Is there something here they weren't saying?

"Franks thinks we can't trust you because you cut out on us," Williams continued. Some murmurs of approval made it seem like it was more than Franks who thought that. "But I trust you, Blanks. Because when an officer is denied their right to resign, when a soldier cannot exercise her right to refuse an unlawful order, the armed services become just another tool of oppression."

Raskin said, "You quoting something, Willie?"

"No," I answered for her. "She always sounds like she's quoting something. She's just smart. If I'm reading you right, Williams, what you're saying is this: you can trust me not to lead you into morally ambiguous or compromising situations."

"Check," she said.

Franks leaned back in his chair. Cheap piece of plastic shit that it was, I was surprised it didn't break. But he seemed to relax, to look at me like a person again instead of like a lion that might bite him in the face any minute.

Raskin said, "The Wizard seems to feel the same way. Hence, Bolivia. Anybody else got beef or can we get into the logistics of this thing?"

Nobody else had a problem, that they were saying. The Wizard being invoked caused some hesitation, some side-long glances at each other.

Raskin put on the display via our contact lens inputs. Some high-quality video loops. A city, run-down and old – the kudzu had gone crazy but the city hadn't flooded yet. They were in good shape. I saw concrete buildings, some brick, lots of graffiti. An open-air cafe. Some cars. People walking by on a street. It was almost like being there, except I could see my teammates through the image.

"There he is," I said.

Williams said, "Holy shit."

Garcia: "That bastard."

"Settle down," Raskin said. "You've correctly ID'd Lewinski. Facial recognition picked him up on a street-level camera, some automated mapping thing. That's why it's moving that way, along the road, scanning the buildings."

"We got something more than a photo?" I said. I was the only one not surprised, because Raskin had given me the heads-up earlier. I cracked a yawn, starting to feel the effects of some mid-day Cosmopolitans and the fact that mid-day was now about ten hours in the past.

"Human intel puts some illicit radioactive material inbound to Bolivia via Venezuela. Timeline is four days. Lewinski is the only one down there with the credentials to handle something like that. Infrastructure, connections for fencing."

"Except the locals," I said. Local governments, out of the business of taxing and spending, resorted frequently to organized crime. A common refrain was that they were already well practiced.

"They're to be considered suspects," Raskin said. "Blanks. Arrest, interdict the shipment. Minimal use of force. Pick a team."

Minimal use of force meant little to us. We didn't do investigations or police actions. We were the One Hundred Thirty-Seventh Special Forces, Charlie Crew, and we blew shit up. "Garcia. Thompkins. Franks. Williams. Good enough?"

"I want a piece of him," someone else said, but my eyes were shut because I was yawning and I didn't catch who.

"Five is good," Raskin said. "Everyone wants a piece of this guy. You'll all have to wait your turn. There will be other bad guys."

Maybe. But nobody as bad as Lewinski. He was the one who set us up in Zaire.

Raskin started in on fuel requisitions, getting a transport plane, money for bullets. Or something. Next thing I knew, Williams was tapping me on the shoulder and Raskin was shouting at me.

"Have a nice nap, Major?" he said.

"Uh?" I wiped drool off my face with the back of one hand. I'd expected to have a uniform sleeve to do that with and only then realized I was still wearing my sun dress from Odessa. The conference room was cold and that felt so good, goosebumps felt so good, that even now it was hard to stay awake.

"Teach you to drink in the daytime," Raskin said. "Why don't you get out of here? We can do this part without you snoring."

"Roger that," I said, and got out of my chair. There was a door almost right behind me, and that led through a well-lit hallway with sheetrock walls to an elevator. I could hear the boredom going on behind me until the elevator doors closed. Up one floor, down another hallway to my room. I was touched: it was just as I'd left it.

Being a Major, I ranked a private room with a toilet attached. I figured I'd shower and turn in. I smelled like rum and fake sand, the shit they made from ground up flint. I stripped down, tossed dress, skivvies, and shoes into a pile in the corner. Stepped into the small lavatory and started the shower. I made it hot, then a little hotter, and stepped in.

The water felt like a revelation. I'd been on the run about three weeks, knowing they'd find me eventually. Nobody really gets to resign their commission, not for long, not from Special Forces. They need us, and they need us in the fold. It might seem weird to a civilian but I felt relaxed for the first time since Zaire. Like I was home, like I knew... not what was around the corner into the next minute, what the next engagement would be, but like whatever it was, I knew I could handle it.

Steaming water ran over my body, carrying with it all traces of my absence from the unit. I brushed my teeth with the brush from the counter, then used a razor from the same place to take the stubble off my head. I hadn't kept up with that. Hair and sweat and fake sand swirled around the drain between my feet and washed away and in a few minutes I was clean again.

Standard-issue body soap didn't make much lather, didn't wash off too easily. It smelled vaguely of limes and vomit – the antibacterial agent did that. The smell was oddly as comforting as the hot water. It smelled like home.

Outside, in my room, the billet door opened. Someone let themselves in. I didn't hear it, but I felt the subtle change in air pressure and temperature.

So much for turning in. I shut off the water and got out, realizing I hadn't brought in a towel. So I just stepped out of the toilet into my little room. Almost right into Raskin. The room was eight by ten with a cot and a dresser and my pile of dirty clothes. Wherever he stood, I was right on top of him.

He watched me, appraised me with his eyes. I knew what he saw and I knew he approved, because he looked away after the once-over. There wasn't any sex in it: I was property, a tool, a machine that filled an operational requirement. I was one point seven two meters tall, seventy-two and a half kilos, all muscle. My breasts were almost totally eroded by exercise, just hard brown nipples over pinches of nearly empty skin. Pectoral muscles rippled there instead. I had broad shoulders, big biceps and triceps. Legs like tree stumps with little triangles of muscle over my kneecaps. Black eyes and black stubble where most women had hair. Even my face was hard: heavy chin, straight, even teeth, thin lips, flat nose.

"You squared away?" Raskin said.

"In a minute. Reach in that drawer and hand me some shorts."

He did. "You know what I mean."

"I know. And if we're doing this, I'm doing it with clothes on. Shirt."

He handed me a black A-shirt. "We need you on this."

"Yeah, I copied that when you set down an assault vehicle on a public beach."

"Don't be an asshole. I'm trying here."

"Yeah," I said again. "Pants."

He handed me a pair of the black cargo pants we all wore. Lots of pockets. "We need you because you passed the test, Blanks."

"What test?"

"You were right. We were there to protect the civilians. They were the locals in question."

"And the fire order?" I said, fastening my belt.

"He wanted to see who would go through with it."

"Did you?"

"Fire on civilians? No. None of us shot anyone. We dispersed the crowd with some warning shots, overhead. They went easy enough. That old lady you mentioned, must've been the same one. She stood by the lorry and crossed her arms, shook her head. Stayed after the rest had run off. Until they had stripped down the truck, taken everything. Then she limped away on her cane."

"That's all?"

"Isn't it enough?" he said. "It was a sort of moral Rorschach test."

"Ambiguous stimuli to provoke response tendencies." I found a black shirt that didn't smell too bad in the discard pile and shrugged into it. "You failed and I passed. That the score?"

He lowered his head, turned his back to me completely. "This one is going to be hairy."

"That's the job," I said. Sleep didn't look like it was going to happen, even if they let me lay down. Well, whatever. I'd sleep on the way to the next job. Or when I was dead.

"This one... The Wizard, he was more esoteric than usual. More... I don't know, Blanks. He explained it, and why it had to be you. I don't like it. Just be careful. And remember Article Twelve."

Article Twelve of the Special Forces incorporation manual had to do with equal inclusion for women soldiers. "*Inasmuch as females have less recourse to violence?*" I said. "That Article Twelve?"

"*A tendency to allow saving of face and to offer aid and comfort...*" he said.

"What does that have to do with anything?"

"Fucked if I know," Raskin said. "But you know The Wizard."

"No, never talked to him." I grabbed a pill bottle from the nightstand. Shook some out, put all but one back. A little white thing, flavorless, that would help keep me on this side of the dirt for four, maybe five days.

"Just be careful," Raskin said. Then he looked me over again, now in uniform except for a beret. Or a pile of weapons. He looked like he was going to say something else. But he just left. Turned, opened the door, stepped into the dark hallway.

I stepped out after him. "When's departure?"

He didn't look at me, just kept walking. "Hit the mess. Get some coffee. Henry's prepping the Truck now. Go is one-hundred hours. Good luck."

"You aren't coming?"

"No," he said, but I'd known already. I just felt uneasy, didn't want to be alone. "I failed the test, remember?" And he started walking again, which made me realize he'd stopped, stopped there in front of me with his head down and his back to me.

He got on the elevator and I let the doors shut, sealing him away from me. I waited for the next one, full of foreboding.

Two

The Truck flew us out to a little base in Turkey. An Ashlifter waited there, a giant gray cargo plane with eight electric turbine engines and a fat body that didn't look skyworthy. It huddled like a toad at the land-end of a runway that stretched out into the roiling sea. Under those waves somewhere was an old Turkish coastal town. Williams would remember its name but I just knew it was gone.

Henry stowed the rotors with some switches and then army grunts pushed us aboard the giant cargo plane – there would be only a single item on its manifest. Henry was a little Black man of maybe Bahamian origin – and word was he was the best helicopter pilot anywhere. Rarely got much chance to talk to him. There was no way into the cockpit from the cabin and he never infiltrated with us. He just drove the Truck.

We boarded up by the numbers. Checked everything was strapped down – guns, food, armor, electronics – and harnessed ourselves into the seats fore and aft, all facing the middle. The red cabin light went dim. I went to sleep as the plane lurched into motion. It was quieter than going under our own power, and smoother, and generally more restful. For a little while.

I was asleep, and then I was awake. Drool hung from my chin and my neck hurt from several hours sleeping sat up with my head nodding. I didn't know just how long. But there was no time to worry about it.

Gravity was all fucked up. The world spun even though all I could see was my team and the walls around us, the red-lit cabin of the Truck.

We'd just fallen out the back of a C226 Ashlifter.

The turbine whined, the starter fired like a rifle-shot, and the rotors kicked into motion. We free-fell maybe ten seconds and then gyroscopic forces righted us, stabilized the world. Williams looked at me, concern in her eyes.

"I haven't puked in years," I said. It was all part of the ritual.

"My recruiter said I'd see the world," she said, and we all finished with her: "But he didn't say it would be all in one day."

The red light went off and the place was dark except for a few instrument lights. An LED here and there, a flashing green light on a weapon not fully concealed by the tarp tied own over the bin in the middle of the cabin, the wrist-implant Garcia had running.

This was going to be a short drop so I started to prep rather than go back to sleep. Thompkins was already unconscious again, snoring so loud I could hear him over the turbines. I checked the count on my sidearm. The radium display said **38**. Thirty-eight forty-caliber rounds should solve just about any problem appropriate to that special solution and, if it didn't, either I didn't deserve the gun or running like a motherfucker was the next order of business.

We were going in without armor for the initial landing. One less thing to do. So I checked com, inputs, my sidearm again (I'd end up checking it four more times, too). Plans, maps – like Garcia, I brought up those details on my wrist implant.

Then the red light came on, flashed: incoming message.

"Raskin will not be with you on this mission," said a man's voice. It was high, thin, pedantic. Like a science teacher I'd had once in college.

"Shit," said Thompkins. I hoped he'd remembered to keep his throat mike muted. You live with the implants long enough, you start to forget about them. "Shit, it's the fucking Wizard."

"This is The Wizard," the voice said, so that he and Thompkins said "Wizard" at the same time. "Yours is a hand-picked team, the best and brightest of your elite unit. Your first stop is Bolivia. You will have two primary directives. First, locate and acquire Petr Lewinski. His information is critical. If lethal force is absolutely required, his brain is not to be damaged and that at any cost.

"Your second directive is to locate and acquire any nuclear material present in Panama with a strength over four micro-Sieverts per hour. Appropriate collection and protection equipment is *en route* to Panama now to be at your disposal.

"Secondary directives are as usual, including zero public perception, minimizing risk to civilians, and appropriate, proportionate use of force. Being who you are, of course that final secondary consideration has some flexibility so long as you maintain moderate optics.

"Your contact in Panama is World Intelligence Agency station chief Rene Aguilera. Questions?"

Williams was first on the spot. "Why can't we shoot him in the head, sir?" I figured she asked because she really wanted to put one right in his forehead. I figured that because I really wanted to, too.

"Classified," The Wizard responded immediately. "But the station chief will know what to do. Anything else?"

"Possible locations of radioactive material?" I asked.

"Downloading to your mobile devices now. Including likely containers and formats."

I couldn't think of any other questions without answers classified above our level. I was apparently not alone. The Wizard signed off.

We braced, arms wrapped around our harnesses. Henry was good but shit happens. The ride started to get rough, indicating low-altitude. The air forced down by the rotors rebounded from the ground, making vertical winds. We'd land soon. For me, the scariest part of any flight was the landing – landing is just a fancy word for a controlled collision with the ground. But we slowed, settled gently as a new mother kisses her baby's belly.

The hatches opened. We piled out, leaving most of our gear where it was. Sunlight poured in, harsh and hot.

"Fucking Summer," Franks said. He meant the Endless Summer, the sick heat that crept over the world year over year. The heat that was killing everything, everywhere.

"Stow that," I said. "Garcia."

"Yes, sir."

I pointed down the narrow strand of beach, away from the struck. Yellow sand, real sand on not reclaimed land, stretched along in front of a dense green forest. Whatever trees they were, they didn't mind salt water. They had leaves so dark they were almost black and roots that grew up out of the sand. The forest itself was only a strip, too, according to the map; there'd be a road just on the other side. "Airport down there, one point one kilometers. Want to secure us a ground car? Something big enough for all our supplies."

She set off hiking with another "Yes, sir."

"Let's unload," I said, and we set to dragging out crates full of electronics, weapons, uniform spares. Mostly weapons, really.

"What country did that used to be?" said Franks, pointing out into the Pacific Ocean. His blacks were already darkened with sweat stains and just talking was making him puff and blow.

"Chile or Peru," I said. "They still exist, just the coastal regions are history. Snag some gear and let's go."

We packed stuff out through about twenty meters of jungle and onto the roadside. A few civilians saw us and what they thought about it was no concern of mine. Garcia rolled up within the hour with a rented cargo van from the airport. It chugged along slowly, solar panels warming in the heavy sun. We loaded up, strapping a bunch of crates to the roof, and piled in.

Garcia drove. We passed a green road sign: "Welcome to Charana." All the signage had been updated to English twenty years ago. Jungle spread out on the coast side, deepening and thickening, and then we angled east and left it behind. Within a few minutes, the city grew up around us.

At the outskirts it was worst. Concrete and corrugated metal – tin, aluminum reclaimed from soda cans, whatever people could get. In some places walls or rooves still had tiny soft-drink logos all over them.

We wanted the police department, which would be downtown. The center of town seemed to be the focus of some renewal activities. Clean-up stuff. There were some lovely old houses that had been restored, candied up for the tourists. Trash cans about every forty feet, painted green. Streets repairs, sidewalks repaved, storefronts gleaming and immaculate.

The department was a little off a shopping strip, a big square building set back in a big lot. Concrete and glass, dark, bluish glass that offered no views inside. It looked like an artist's rendering of itself. There was a wide parking lot full of junky old vehicles, some of them still gasoline cars. Garcia pulled into two slots and we piled out.

"Who's our contact here again?" I asked Williams.

She had the relevant information on her wrist already. "Aguilera," she said. "Rene. She's the station chief here."

"Copy." I strode towards the building, inside wishing I could just slump and melt in the heat. But it didn't do to show human frailty. The others followed behind, fanning out. We pushed through the front doors, walked right by a startled receptionist. Secure doors opened for us: local governments were required to switch to electronic locks and they were all keyed the same. Thompkins' wrist device popped all the locks ahead of us.

I came to Aguilera's office downstairs, me taking up most of the doorway and my squad crammed into the hallway behind me. The elevator was broken and the air conditioner was not running. Aguilera looked up from a little desk in a closet-sized room, sweat dripping off her face. She stood, panic crossing in front of her face – information that I stowed for later. She had on khaki shorts and a gray halter top, khaki shirt thrown over the back of her chair. Shiny shaved head. Her chest was slick with sweat. She had a thick waist in a place where people were hungry, and I stowed that, too.

"Help you?" she said.

I replied, "Lewinski."

"Ah." She seemed to calm a little at that. "Let's go to the conference room. Cooler." She grabbed her shirt then pushed by me into the hallway, through my team to a stairwell. We went down more stairs, tile over concrete, into a sub-basement. She led us into a room maybe four meters by three. Padded walls, padded ceiling. Small table with rings for anchoring cuffs or shackles. Cool air poured in through a vent in the ceiling, dropping the temperature to a tolerable thirty Centigrade.

"Good thing I trust you," I said, eyeing the shackle rings. Trust wasn't quite the right word for what I felt.

"That's not mutual," she said. Her accent shouted native. She remembered that she still had her shirt in her hands. She looked at it as if considering putting it on, but we'd already seen all there was to see. The shirt landed in the table with a puff of warm air.

"Bolivia was never in favor of the One World Government initiative," I said. Probing, observing.

"No."

"And you're sure I'm just a goon."

"I wouldn't say that."

I nodded. She wouldn't say it. She'd think it, though. "Business, then."

"The guy you want. He's a bad guy. Locally, he just employs a bunch of kids to do lookout work, gets a couple to be trigger-men. Or boys. Or girls. He's no worse than any other gangster. But."

"But he's not just a local problem," Williams offered from nearer the door.

"Right. He's got ties to the Peruvians. We're sure he's into drugs. Never guns or human trafficking, but the drugs tie into all the rest of it. We've never been able to connect it all together and put him away, not directly. But we think if we keep watching him..."

"You'll grow old and die," I said. "He's too slick for you."

"But not for you."

"He's a slippery sack of crap, that's for sure. But we don't plan to bring him up on charges or deconstruct his criminal empire. We plan to shoot him in the face."

"After a fair trial, of course," Rene said. She didn't pale or quaver. She knew what kind of people we were. "I have the address of his biggest warehouse operation. And the times he usually visits. Maybe you'll get lucky. Do me a favor: don't shoot him right away. Bring him here and make him talk. We're on the same side here, you know? And he's into even more than drugs."

"Cesium," I said. "When and where?"

"That's what we need him for." She handed over a credit card. All the data we needed – address, layout, blueprints, names, dates, bank account numbers, everything – would be encoded on its magnetic strip. Used to be high tech, the in thing, except credit cards were nearly obsolete. Only old people used them anymore.

"You're One World too," I offered. It was almost true, too. The local force had changed the names on the buildings but not much more.

"Yes, one big family." She said that on her way out. I stuffed my foot in the door as it was swinging shut, not completely certain it wouldn't lock behind Aguilera.

"Thank you for your cooperation," I told her broad back as she retreated.

***

I was in civilian clothes again for the second time in fifteen years.

Garcia and I sat outside a bodega. A bunch of towns had grown together here, a population rush fueled by land loss, by ocean growth. The air was salty and tasted like petrol fumes, trash, rot, and spices. A lot like home, come to think of it. We had wrought-iron chairs at a table of the same material with a little iron fence around the outside. This place had been here a long time, then. The rest of the neighborhood was concrete and corrugation. People milled around: walking with purpose or just ambling, going into stores, doing what people do.

Bright paint livened the place up a little and people here were poor rather than totally destitute. We didn't do undercover work so I couldn't have said whether my jeans and silk shirt or Garcia's cargo pants and jacket looked out of place or not. The heat did not encourage a lot of clothing, for sure, but we had to conceal our weapons and armor somehow – or leave them behind. We'd decided to overdress and armor up.

Killing time. "You got plans for after?" I said.

"There ain't no after. You know that," Garcia said.

I guess I knew better than anyone. "Yeah. But if you weren't doing this, what would you be doing?"

"Dying slowly, I guess," Garcia said. She was young and from a place just like this: crowded, hot and hungry. "Careers and stuff, that's for old people, you know? Ain't nothing in the world for a younger person. They tried to tell me I could be a doctor or a lawyer or something but all I ever wanted to be was this."

"Why?"

She pointed with her chin, a little backwards nod. I looked where she aimed my gaze, saw two girls wearing even less than the usual locals. They leaned up against a tin wall and made eyes at passing men.

"Them, they're what's left for girls to do. Or boys, really. My brother... I didn't want to do that. I wanted to do something important."

"Is this important?" I said.

"It's the only thing left," Garcia said.

Then Franks spoke in my ear from the control room, a scuzzy hotel about a mile away. "Radar calls one inbound."

"You might have just said there's a car coming," I said, as if to Garcia. She smiled and took a bite of her jellyfish bar. We'd been in the same place about half an hour, which I marked as about twenty minutes too long to sit and eat a bar of food and drink a cup of coffee jelly.

Franks said nothing.

The streets were pretty empty of vehicular traffic. The petrol smell was ground in, visible in grime on the walls. You needed a special permit for gas powered vehicles and nobody here could afford an electric one. So when the truck rolled up, it was conspicuous.

It was a dirty tan and it rode low. Dented hood, bumpers that had been chrome once and now were mostly rust, missing a wing mirror. But the windshield was unchipped and tinted dark. And the tires were new.

I watched it roll by without looking right at it. Maybe that was a mistake: everyone else looked. It made a right turn about twenty meters in front of us, onto 17th street. Slow, stately, but not wallowing – the suspension was good.

"Driver is female, thirty to fifty," Garcia said. "Passenger is masked, surgical mask, hair concealed under a hood. ID impossible."

"Yeah," Franks confirmed. "Facial rec doesn't have enough to work with. Car is registered under a front, no surprise there."

"It's him," I said.

Thompkins chimed in from probably right next to Franks. "Why?"

"Look at the truck. Sits really low but not on bad springs. The cosmetics are right but the mechanics are all wrong: new tires, engine sounds sweet, and that glass is bulletproof. That's why she's riding so low. Bullet-proof glass, inserts in the doors, maybe the floor too."

"So let's go get him," Garcia said, and we stood, tossed our trash in an overflowing can, and headed out. We headed the opposite way from the truck – we knew where he was going, if Aguilera's intel was any good. Garcia matched my stride, trying to look casual. We circled the block, came around behind the warehouse where Aguilera said Lewinski did most of his local business.

The warehouse was like the truck. The exterior walls were concrete. Cracked, chipped, sooty, heavily and illiterately decorated with spray paint. The roof was covered in big tin panels that looked vulnerable to any strong wind. Trouble was, strong winds came through here all the time. Ninety, a hundred kilometers an hour was totally mundane anymore. And under the tin, hard to see from down here, was armor plating.

Then there was the door. We were in back of the place, staring down a steel door that looked pretty ordinary except it had no handles. And there was a drive-in door that looked like a regular roller, except for the booth next to it. Bullet-proof glass, tinted out, with a shadowy figure just barely visible inside.

And they'd been sloppy with the concrete. Where the roller door joined the exterior wall, I could see the edge of a steel plate.

Now what kind of warehouse has steel plates in the walls?

"In position," I said.

"Standing by," said Williams in my ear.

"Go for extraction," Franks said, meaning he had the van nearby.

I nodded to Garcia. We stepped up to that ordinary-looking steel door. She planted a charge on her side and I planted one on mine and we backed up. The two charges popped and the door fell out of its steel frame, sparking from some non-standard wiring. We stepped over it, into a dark stairwell. There was another steel door at the top of a flight of stairs, and a security camera peered down at us from a fixture in the corner.

I ran up the stairs, slapped another charge on the wall by the door, jumped back down to duck and cover. Garcia blew the charge.

"Good enough?" she said.

"Play it out," I replied. We needed confirmation. It would take another thirty seconds, maybe.

The door buckled but did not blow out. I didn't want it to drop, or I'd have used two charges. Someone started to hammer on the other side, kicking hard, trying to pop it. I pulled a single-charge pulse pistol. Timed the kicks. Fired as the next kick should land, electrifying the door for half a second. I don't know if it worked; I just know nobody burst through that door to shoot me.

"The Admiral is on deck," Franks said.

I think code is stupid, but Franks loves it. I just figure, if the enemy can hear you, they know what's going on and silly code phrases aren't going to conceal much. Much better to scramble your channels and trust them. Anyway, it was time to clear out. I nodded to Garcia and we faded. A block away, we piled into the rental van.

In the back, between Thompkins and Williams, was an unconscious man. He was fairly nondescript. Brownish skin that might have looked at home on any continent, black hair, a flat nose, good teeth. Dressed in a suit, indicating wealth – only people with air conditioning wear suits. He had loafers on his feet, impractical for almost any line of work other than looking good.

"He doesn't look so bad," I said. "Give you any trouble?"

"No," said Williams. "Just like you said, you made a bunch of noise and flashed the stairwell cam and he jetted out the side door. I punched him in the neck, like you taught me. Cairo, remember? Blood pressure spiked, he went away, and we stuffed him in here."

Thompkins gave Lewinski an injection in the meaty part of his thigh as the man showed signs of resuming consciousness. "What's that?" I said.

"Home brew," Thompkins replied. "It'll do the job."

The job I wanted to do was to shoot Lewinski. We had enough reasons.

"Maybe just in the kneecap," Williams said, as if reading my mind.

I nodded slowly, but said, "No, Aguilera's right. We need him to get the rest: the drugs, the cesium."

"Maybe later," Williams said, and turned around to watch the road.

"Take him to Aguilera?" Franks said. If I had my bearings right, we were going in that general direction already.

I looked at him back there again, quiescent, harmless-looking. Vulnerable. "Yeah, there," I said. We could have taken him to a hotel room, to an abandoned building, all the way back to Liverpool. Anywhere. I wanted to do the right thing, though.

Mistake.

We got him there all right. Dragged his inert body across the parking lot, through the front doors, down into a holding cell in the basement. God, it was hot down there.

The day just cooked and cooked. Aguilera showed us where to go, her interrogation room. It had a small table, two chairs, one bolted down with cuffs on that side of the table. I clicked the cuffs shut myself. He was still out and his head rested on the table top, drool ticking slowly from one corner of his mouth.

"Leave me with him," Aguilera said. A request.

"One hour," I told her.

There was one-way glass and a com. I patched into that – Thompkins showed me how – and listened. Thompkins gave Lewinski a wake-up shot and joined me back outside.

Lewinski went from sleep to wake in about twenty seconds. He was like a machine that had been turned off and then on again. His head came up, his eyes opened and then focused.

"You," he said. Then he looked at the one-way glass, and back to her again.

"You're in deep shit," Aguilera said.

"I thought you had some finesse," Lewinski said. "Straight out with the threats?"

"I'm not threatening you, man. I have you already. Strapped down in a basement, where nobody knows you are. You dodged me for weeks but One World is here for a single day, and here you are."

Lewinski smiled, said nothing. Glanced at the glass again. A game? What was he not saying?

"I hear you're into something a little more than your mandate," Aguilera said next.

"Who is listening?" He leaned back as far as the shackles would allow, crossed his ankles.

"Who do you think? Maybe you give me whoever sold you the cesium, and whoever you're selling it to, and we make some kind of arrangement. I mean, it's the end of the world anyway, right? Who really wants to spend it like this?"

Lewinski smiled again. "It's for a clock."

"Bullshit. It only takes one single cesium atom to make an atomic clock. You've got what, twenty tons of the shit coming in?" Aguilera drummed her fingers on the table for a second. "Who wants it?"

"I'd like to talk to a lawyer," he said.

"And I'd like to talk to whoever made it so goddamn hot," Aguilera replied. She wiped her forehead with a sleeve. Lewinski seemed pretty dry to me, and pretty unfazed. "A man in your position," she started, but Lewinski cut her off.

"I am happy in my position. You are the one who should worry."

"Yes?"

"As you said, it's almost over anyway. What does it matter if a few extremists accelerating things by a few years? Maybe you let me out of here and I forget where you live."

She sat back, surprised. "I thought you didn't like threats."

He laughed at her.

This was going nowhere. "Thompkins. Round up the team. Let's go through that warehouse."

"Yes, sir," he said.

An hour later, we were back in the warehouse, this time with warrants and seals and the whole thing. Some of Aguilera's cops had been here ahead of us but they didn't look to have touched anything.

"Cesium's not here," Thompkins said.

"That would be too simple, wouldn't it?" I said. "How can you tell, anyway?" I didn't even know what cesium might look like.

"Geiger counter in your wrist device. It isn't very sensitive, but even a low-grade radioactive in much quantity should trigger it."

"Show me how to work it."

He did. With the touch of a few virtual buttons, I was scanning around the building. It clicked really slowly, indicating just background radiation. Fun. I worked the area around a loading bay while Garcia and Williams nosed around big crates in the middle of the room.

"I never understood," Thompkins said, "how you managed to never learn computers. Half a million dollars of technology in your body and you're still a complete Luddite."

"A what?"

"Never mind," he said.

"It should have left a residual if he had it here and moved it out, right?"

"Right," Thompkins said.

"This is a problem, though," Williams said. She had one side of a large crate stripped off, revealing some esoteric machinery inside. I came over and gawked, Garcia too, and Thompkins watched from where he was. "Aerosolizer," Williams said. "Right, Tommy?"

Thompkins nodded. Garcia shuddered.

"Somebody want to fill me in? Assume I'm just a dumb-ass soldier?"

Williams did. "Cesium. Low-grade but persistently radioactive. If you aerosolized it, you could raise the background radiation over a large area. Slowly, maybe, but didn't Aguilera say there was essentially a shit-ton of the stuff coming in?"

"What's this mount to?" I said. It looked like a pretty big piece of equipment to me, maybe the size of an industrial laundry machine. A three meter cube.

"Stick it in the back of any old cargo plane," Thompkins supplied. "Ashlifter could mount four of them, no problem."

"Shit."

"Blanks." Voice in my head. I looked around for Raskin, knowing he wasn't there. That's the trouble with piping voices right into your cochlea: you can't tell them from the people around you.

"What?" I said.

"Trouble," he said. "You miss Lewinsky somehow?"

"No, we've got him stashed at the police station. Why?"

"Sighting," he said. "Antarctic station. Face recognition confirms it."

"He's wrapped up tight," I said. "Double-check your source or your time-stamp or something."

"I did," he said. "Seems righteous. I'm sending."

I stopped moving because he was about to send a picture right into my eye via my contact lens. He did: it was a man in a truck with big balloon tires. Driving out of some muddy place, into what seemed like maybe a dock: there were cranes all around. The picture was through glass, into the cabin of the truck, but it sure looked a hell of a lot like Lewinski.

A chill crept up my spine. The sweat on my forehead did double-time. "Drop everything," I said. "Back to the station house, right now."

"What is it, boss?" Garcia said. She was moving already, we all were.

"I don't know. But this one is going to get weird." And I remembered Raskin trying to tell me just that, back in Liverpool.

We ran outside, pushing cops out of our way as we went. Charged at the van and tumbled inside. Franks drove it, taking corners so fast two wheels came up off the pavement at times. In back, we were tossed around like we were in The Truck during a drop.

"Williams. Try to hail the station."

"Yes, sir." She looked for channels on her wrist device, patched them in one by one. "One World calling, this is One World Government agent Captain Williams. Please advise current status." Over and over, no response.

Then we were there, twenty minutes across town in less than ten, tires squealing and smoke pouring off the overtaxed electric motor. I led the way, stampeding out of the van towards the station house.

Something was wrong and I could just about smell it from the baking parking lot, see it through the lines of haze rising from the hot asphalt that half-melted and gripped at the soles of my boots.

It was quiet.

I shoved in through the front doors and came up short at the interior security doors. Thompkins had the key code and he was about twenty steps behind me. But there was nobody at the desk, nobody in the hallway you could see by stretching over the counter and looking left. No sound but the hum of computers.

Thompkins caught up and the doors clicked and I charged through them, pushing so hard they bounced off the wall. I heard something break. I had a pulse rifle in my hands and didn't remember picking it up but I checked the charge while I ran. Eighty percent. Six or eight good bursts, then. I skidded to a stop in front of the elevator, staring at the floor.

If I hadn't glanced down at the charge counter, I'd have missed it.

Williams ran into me, and Garcia into her, and Thompkins and Franks dragged up short of them. "What?" Franks said from the back.

"Footprint," I said. "Williams, collect it."

She looked, pressed a key on her wrist. Her contact lens captured the image for later: a single footprint in rusty red. Not a rubber sole with patterns in it, like a sneaker; not a wide, flat bootprint like a cop would wear. A loafer.

"Downstairs," I said. We hit the stairwell at a run, me leading with my body and my pulse rifle. There was a lot of hardware ready behind me and I hoped like hell this didn't turn into a firefight.

We emerged onto the holding level, our ears telling us right away we were in the right place. There was screaming, shouting. Commands being given in Spanish. Good soundproofing had kept the noise down here. We ran up on a scene that told its own story.

Aguilera had been torn apart. She was alive. In fact, she was the one screaming. Her torso was propped up against one wall, legs splayed out in front of her. Her arms, though, were missing. Well, not missing exactly: they were piled up against the opposite wall. Cops were all over her, uniforms saturated with blood, doing emergency things to keep her alive that would certainly cost her any hope of having those arms surgically reattached. I saw needles from sewing kits, a propane torch, a bottle of whiskey that was certainly black market. All the sewing and cauterizing would ruin any veins, any nerve endings. A woman in her underwear had found a cooler full of dry ice, probably from a specimen room, and was trying to fit the arms inside. They were just a hair too long.

Aguilera didn't notice us. If the cops did, they didn't acknowledge. They had their hands full.

"What is this?" Franks said.

"The end result of a set-up," I replied. It was at least fifty Celsius down here but I felt cold. There was an icy finger on my spine, and two more digging into my temples. "We got played."

"Lewinski?" Franks said.

I just nodded. I turned and walked back to the stairs. When Franks caught up, the rest of the team in step, I said, "This was a gang hit. Aguilera looks like a cop but she's really a gangster, a rival crime syndicate. Black market food she could tolerate, and black market drugs. But what she was into was weapons. When Lewinski started moving weapons on her turf - cesium, aerosolizers - she had to do something about it."

"How do you know all that?" Franks said.

"Easy, Franks. Because local governments are always into crime nowadays, and Lewinski operated here for years. You heard what Aguilera said. *A respected member of the community*. Why did we get called in?"

"The terror shit?"

"Damn right. That's where she drew the line and so there was a reason to draw it there. Well, while the whole station house is busy trying to patch her back together, I guess we'd better raid this place. Fan out, search every office. Thompkins, maybe you should set up everyone with that pass-key ap." Maybe should have thought of that earlier but we didn't usually do investigations and police actions. We killed people and destroyed things.

"Yeah boss," he said. We crammed into the narrow stairwell.

"Wait," Franks said. "I still don't get it. Aguilera set us up? So why's she the one bleeding?"

"She didn't set it up. Lewinski did. He got into weapons exactly so that she'd call in One World and we'd bring him here. He knew she wouldn't want to kill him, only get his connections out of him and put him back into circulation. But he didn't show for the meeting. He sent... something else."

"What?"

"I'm not sure. But whatever we brought in here, it wasn't Lewinski."

***

I leaned against the van, sweating. The asphalt gave off sickening fumes as it cooked under the sun. Raskin was in my ear.

"Next stop is Antarctica," he said.

"That's hardly a good lead, boss. Lewinski manipulated this whole thing. If he's even there, it's some kind of a trap."

"Nevertheless. They don't send us to garden parties, Major."

He had a point. One he delighted in making. "So you think the cesium thing is real."

"Sure. He brought it in to get our attention, maybe, but a businessman like Lewinski would certainly get someone else to pay for it. Meaning there is a buyer somewhere, for some reason."

"It just doesn't make any sense," I said. "Cesium is much too low grade to cause much harm, especially when spread thin through the atmosphere."

"We think it was just a place-holder," Raskin said. "Something just hot enough to track by satellite, just hot enough to alert us. There is a real threat, a real radioactive, and we think you'll really find it in Antarctica."

"Roger that," I said, and Raskin was gone from my head.

In front of the station house, Williams brought out a crate of fragmentation grenades and set it on a pile of similar munitions. I could see them shifting around between the wooden slats. Dangerous. There were about thirty such crates, most with grenades, some with pistols. Two contained broken-down pulse rifles.

Bad shit.

Garcia brought out one of the local cops. He was in dress uniform and his hands were cuffed behind his back. She asked him to kneel but the guy just stared at her, mouth slack.

"Just do it," I said.

"Williams?" Garcia asked.

Williams came away from what she was doing and looked the guy in the face. She was taller than him and she came in close. I couldn't hear what she said. But I'd heard it all before.

"Under One World Government article fifteen, section two, you are hereby convicted of racketeering, corruption, black market operations, and abuse of authority. Summary justice applies."

Garcia pulled out her sidearm and shot him in the back of the head. His brain turned to instant pulp. Some of it leaked out his nose even as he slumped to the hot ground. Garcia turned away, stalked back into the station house to get the next one.

Garcia repeated the procedure nine times, Williams reading the sentence each time. By the seventh, the first bodies were cooking against the hot pavement, searing, smelling meaty and foul. The odor mixed with the petroleum fumes from the asphalt and turned the stomach. Then the job was done, the corpses left to cook and rot as an example. Everyone but Aguilera.

I went inside, down into the hot basement levels, into the one room that passed for cool. The conference table held Rene Aguilera's body. She breathed on, shallow and frail. Her wounds were totally grievous, among the worst I had ever seen someone survive. For what good that would do her.

I called in Thompkins. It took him a minute to respond; he was sterilizing paperwork on the admin level. When he came in, he looked harried, hands and face sooty, a desperate look in his eyes.

"I need her to talk," I said.

"Unlikely," he replied. "Shock. Not enough blood left to supply the necessary oxygen for consciousness. I might be able to bring her up for a minute, and she'd probably die after that. Move blood into the brain, move it away from the heart, cardiac arrest."

"I'm going to shoot her in the head anyway, Thompkins. Do it."

He sighed. He was always the sensitive one, the reluctant one. I could see he wanted to touch my hand as he studied my face. Did he want comfort or did he think I needed it? Or was there something else I wasn't grasping? But he went for his medkit. Came back with some syringes ready, started loading Aguilera with drugs. "These ones will close off veins and arteries," he said, carefully injecting drugs into her legs. Top of the right thigh. The veins in her crotch near the big arteries there. "These ones will open them up," working on her neck. Finally, "This one is adrenaline. Her heart will set to beating faster. It will do what you want. But she can't sustain it."

"Why aren't you a doctor?" I said.

He thought about it for a few seconds. Looked at his hands. They were big and grimy and flecked now with blood. "Well," he said at last, "I suppose because I hate her. Doctors aren't supposed to hate their patients." Then he left, back to the job of stealing all the electronic records and burning all the paper ones.

Aguilera opened her eyes, winced. Groaned. He hadn't given her anything for pain, and she must have a great deal of that.

"What happened?" I said.

And she gritted her teeth and told me. Every word.

When she was done, I shot her in the head. Between the eyes. Then I left her down there in the cool conference room.

Three

I didn't puke.

That's all the good I could say about these drops anymore. By now you know the drill: dark cabin, red light to warn us gravity was about to take a short vacation, spinning and noise and inertial chaos. Someone asked me if I was all right and I said, "Shit, I haven't puked in years." Ritual.

The Truck righted itself as it always does, the engine caught. I knew it would. Still, my heart straightened out and my breathing eased, just a little. The cabin went dark again and we had survived being dropped out of yet another cargo plane over yet another place on Earth. And here came the next part of the ritual.

"My recruiter told me I'd see the world," Garcia said, and we all finished for her: "Just not all in one day."

I checked my gear. For this one, we were in Arctic gear, civilian issue. Thick, down-filled coveralls, heavy coats rated for forty below, moon boots. Plenty of places to conceal small arms and I had plenty of those, as well as discrete body armor. I checked the counter on my pistol. More ritual. I knew how many rounds it held.

The Truck landed, Henry setting us down easy. No reason for a quick turn so no bouncing around. Hostiles were not anticipated.

The hatches opened on both sides and, for once, the air outside was colder than the air inside. I had on a balaclava, green. So the only part of my face to feel the full smack of cold was lips and eyes. The balaclava smelled of wool and vomit – the antibacterials it was treated with, just like our standard issue body soap.

We piled out of The Truck, shouldered duffels. We'd look just like settlers.

Garcia had her balaclava rolled up to her brow and found out right away that was a bad idea. "Who the fuck would want to live down here? Jesus H, it's fucking cold."

"You're from Rio or something, right?" said Thompkins.

"Close enough," she said.

"And how old are you, twenty-four?"

"Twenty-five."

"Jesus," he said. "You were born after the Endless Summer. After there were seasons."

"It's Endless, dipshit," she said.

"Endless as in never ending, not as in never beginning. Anyway, this is the last place still cold. Some of us remember what it was like to not be broiling hot all the goddamn time." Thompkins got right into it. He settled his pack and set to hiking. There wasn't snow out here but the ground was frozen this early in the morning.

Well, what passed for morning, with a sun that sat on the horizon for four hours then wallowed back under it.

Mud, brownish grass, and nothing. A flat ground bare of buildings or people all the way to every horizon.

"I did boot in Reykjavik," Garcia said, her mask down now. She got in step with Thompkins. "One morning the DI, he gets on the intercom and goes, 'PC condition three, it's seventeen below out there. Christ, it's cold.' And I was like, below what? Fifty?"

That was an old joke. Far older than Garcia. The joke was so old it used to be in Fahrenheit.

I paired up with Williams. Franks paired up with Garcia, and Thompkins with Hull, a new addition since South America, flown in from the main unit in Liverpool. Short guy, wiry, light brown skin. Hazel eyes. Each pair of us headed off in a different direction, to come at New City more discretely.

Like Charlie Crew does anything really very discretely.

"I don't like this spy shit," I told Williams.

"It's within our mandate," she said.

That was it for conversation. I liked her.

We trudged for a few miles. That's half a soldier's job, it seems to me: trudging. After a while, she pointed out to the horizon, said, "What's that?"

It looked like a ground vehicle. I patched in Henry in the Truck, mostly by intuition since my wrist implant was buried in my coat sleeve. Design flaw, and the main reason I wasn't fluent in using the thing: I preferred to keep my body armored and my hands on my weapons. I said, "Stand by, Henry. Possible hostile." The implant in my throat wired my voice through the implant in my wrist and on out into space via radio.

"You're solo, boss," he said back. "Fuel and distance."

"Shit."

He didn't answer, because I'd patched him back out.

Whoever was out there, they clearly saw us. The vehicle executed a sloppy turn and rolled our way. As it closed it resolved into a tracked vehicle mostly suitable for snow, sort of a snowmobile with a body like a pick-up truck. Two people sat behind the glass. The thing must have lacked cabin heat because they were swaddled up like we were, layers of down-filled clothing.

The vehicle got within five meters and stopped. I stopped, too, Williams beside me. I kept my hands in the open, fingers freezing because none of my pistols were especially easy to operate with thick down gloves on. A man got out on the left, a woman on the driving side. They had rifles but kept them across their backs.

You're getting paranoid, Blanks.

The woman said something I didn't catch. Sounded Slavic. Almost Russian, but not quite.

Williams answered. She seemed to speak the lingo. The two chatted a few minutes, then the soldiers got in their vehicle and we continued on our way.

"So?" I said.

"Just checking credentials."

"We don't have credentials."

"Which is a credential in itself," Williams said. "Nobody brings paperwork down here. This is a Free Zone."

I hadn't thought of that. "What does that do for our jurisdiction?"

"We'll work that out later," Williams said.

"I don't like this spy shit," I repeated. Even though New City was well outside the purview of One World Government, if there were radioactives stockpiled down here, we needed to find them. The world was already one huge clusterfuck and who knew what would happen if that shit got on the wind? Jurisdiction be damned.

The sun edged down under the horizon, about four points to our right. It was a slow process, slower than we walked. Down here, the air was still clean. Stars came out long before the sun was really gone. There was no sunset. Pretty sunsets, the reds and oranges and so on, they're all about dust and smog and pollution. So we didn't get a show like that. We got the beauty of purity, of clean air that didn't look like anything.

On the horizon now were the lights of New City.

White lights and yellow, halogen and sodium bulbs respectively. Still too far know much about it, except that this walk, unlike the Summer, would not be endless.

"I wonder if they hassled Franks and them," Williams said.

"Guess they would have squawked," I said.

"Yeah."

Now she had me worried. Franks and politics, or even basic human decency, they didn't go together in one sentence. Anyway, soon enough we were at the edge of what passed for town.

We passed a feed lot. Bunch of cattle, rare sight these days on Planet Earth. Too hot for cows or anything they would eat. They stank and that was kind of good, a new thing in a world that all was starting to look the same: brown and burned and dry, or brown and rotten and wet. Some warehouses, tractor supply store, heavy equipment. Camping and outdoor supplies for noobs and rubes. "Let's try there," I said, pointing at the outfitter.

"Bet everyone tries there first," Williams said.

"Yeah, so that's who we want. They'll know everyone, especially newcomers, and it would look weird for us not to be rubes to start with."

"I guess," she said.

We found a door, glass, like a regular store in the real world. It was warm inside. Well, compared to outside. I'd gotten almost used to temperatures in Centigrade that would've looked OK in Fahrenheit. A bare plank floor was filled with rows of garments hung on bars. Khaki, canvas, down-filled stuff like we wore already. On the walls were tents, sleeping bags, Coleman lanterns from a previous age. Black market if not just antiques.

A youngish woman dressed in khaki appeared from a back office. She rattled off something in Russian. I stared and shook my head.

"Not English, surely?" she said in a thick accent. United States. The South.

"English will do," I said. "My partner can handle the Slavic languages if that's better for you."

"Oh no, Honey, I'm from Tennessee," the woman said, and when she spoke she was pretty. Red hair, expressive lips. "Everybody here speaks Russian, though. Or Belarussian, which is just about the same. Now aren't you two about the cutest couple. Are you together?"

I glanced at Williams. Willed myself not to blush. Not that I could stop it. I guess Williams must have looked really femme to my butch, even wrapped up in winter gear.

Williams said, "Not *together* together. Partners, not *partners*."

"OK, but you are cute. What can I do you for?"

"I think we're about set for gear," I said, and cleared my throat. And I wondered if that was at all a giveaway, worried much more about Williams than the shopkeeper. "What we could really use is work. We imagined most folks checked in here first and maybe you'd know just about everyone." I found myself slipping into her manner of speech, unconscious and unwilling. It was contagious.

Like foot fungus.

"You sure thought right, I guess," she said. "My name is Annie. Like you said, everyone comes here first, so we have all the help we need. My husband and me own the place and do most of the work ourselves. But Stanislov, he runs the warehouse. About a quarter-mile back on up the way, here. He goes through drivers like nobody's business. You all can't drive big rigs, can you?"

I lied through my teeth. "Sure can, miss." I had in fact driven one, once. An old one with a bunch of gears and peddles and so on. That hadn't gone at all well. They told me then that the new ones just about drove themselves, and that was what I was hoping for.

"You know what? You just about look like a truck driver. Or a soldier, bless your heart. You aren't a soldier, are you?"

"We're retired," said Williams. There was no way to hide the fact that we'd done time so we might as well embrace it.

"Honey," Annie started, "You ain't no way old enough to be retired from the *army*."

She obviously meant Williams. I had plenty of miles on my chassis. "Let's say," I said, "we didn't leave on exactly the greatest of terms."

Annie tapped herself twice on the side of her nose. "Leave me your names and I'll call Stan in the morning. Don't tell him I call him Stan, either, he don't like that one bit. Now you go on down to the hostel, I guess you all will be staying there? And check in with me first thing, OK?"

"Thank you kindly," I said, hating myself. We poked around a little like we were interested in the wares. Then I got inspired. "Why?" I said.

"Why what?" said Annie, watchful.

"Why Russians?"

"Oh," she said. "First few farms that opened, the Americans chased everyone off like those old treaties were still laws. Remember those? But you're both so young. Anyway, soon there were more settlers than they could keep out, and as soon as that happened, bang – a bunch of Russians. Or, you know, Belarussians."

"So, why?"

"Well, because this is the last arable land, sweetie. And the last clean water. You know how those people are.

Horning in on the North Pole oil after the thaw? All of that?"

"Yeah," I said. "I remember." That particular pot had been close to boiling for forty years. We said our goodbyes. The door shut behind us.

"That was easy," Williams said when we were a few paces out of earshot.

"Yeah," I said. "That's what worries me."

"I think she's right. About the Russians."

"Nationalism?" I said.

"Not everyone was big on the One World business," Williams said. "The Americans were against it so the Russians were for it, which is probably the only reason the Americans were against it to begin with. They knew the Russians would love it if they hated it."

I stowed all that away for later.

***

Annie had called it a hostel but it was more of a bunkhouse. A common room held rough tables and chairs. No TV or amenities. It was warm enough to take off our coats. And there was stew in a pot that seemed to be always half-full, the kind of pot that was never really emptied out and washed, just continually replenished.

It should have been terrible but I'd been on rations for fifteen years. Dried jellyfish, protein powder, vitamin supplements and flat water. And that was when times were good. This was stew, by-God stew. Real food. Flour and milk and meat and even some vegetables, celery and onions. I paid for a bowl and then another and one more, and was considering a fourth only Williams looked at me and shook her head.

Yeah, don't draw attention. My belly didn't need it anyway, only my spirit, my soul, and One World

Government assured us that the soul was imaginary anyway.

We ate, rubbed shoulders with the locals, listened. Williams listened, anyway. I didn't have any of the dialect. It was warm and there was nothing to do but wait: to check in with the team later, to check in with Annie in a few hours. So I did what any soldier does when her belly is full and she doesn't have to piss right away and nobody is yelling orders at her.

I went to sleep.

The dream started right away. I knew what it was.

Rene Aguilera had died badly, ripped to pieces by something we'd thought was Lewinski. He'd set us up in Zaire, and he'd set us up again in Bolivia. I wanted him bad.

In the dream, I was Aguilera. She'd told me what happened, how Lewinski had escaped. It was impossible, the ravings of a woman dying with her arms ripped off, so I'd watched the video. Listened to every word, watched it all unfold.

I was her, but I was me, too.

Lewinski sat across a small table from me. Formica top, cuffs bolted to the tabletop, chair bolted to the floor. They should've restrained him better.

"You ready to play?" I said. We'd started an interrogation earlier but he'd just smugged through it.

"Maybe," he said. "You?"

"Me?"

"Don't be coy," he said. "I know who you are, you know who I am."

Can you get a chill in a dream? Like someone is looking through the dream-you into the real you? Shit, I hope not. I hoped that was just the creeps upon waking coloring the memory of the creeps while sleeping. I hoped that like nothing else.

In the dream, I glossed it over. "We've got you on some serious shit. The food smuggling, you know, we don't care about that so much. Drugs, well, it's almost over anyway. Let people die high if that's what they want to do, that's my approach. It's the weapons I don't understand."

"No," he said, and leaned back as far as he could with his wrists chained down.

"Tell me about your buyer," I said.

"And then you make this whole thing go away?" he said, smiling.

"Not exactly. There's still Zaire to consider." Rene hadn't been in Zaire. I had. Was I me, really, all the way?

"As you say," he said. "It is almost over already. That's what you don't understand, right? Why a dirty bomb, why irradiate a planet that's already poisonous. Especially when you're an organism vulnerable to radiation. That's it, isn't it?"

"Yes," I said. "So assume I'm a dumb-ass army girl and explain it to me." He wanted to, I knew he wanted to.

"What you have," he said, "is a Soviet problem."

"Ain't no Soviets no more."

"Right," he said, and then he leaned forward again, something in his eyes. Something... inhuman. Mechanical. Cold and calculating. "Machiavelli," he said. "And Sun Tzu."

That got my attention.

Those were standard reading. *The Prince*, *The Art of War*. Every officer read them early in training, young. The early United States race war. The Civil War, they called it. The North won by a psychopathic strategy of murdering civilians and burning the land, burning the means of production, burning everything. Scorched Earth, they called that. All this in a rush, in an eye-blink. And then I understood. About the Soviets.

"Now you see," he said.

And I should have awakened then. I wish I had awakened then. I had the revelation, knew what the dream-self wanted to tell the waking self. But the dream rolled on, back on-track with the video recording and Rene's story.

It laughed. Lewinski threw its head back and laughed. I stood up to leave: this interview, like the last, was pointless. Not-Lewinski needed more time to get thirsty. But it grabbed its left hand with its right, twisted, pulled the hand off. The cuff dropped to the table with a wet *clink*. Blood and something blacker than blood pooled there, dripped to the floor.

It put the hand back on and did the same trick with the other hand. Then it stood and faced me.

I tried to run, to get through the door, to put wood between it and me. It beat the door into matchsticks, smashed my chest with a fist. Ripped my right arm clean off and used it to beat me down, although shock from blood loss left me half conscious. I was too gone to feel the second assault but I felt it anyway, the tugging, searing heat of muscle tearing, of cap sucking away from ball, of arterial spray, of horror.

I woke with a start, not knowing if I had screamed or not. Williams looked at me, alarm in her eyes.

"What?" I said.

"Let's go for a walk," Williams said.

No way to talk operations in the crowded common room. I was practically holding hands with the people next to me. We stepped out into the cold. For my part, I relished it, watched avidly as my breath coiled into steam and swirled around. We got far enough away to talk if we kept it quiet. "What?" I repeated.

"It's Franks," she said. "He's missing."

I blinked, awake all the way. It's a skill soldiers acquire: shaking off the dream-world because if you're awake, someone might be trying to kill you. And the dream, the meaning of it, slipped away. Lost quietly in the needs of the moment, in the emergent situation. "Go," I said.

"He told Garcia he needed to take a leak. Went into an alley between an engine parts supply and a feedlot. Didn't come back. Garcia went to check on him, didn't find him. Reported in and I woke you."

"You did? Never mind. Drop in his last-known, distribute teams. Spiral search pattern. Keep it quiet."

She had the sense to not "sir" me in public. She sent it all out by wrist, text format. And we set off at a brisk pace towards the other side of the settlement.

It was a weird place for Summer folk. A lot of wood construction. Trees had arrived here naturally as the Antarctic started to thaw. So, wood. Lots of wooden buildings. Mostly long-halls, Viking style, for efficiency. Wood fences, large pastures for animals. Noise and smells not found in modern cities. And with the sun down, not many people were out. Too cold. The few people with places to go went there in a hurry, with hands jammed inside coat pockets, bundled up from feet to head.

I'd left my coat at the bunk house. It felt good to be cold and I guess that marked me out as a noob or a rube, a novelty-seeker not yet long enough in the environment to wish for warmth.

We circled around, going wherever Williams' search algorithms led. Between two buildings made of first-purpose corrugated metal, still shiny, we got the call.

Williams stopped still for a minute, listening to a voice piped straight into her cochlea.

"Got him," she said. "Garcia says he was mugged."

"Mugged? Like a coffee cup?"

"Man, don't you have muggings in Brazil or wherever you came from? When he had his thing out, someone came up behind him. Knocked him out cold, dragged him off. He's been in a hayloft since then."

"Oh," I said. We had muggings in Brazil, we just didn't have that word. And Brazil was a long time ago, when the sun had still been kind. Hot chocolate with cinnamon, monkeys that lived on the balconies of the high-rise where I lived. All gone now.

"They took his clothes, left him his skivvies only. Got his gun, everything. Looks like they even tried to pry out his wrist implant."

"He good?"

"Red in the face, Garcia says, but he checks out. Thompkins is with him now."

That all meant whoever had assaulted him had his gun. Wouldn't do them much good: it was biometric. They might could salvage the ammo is all. Except...

"So they know who we are," I said.

"If 'they' mugged our boy, I'd guess they knew already. But if it was just some crime of poverty, then they know now."

"The gun's as good as an ID," I said. And in the right hands, it was. They could trace back the biometrics. In the right database, that would give them a name. "Well, we'd best get some rest."

Williams was a soldier, too. Maybe most people would have worried about it, stayed up late fretting. But we went back to the bunk house and bedded down.

***

Morning. Or at least a few hours after what we had called night. I rolled off my bunk, a narrow strip of canvas on a rolled aluminum frame. Dropped to the ground and headed straight to the head. An outhouse in back, of all things. At least the shitter was nominally heated.

Huh. Guess the novelty of being cold is wearing off.

Williams joined me in the common room and we paid for stew out of that never-ending pot. I helped myself to a single bowl. When we went outside, it was still dark. The sun would peek up again in a couple more hours, loiter on the horizon, and then drop away once more. Around here, one did not wait on daylight.

This time I had my coat. We stalked through town to the outfitter. It wasn't open yet, so we waited outside, stamping our feet as if that would help warm us up. Then Annie unlocked the glass door. I stepped in first, Williams right behind me.

"You all sleep enough? Get enough to eat?" Annie said. She looked pink, like she'd only just stepped in from the cold herself.

"Yes," Williams said. "Thank you. Ironically, we're eating better than ever."

Annie almost pouted. "Oh, the world is such a mess. If we just all went back to basics... well, I suppose there just isn't room for everybody down here, is there? Anyway, Stan was delighted to hear that you could drive a rig. He wants to meet you first, but he sure can use you. If he likes you."

"Where?" I said. "His yard?"

"No ma'am. He prefers someplace public. Go on down to the lake and he'll find you an hour from now."

"Lake?" I said.

Now she went from pouting to amazement. "You don't know about the lake? Why, it's only the whole reason there's a town here and not someplace else. People come from all over just to see it."

Williams nodded. "On the map. Right in the middle, remember? Antarctica has been frozen over just about forever. When the glaciers melted, some of them were miles thick. That's why the land down here is so flat – it's been squashed flat by ice. And sometimes they covered over lakes that hadn't seen the light of day for millions of years."

Annie continued, "And we've got one of them, right in the middle of town. Oh, you just have to see it. Go on, now. Hurry, before the sun comes up. It's prettiest when it's darkest out."

She just about shooed us out the door. Then there was nothing to do but to hike back to the center of town, right back the way we had come. We smelled the lake before we saw it. More rightly, we stopped smelling anything else so much. The water, as Williams had said, had been there millions of years and what it smelled like was nothing at all. Then we saw the glow. There were lights around town, at least minimally, but the lake was lit up from under the surface, and gave off a soft white light we could see from about a kilometer out. Then the buildings faded away: nobody built too close to the water. And, finally, we came to a rough waist-high guardrail made of tubular steel, and saw the lake itself.

It stretched off into the distance and the town curved around it. The water went on for three or four kilometers. The surface reflected the sky full of stars, saturated with them, thousands of them. It was still, glassy, a perfect moment. A windless idyll, just for us. If we were lovers, me and Williams, it couldn't have held more romance. For a minute, I looked at her instead of the water. Might-have-beens rolled around in my head until she saw I was looking and glanced up to see what I wanted. By that time my eyes were back on the water.

The lake was deep and perfectly clear. There were no boats, no activity. There was enough groundwater to leave the thing alone, let it sit in beauty under the grand sky. Somebody had rigged up submersible electric lights and dropped them in to rest on the bottom, and you could look into the water, see them down there. Three, four kilometers down, through water so clear it hardly existed, there were the soft white lights.

Williams put a hand on my shoulder and it was then I realized I was crying. My tears had none of the purity of the water, none of the beauty, but they were for it. *This is the last pure thing,* my tears said to me.

"I know," Williams said, and there was room in my head to wonder: how much? All of it?

"Is beautiful, no?" The voice was male and deep. "Oh, I am sorry," the voice said. "I should make more noise when I walk." Neither of us had jumped. I'd barely shifted my eyes. We're paranoids by profession, difficult to surprise. "I am Stanislov. Annie told me to find you here. Is beautiful, no?" he repeated.

I wiped tears from my face before they could freeze there. "Mr. Stanislov. I'm June, and this is my partner, Willie. The lake is... a revelation."

"Yes," he said. "Good to meet you. Anyone who can still weep for to see beauty is OK in my book, I think. And look, it loses already." He pointed, deep into the lake, off to the right of the lights. Down there, when I focused just right, I could see what he meant: a foggy patch in the water, yellowish. Agricultural run-off, most likely. The inevitable consequence of proximity to humans. "I am Russian," he continued, "and we know something the Buddhists always say: everything is impermanent."

"I hear you need a driver," I said, turning my back on the lake. I looked right at Stanislov for the first time. He was taller than me by four or five centimeters and about the same weight. Sixtyish, gray hair under a fur-lined parka hood. Good boots. Thick nose, thick lips.

"Always need driver," Stanislov said. "Town grows. Ten, twenty people each day. Need plastic and clothing and food, always more food. Though soon food goes out and not comes in. Lights and heaters. Sometimes drive truck a few days to pay for supplies, then start to farm. Always need drivers. Come with me, I will show you warehouse."

He started to amble away. Williams followed and I walked alongside him. He didn't have much to say until we came to his place. He had a large yard fenced in with chain-link. The fence had plastic strips between the links, obscuring the view. He let us in a padlocked personnel gate. Inside, a pair of trailers sat against a warehouse wall, backs open to the interior, muddy balloon tires dripping muck into the yard. Two women and two men busily unloaded cargo, crates of unknown goods, bales of clothing.

A rig stood ready by a sliding vehicle gate. It was for sure newer than the trucks in Africa had been. It had three axles, giant balloon tires like the trailers. Presumably good for tundra driving. I hadn't seen roads out there. The cab was ovoid in profile, the back red aluminum, the front glass tinted reflective blue. It looked like an exotic mantis, ready to spring.

"You can drive XL four?" Stanislov said.

"Last thing I drove was an antique," I admitted. "Gears and clutches and so on."

"Then you can drive XL four. Mostly is just push buttons and wait to arrive. Driver is for emergency. Flat tire, attach trailer, such as this." He walked around the rig with us, showed us the various features. Cables, hook points, gearbox, indicator lights. The cab looked like a spaceship with digital displays that lit up green and red.

When the tour was done, he said, "OK, you drive now."

I didn't let my surprise show. "What's the load?"

"You go out empty," he said. "Take trailer six. Here. Is empty. At dock, cargo man will give you container. Bring back."

"OK," I said. "Coordinates loaded?"

"Da," he said.

"All right, Willie. Let's pee first and then hit the road."

"Toilet is around corner," Stanislov said, and then he went indoors, apparently satisfied.

Civilians are weird people.

Williams came back out, did one more walk-around of the vehicle. Then we boarded up. There were five-point harnesses and an array of controls. Lights, gauges, knobs, levers, a tiny steering wheel. I found the *engine start* button and gunned it. The truck started up first try. Electric motors are much more reliable than gas. I backed it under the trailer Stan had indicated.

"Now what?" I said. "You ever drive one of these?"

"I only drove until they found out I was better at stabbing people in the neck," Williams said. But she reached past me and pushed a small brown button labeled *Acquire load*. "Good thing these aren't in Cyrillic."

"I thought you spoke Russian."

"Yeah, but who can read the alphabet? Anyway, it's all automatic. Light's green, you're good to go."

A couple of men pulled open the rolling gate. I got the truck moving much more easily than the rig in Africa: no clutch, no gears, just a light touch on the accelerator. That, and remembering to take off the resting brake, and we were good to go.

I swung the whole rig out onto what passed for a road, sort of a boggy, frozen-over trail leading out of town. We passed the same stuff we'd passed coming in but now from a higher perspective. The view was not much improved.

Out of town the road got worse. It was hard to tell there was even a trail at all, just an area with less dead grass. The heads-up display showed me some green lines to stay between, and the autopilot (when Williams reached over again to switch it on) did even that for me. The truck eased itself up to a comfortable cruising speed of about eighty kilometers an hour, and it didn't seem to care that that speed over rough ground with no lights and no control made me want to scream.

About twenty minutes into this hellish flight through the tundra, one of the tires exploded.

The rig shuddered, slid a little to one side, righted its course. I hammered the brake, probably a rookie move, but the truck compensated for my incompetence. It understood I wanted to slow down and took the appropriate measures. We ground to a silent stop about ten meters outside the green lines on the HUD.

"Guess we'd better take a look," I said, and slid out of the cockpit. Williams met me around by the damaged wheel. It was shredded up pretty good. "I don't think we can run on that."

"You know," she whispered, "a little C4 in the right place at the right time can create opportunities."

And that explained the second vehicle inspection at the yard. "As can the need to urinate?" I said.

"That's affirmative. Low-level radiation present. Concentrated in the yard. If something was there it's either long gone or was never very strong."

"You want to RF sweep this vehicle or just search it?" I said.

"A sweep would almost certainly alert any electronic surveillance on it," Williams said. "Geiger is passive."

"Roger that." We walked around the truck, wrist devices set to radiation sweep. When we met back at the flat, I said, "Nothing too unusual. Looks like background only."

"And the trailer really is empty," she said. "Deadhead run."

"Plausible," I said. "No exports from here. That's what he said, right? Soon they'll start exporting food, but not yet?"

Williams nodded. "Let's get this fixed."

"Fixed? Is there a spare, or did you bring a shit-load of duct tape?"

"Well, there are enough wheels to run with one down. We can just take it off and toss it in back."

That turned out to be quite a challenge. We found an old-fashioned tire iron, took off what seemed like a hundred lug nuts. The weather was cold and running to colder and I smashed up my knuckles pretty good getting those lugs to turn. My hands oozed blood – and I was almost due for a pill. Those were in Liverpool. And then the wheel came off and it was heavy. We rolled it around back of the truck, brought up the door and brought down a ramp, sweated and heaved until the thing was on board.

"Best get moving again," Williams said. "Sweat and cold don't mix."

And they didn't. I stank, she stank, and the chill was gripping at my skin through the layers of cold-weather gear. We got in the cab, started it up, and got rolling. Williams found a temperature control and racked up the heat.

A proximity alarm beeped at me. I looked at a radar scope, saw another truck coming in fast. Our rig, now up to about forty kilometers an hour, turned on lights so we could be seen by the other driver – although their truck would coordinate with ours to avoid a collision. We passed each other so fast the wash of wind between us rocked the cabin.

"Trailer," I said, and Williams nodded. I wanted to check in with the team but there was almost certainly radio surveillance in the truck. Even a coded message could be intercepted. And the hell of it was, I figured we'd been made a long time ago.

In the distance, across dark tundra, lights started to appear. There was some kind of complex out there. Familiar looking, too. The sun finally started to scrape above the horizon, providing an eerie blue glow to the day, and we could see scaffolding. No, not scaffolds, cranes. Dozens of cranes. A whole complex of cargo containers, cranes, huge ships standing off in an artificial harbor, white lights everywhere. Outside the harbor was the ocean. Great waves, impossibly huge waves to be seen at this distance, seemed stationary until they broke against harbor walls.

Another ten minutes and we were there. The truck rolled through an archway made of broken crane parts. It cruised to a receiving area and dropped its trailer on command, and then the HUD indicated we should go back out.

"No new load?" I said.

"Let's ask the harbormaster," Williams said.

I asked the truck where to find such a person but it didn't know, so we rolled around looking for a likely spot. Ten minutes of driving between stacks of orange, brown and yellow shipping containers, artificial valleys of consumer goods, we found it. Might have missed it except I turned on the lights and accidentally caught a reflection off a window.

The office was, naturally, a converted shipping container. One among thousands except for that bit of glass set into a door.

I stopped the truck and got out. The temperature out here was a little warmer than inland but not by much. My knuckles stung with the cold. Inside, through a door held shut with a spring, was a cozy office. Wooden table, lounging chair upholstered in horrible orange, and an old guy who looked like he belonged there. He had on a pea coat and a black wool hat, jeans and fingerless mittens. He looked up at me over a clipboard, surprise in his eyes.

He thought for a minute. "Stanislov?" he said.

"Yes," I said. "We-"

"You are late," he said.

"Sorry. Flat tire."

His surprise magnified. "Tire is very strong."

I just shrugged. "You have a load for us?"

"Envelope," he said. He went into a back room. He was gone so long I almost went in after him. Williams restrained me with a hand on my arm and he came back out, quiet as a slow leak. He had a manila envelope, document sized, all taped up.

"He sent a truck for an envelope?" I said.

"And to leave trailer. Have nice day."

We seemed to have been dismissed. The fellow went back to his clipboard. But I've been around a long time. I mean, I've survived a lot of places – firefights, fires, bombings, knife-fights – and I've done it by watching people. He wasn't looking at the clipboard. His eyes were on it, but his focus was on me and Williams.

"Still down a wheel," I said.

"What?"

"You got someone who can give us a spare?"

He seemed to calculate for a minute. And I knew we were never supposed to leave. This was a dead-head run, pure and simple. Dropping off empties, taking out the trash.

"I call crew. Go and wait with vehicle."

I left with Williams. We waited by the truck for a few minutes. When the crew showed up, six men in black turtlenecks and longshoreman's caps, they didn't look at all like dock hands.

They looked like soldiers.

They showed up in a half-track suitable for varying conditions, with a big balloon tire and wheel dragging behind. I watched them affix it with cold efficiency. No bruised knuckles for them. Then they got in their truck with no conversation, drove back off again.

"What was all that about?" Williams said.

"I don't think we were supposed to see them. I think your C4 saved our asses."

"Huh?"

I said, "We were supposed to just drive out of here, and those guys were going to jump us. Take us by surprise. No surprise, they won't try anything now."

"There're still six of them," Williams said. "That we can see. There could be any number of them out here."

"Yeah," I said, "but they know who we are. So they know what we saw is recorded through our eye pieces and maybe transmitted all over. They can't do anything now, not and keep a low profile."

She thought about it. "Maybe. And what's in the envelope?"

"Nothing. We surprised him by wanting something. Fuck-up in the set-up. Nothing in here but bubble wrap, a hundred to one."

"We should go."

"Yeah." We saddled up. The engine started turning. The batteries were still warm and a trickle of solar now kept them topped off. I got the thing pointed in the right direction, back towards town, towards whatever trouble waited.

The truck did the work. I was extraneous, a brain in a machine that had its own brain.

Predictably, I went to sleep.

***

I'm getting predictable.

Yeah. It was getting to be like the drops. I tell someone it's been years since I puked. Someone says the bit about the recruiter, about seeing the world all in one day. And when there's nothing happening, I have a weird dream that ties everything together in my head.

Or doesn't.

I had a picture of Joseph Stalin in my mind. Brown uniform, red rank insignia, white face, big black soup-strainer mustache. If facial hair were masculinity, this was the manliest of all men. He stood over a game board, a map of the world. It was covered in trucks, little tiny models of the thing I was driving. Or was driving me. Whatever.

In one hand, he held a fistful of nuclear missiles.

"Catch," he said, and tossed the things at me. They went everywhere. I tried to catch them but how do you catch forty missiles? I got a few. The rest dropped onto the map.

Where they hit, the ground turned black. I imagined flames and fall-out, wasted ground, pure destruction. A flash of white light and you're dead, not even meat, only ashes on the wind. Some of the walls at Nagasaki retained shadows on the walls, of ashes blasted into brick or concrete. Shadows of people who exist no longer.

People. All the people gone. When I looked up, Joe Stalin was gone, too, a cloud of ash where he had been.

But down on the map, the trucks remained in place.

And I understood.

***

Awake again.

This time, I told Williams before the revelation could dissipate.

"The Soviet strategy," I said.

"What? Like the Cold War?"

"Yes," I said. "The Cold War. The United States and the Soviet Union, each stockpiling weapons. We've not yet had a nuclear war, not a full one. Why not?"

The truck rolled on and on through the dark. Another vehicle shook us with a wash of air as it rattled past.

"MAD," Williams said.

Right. "Mutually Assured Destruction. The hegemony would have to await either total cultural assimilation or some weapon that could kill selectively."

"You think they really wanted to kill everyone on Earth but themselves?" Williams said, yawning and stretching.

"Yeah," I said. "That's why the bombs never went off – the 'but themselves' part. And why we worked so hard to contain nuclear proliferation when the U.S., and India and Pakistan, all went under."

"So the Soviet problem is how to murder everyone and remain alive."

"Yeah," I said.

"What's the solution?"

"Don't be a human being."

She looked at me like I was crazy. But then I got a signal in my ear. "Urgent communication from headquarters."

That sounded like Raskin. I figured the op was about as blown as it could get, anyway. "Go."

But the voice that followed was The Wizard. "Please update regarding Antarctic investigation."

"You're killing me, chief," I said, and I meant that.

"Trust me," he said. "We're on an encryption algorithm such as the world has never seen. Update."

"I think we're compromised. Probably always were. This was a long-shot from the start. Met some soldiers, rough looking bunch of fellows. We accidentally made them before they could do any murdering. Insufficient evidence of radioactive materials here. Lewinski wanted us here for something, I'm sure."

"How sure?" the Wizard said.

"Pretty sure. Please advise. We're out of our jurisdiction here and have nothing to go on."

"Stay on mission," he said.

"What mission, boss? Nothing to see here."

"Stay on mission. Out."

And that was that. "You hear any of that?" I asked Williams.

"No, only your side."

I filled her in. "What do you think it means?"

"Sounds like a coded message," she said.

"Why?"

"You ever know someone like The Wizard to make contact if it wasn't important? Me neither. But did he say anything that sounded important to you?"

I shook my head. "So what's the code?"

"I don't know," she said. "But he repeated himself. 'Stay on mission,' you said he said, and you said he said it twice."

"Yeah."

"So what does it mean?"

I shrugged. "Trouble with codes. They have less chance of obscuring things from your enemies than they do from your friends."

"So what do we do?"

"We stay on mission," I said. Then I went back to sleep, and the truck drove itself home.

***

Stanislov looked surprised. The truck had rumbled up to the gates. Williams was out there dragging them open, and Stan stood there in the courtyard, perplexity slipping across his face and off again. Communications out here really were shit for some reason: there was no logic in him being surprised or showing it.

I parked the truck. Or, more accurately, told it to park itself. When the engine was off, I slid out.

"You make poor time," Stanislov said.

"Not bad for a flat tire. What kind of outfit are you running here, chief? Looked like someone blew it up with C4," I said, and Williams turned away to hide a grin.

Stanislov's eyes narrowed. Then he smiled and reached into his pocket. My fingers twitched, wanting to snatch a weapon out of my coat, but he only brought out a roll of greenish paper. "Pay," he said. "Sixty dollars each."

"Dollars?" I said. "Why greenies?"

"Onesies spend not so well here," Stanislov said. "Nobody trust One World Government."

"But you trust Americans?" Williams said, arms folded.

"You want tanks and bombs, you ask Russians. You want dead bodies, you ask One World Government. You want soldiers, you ask Indians. You want capitalism, you ask Americans. Each to skills." He counted bills into my hand, then into Williams'. "You come back tomorrow, drive again. But don't blow up any more tires, they cost much. Very greenbacks, yes? You want to look around, just look around. Nothing funny here."

I was momentarily sorry for my suspicions. Maybe these people were just what they claimed to be: pioneers seeking freedom on the Antarctic tundra. Helping out people deserting the One World Government's forces of oppression.

"Let's get out of here," I told Williams, and she agreed. We headed back towards the lake. "Call a confab," I said. "Neutral location. There's got to be some kind of bar or pub or hangout, right?"

"Anywhere you get more than four Russians together, they're going to make vodka out of something," Williams said.

There turned out to be a sort of frontier saloon, about a kilometer from our bunkhouse. Sod walls reinforced with corrugated tin in places, dirt floor, furniture made of salvage. Garcia was already there with Franks, Hull and Thompkins arriving right behind me and Williams. They had seats around a table made from a broken tractor wheel, chairs from mechanical parts that had not survived the conditions.

Once we had drinks and were safely camouflaged by the noise of thirty or so other patrons, ruddy people with light skin and light eyes and booming, buzzing voices, I said, "What do you got?"

"Zippo," said Franks.

"Bupkis," said Hull.

"So what the hell are we doing here?" I said, nearly angry.

"I got a job as a handyman," Thompkins said. "Cleaned out some stables, fixed some wiring. They use heaters down here."

"Great."

"Actually," he said, "I could stay here. They have real food."

"I feel like we've been shuffled off out of the way of something," Garcia said.

I thought about what The Wizard had said. And that he had said it. Codes, implications. If it was important enough for him to say it at all, directly, and to repeat it... "I have a bad feeling," I said. I glanced at Franks. He had a black eye, a slightly glazed look. New clothes from the outfitter didn't suit him: nothing really was his size. He was too short and too wide.

"What?" he said.

"You squared away?" I said.

"I got caught with my dick in my hand. Won't happen again."

"What if you weren't the problem?" I said. The team all looked at me now. Thompkins had a glass half-raised to his mouth, stopped there as the new idea crept across his features. "We were all pretty quick to put it off to desperation and surprise. But what if there's someone in town actually better than Franks? Sneaky, light-footed, who knows how to hit hard and with precision? Not some hungry pioneer, but a trained, competent, dangerous agent?"

That sunk in slowly. Thompkins finished his movement, sipped his beer. Franks went through the same motion but the glass went back just as full as when it had come up. A waitress wandered by, saw we weren't really big drinkers, kept busy elsewhere.

"So why not finish it off?" Garcia said. "Knife in the skull, busted neck, like that?"

"Because there's a longer game going on here," I said. "Williams."

"Yes, sir."

"Get Henry back here. We need The Truck."

"Jurisdiction-" she said, but I cut her off.

"Can wait. There's a global security issue here. We need to sweep the place fast and bug out. We're going home."

***

It took Henry eight hours to get in position. Fuel, speed, distance, ongoing transportation needs. The Truck couldn't fly direct to Liverpool.

He came in high, infrared sweeping the place for hot spots. Radiation isn't just heat, I know that, but it does produce heat. I packed my duffel ready for departure, which took basically zero time. Hadn't pulled anything out but a change of skivvies.

We met about a kilometer out of town more for safety than cover. Secrecy was a secondary consideration at this time. One World Government really only tolerated the Free Zone rather than condoning it. The Truck swept down in a blur of flying dirt and broken grass stems settled into the hardened mud. The hatches opened. Everyone boarded quickly and I patched into the internal com as The Truck lifted back off.

"What have you got, Henry?" I said.

"Same as you," he said back. "About six hundred little farms, all of them with artificial heat but nothing that looks like large quantities of radioactives."

"Why didn't we just sweep from the air to begin with? Or satellite?"

"Not a lot of polar orbiting birds with the sensors you want, and the ones we have tend to zip by pretty quick in low orbit. Easier to see things nearer the equator. But that's all secondary."

"Primary?" I said, losing patience.

"Orders," Henry replied.

"Fine," I said. "Next stop, the port on the coast. Only logical place. It's where Lewinski was seen. Lots of goods in and out. Absolutely no logic in storing your WMD in a farming village miles from anywhere."

"Unless they are the target," Williams said.

"What?"

"The Soviet problem, you said. And, why bother? Isn't that right?"

Yeah. In the dream, I'd asked Lewinski, *why bother poisoning dead people*?

"Finish the thought," I said, but I knew where she was going.

"These are going to be the last people left alive, aren't they? How long can they live down here, in increasingly temperate conditions, while the rest of the planet turns into a burn scar?"

"Henry?" I said.

"Yes, Boss."

"Change of plans. From where could one launch a high to middle altitude chemical attack?"

"Range," he said. "Solar voltage motors, if you can get your load airborne... anywhere, Blanks. It could come from anywhere."

"Thompkins. Can you patch into those satellites? From here, the ones with heat sensors?"

He stripped off his coat to expose his wrist device and tapped on it furiously. "Need authorization," he said after a minute.

"Get it, fast. I need a scan, everything we have, for high-altitude vehicles with anomalous heat signatures."

The crew stared at me. I ignored them, and played another hunch. I cut off transmission to the cabin circuit so nobody inside could hear me over the engine noise. Then: "Wizard, we could use a hand here," I said.

"Make it quick," came a voice in my ear.

"Whatever Thompkins is working on, I need it to work," I said.

"That's a lot of red tape to just cut through," The Wizard said a few seconds later.

"But if you're watching and hearing everything, you know why it's important," I said back. "Patched into my eyes and ears, right? Through my implants? We'll talk about that later. For now..."

Thompkins *whooped*. "I don't know what you did, but I've got it, I've got everything. Scanning now, starting close, radiating search pattern... There it is, shit, it's right on top of us!"

Henry's voice came in now. "Radar signature, six kilometers, altitude eighteen thousand meters. Transport, C88 type. No radio identifier."

I patched back into local comm. "Can you hit it from here?"

"Are you willing to take that on yourself?" Henry replied.

"No time to think this through, Henry. Take out the target."

A dull thud ran through The Truck's superstructure as a missile kicked off.

***

The dock master's office was warmer than on our last visit, and it was crowded. Me, Garcia, Williams, Hull, Franks and Thompkins. Henry stayed with The Truck. He always stays with The Truck. The little dock master was there, eyeing us over a cargo manifest, and eight dock workers all dressed in black.

"Are we under arrest?" one of them said. He was tall, built heavy. Like if Franks spent some time on a rack.

A second man had a tooth missing in front and sandy brown hair that hadn't really all grown back yet. He said, "You said we'd be safe down here. They wouldn't come looking for us down here."

"You're safe," I said. Williams shot me a look but I ignored her. "Our time is almost up anyway. I mean, who am I to drag you back up there, to fight for people who're going to be dead anyway in a year or ten years?"

"Desertion is a summary offense," Williams said.

"They didn't desert. Did you, boys? You resigned, right? And we just lost the paperwork."

There was a lot of nodding and head-shaking.

"Just tell me one thing," I said. "You were going to kill us, weren't you?"

"Yes," said the guy with the missing tooth. The other guys hissed at him to shut his mouth but he went on. "Only Davy said there was no point. Once you'd seen us, everyone had seen us. We wore the same gear you wear, once."

"You must've wanted out pretty bad," I said, and pointed at gap-tooth's arm.

"Yeah," he said, and rolled up his sleeve. There was a big chunk missing out of his forearm, a huge, messy scar twenty centimeters by ten. "Walls worked in medical, got the supplies we needed. Not all of us lived through the procedure. The ones in our eyes and ears we couldn't help, but they all run through the arm com anyway."

"All right," I said. "We're done here. Saddle up."

"You're really not taking us in?" tall man said.

"Really," I said. "Stay. Make a life. Soon, you'll be the only ones left who can. And tell Annie we said thanks." Then we split that scene. Henry had the truck warmed up.

Back in the air again, with a rendezvous arranged for transport out of Argentina, I got Henry on the comm. "Damage assessment?" I said.

"Did more good than harm," Henry said. "Target continued sixty kilometers due to high altitude and velocity. Failed to deploy weapon system. Held together pretty good, dispersal minimal. There's a big patch out in the tundra that's going to need cleaned up."

"We getting a team on it?"

"Above my pay grade," Henry replied.

"If we don't that's it for this settlement," I said.

"Still above my pay grade."

"So was taking that shot," I said.

He didn't answer.

So I did what soldiers do when nobody needs killing right away. I ate powdered jellyfish, washed it down with jellied water, and slept. I'd saved a lot of people and that felt good. But we were still no closer to Lewinski.

I was going to go home and brace my boss with some very serious questions.

Four

The flight wasn't long. We all slept through it. Sleep when you can, eat when you can. It was too noisy for conversation anyway.

The nearest airbase was in the Falklands. We barely made Argentina, though. Henry got us refueled at a standard gas station, somehow without ever leaving the cockpit. Then we got in the sky again, another couple hours to the islands.

We didn't see anything of the Falklands except the airfield, where we were shoved aboard another cargo plane. I slept the rest of the way to Liverpool.

We managed to skip another one of those chopper-drops. No need: no infiltration. In fact, from the airport we rode into headquarters in a motorcoach, an old one converted to electric.

Headquarters: a hospital building abandoned in the 2000's. Budget problems, flooding and high winds. The sea had crept up within a few hundred feet of the parking lot and a constant howling gale etched the west walls with salt water.

But the place had everything we needed: keep-out fences, electric generators, independent food-sourcing, a hardened basement. That used to be a morgue but what did we care? The unit was a bunch of killers. None of us was afraid of spooks and at least it was cool down there. We just put up fabric panels like it was a basic cubicle farm.

We got into the briefing room right away, no comfort stops. I had to piss like a racehorse but it would have to wait.

"Nobody else coming?" Garcia said. "If it's just gonna be us, I gotta take a leak like nobody's—"

A voice from the tabletop cut her off. A little speaker disgorged The Wizard's virtual presence into the room. "Save it a minute. We have to talk."

"Yes, sir," I said, not quite coming to attention.

"We're not secure here," he said.

"Bullshit," Franks said, snatched his pistol and field knife into his hands.

"No bullshit, but you won't need the weapons right now. New orders: get squared away, then you're heading to Kamchatka to talk to a gentleman called Fyodor. You won't need his last name."

"Is it Dostoevsky?" Williams said.

"Let's assume yes," he went on. "This guy is into sentience."

I looked sidelong at Williams but talked to the radio box. "What, am I supposed to pick him up?"

"I thought you said you were ready."

"Sorry, Boss. Go on."

He sighed. "Artificial intelligence is passé. His work is machines that can not only think but that can reflect on the nature of existence. Have a sit-down with him. Kamchatka. And... ask him about the singularity."

"What happened out there, sir?" I asked.

"That's classified," he said.

"Bullshit." I wasn't the one who said it.

"Be that as it may. There is a lot going on here even I do not understand."

The line went dead.

"Shit," Franks said. "Fucking Russia. And the far side. We'll be in the air ten hours."

Garcia said, "That recruiter said I'd see the world..."

The rest of us finished for her: "He didn't say it would be all in one week."

No chance to sleep or eat or even shower. I at least picked up my pills from my billet downstairs. Rather than take any chances about being in field too long again, I pocketed the whole bottle.

***

"A church?"

"That's what the man said," Williams replied. She pointed at the door.

It was a little Byzantine thing. Old stone walls were covered in layers of paint, bright primary colors. It had a steep sloping roof in blue tiles and a minaret wearing a bright yellow onion hat. Inside, pews jammed together in the small space. The walls were close and gaily painted, with crude icons drawn into niches and stained glass everywhere. We just about filled the place up. Thompkins went all the way front and left, Franks took up half of the back right pew. Garcia and Williams were smaller but stood out in Russia as I did, dark faces in the world's whitest place.

A little man, middle-aged but hale, sat at the right front. Since he was the only local (aside from a scared-looking priest who wandered in from a side door and scampered right back out again) I assumed he was Fyodor. I plopped down next to him.

When he spoke, I imagined I could see his breath. The temperature was sweltering, but that little church screamed winter. No, that wasn't right. Cold, isolation, death. My emotions clawed at me, futility shooting waves of despair through my chest like a heart attack. No reason.

"Sorry," I said. "No Russian." No time for difficult, inexplicable feelings.

He nodded. "English will have to do, then." His English was unaccented. He had a gray face to match his gray shirt.

Dour lips and epicanthic folds that made him of Mongol stock, from that borderland where white people sometimes were culturally Chinese and Asian-looking people Russians. His appearance was as disheveled as it was chaotic. His shirt lacked a button and there was a stain on one pocket.

"Is there a message in this meeting place?" I said.

"Don't you like my church?"

"Me, I'm just a dumb-ass army girl," I said. "I don't know why they schlepped me halfway around the damned world but I assume it's because you have something important to say. So maybe we could skip the small-talk and get to it." That weird feeling of despair wasn't going anywhere. I could hear it in my voice.

He half smiled. "A pragmatist, yet. We'll all be dead soon so let's get to business. Is that it?"

"In a nutshell."

Now he did smile. "So what do you think of my little church?"

I didn't smile. I did stop and think. Looked around. Saw the podium up front, carved with symbols from various religions. Looked at the stained glass: here, a window depicted Buddha under his Bodhi tree; there, Shiva kicked the asses of some ancient demon-gods; there, Christ made sad eyes as a Roman stabbed him on his cross – brown Jesus, white Roman.

"You're pacifists," I said.

"Yes."

"There isn't really time left for that," I said. "Any lessons we've failed to learn will have to wait for the next life. So, what am I here for?"

"That's the question, isn't it?"

That was really my limit. I was no novice to sit at the feet of the inscrutable master. He must have seen the set of my mouth, some other sign of my intentions.

"No, don't get up, it all pertains. What your Wizard wants you to know is, you are looking for a machine capable of asking such questions."

"And he couldn't just tell me that through my implant? Voice from God, like that?"

"Maybe you have to be in a church to really hear it," he said.

"Look, like I said, I'm just an army girl. Theology is for those who can afford the luxury of clean hands. Just tell me where I'm supposed to go and what to do when I get there." My voice must have been getting loud: Williams looked at me sharply. Annoying riddles and inexplicable grief warred for control of my body.

"You are looking for a place capable of making very sophisticated machine parts, ultra-clean and bio-synthetic. So sophisticated they might pass as organic, might even be organic by usual measures of the word."

I thought of Lewinsky in that Bolivian interrogation room, pulling off one hand, cuff dropping to the table in a puddle of blood. Putting the hand back on, doing the same with the other hand while Rene Aguilera just watched in horror, her life about to end. "Antarctica?" I said.

"No red herring. Nor any great waste of time," he said. "The last people to live on this world will live there. Now who could want them poisoned, the land made radioactive?"

"People who can survive radioactivity, or just plain nihilists." I said the second thing just to be difficult. I saw now where this was going. "The Soviet problem," I said.

"Here we call it the American problem, but yes."

"Artificial people, immune to climate change and immune to levels of radiation that would kill mortal humans. Uploaded intelligences?"

He showed me his teeth, one of nature's least charming smiles. "The ultimate solution to the problem, yes? But something has gone wrong."

"And if I destroy the fabrication capacity, nobody has any further cause to accelerate the end of time. Fine. Where to start looking? That's what you really know, isn't it?"

"Yes," he said.

"I'm sorry about your wife," I told him. It was mean, a shot to unbalance him, so he'd feel like I felt: adrift.

"My wife?" he said, eyebrows moving together. "What about her?"

"You're losing her or you've lost her. You tech people are all the same. Without a spouse to care for you, you fall to pieces. That shirt needs to go into a trash can."

"Cancer," he said. "It will be over soon. Forty years... Well, if your concern is sincere, I am grateful for it."

"Sorry." I didn't mean that yet.

"Not your fault. No, no message in the choice of place – except that I prefer public places when meeting One World Government officials. Is 'official' the right choice of words for an assassin?"

"I can't deny that," I said. "I've killed people before and I don't regret it. What I need you to do is tell me who to kill next."

"That," Fyodor replied, "is well outside my interests or expertise."

"Of course. My boss sent me to ask you about a few things, though. First, the singularity."

He smiled. "That's above *your* interests or expertise. It is the time when artificial intelligence is so successful that actual sentience is inevitable. Sometimes also referring to the future time when humanity merges with technology. Becoming a self-selecting being."

"Intelligent selection?"

"If you credit people with intelligence, yes." He laughed at his own joke. Usually when meeting new people you feel the urge to laugh with them, a bonding social experience more than a reaction to humor. But Fyodor's laugh had nothing to do with bonding or humor.

"Can I trust you?" I said, not really sure why.

"Of course not. Have a nice day, it was nice to meet you." He stayed in his seat, but the message was received loud and clear. And there was something in his face, in the way he held his hands. Regret? He made eye contact briefly but then let it slide away.

"Five by five," I said. "I don't see what that has to do with anything. The singularity."

"Can't help you with that, I'm afraid. Most of the things I know are fairly abstract. Esoteric, even." That slide of the eyes again: touching, making contact, slipping away.

"Well then, seeing as I'm more of a practical sort, how about this: where would be the best place to set up shop making people?"

"Bedroom?"

"Not babies. Synthetic people."

"Well, there's your connection," he said. "The dividing line between human and artifice would be narrow indeed if we could make people without sperm and eggs. Where, you said? Well, nowhere, really."

"I'm going to need a little more than that to go on," I said.

"I'm not being obtuse. It's just that there isn't really one great place in the world to do what you are saying. I suppose I would want a certain degree of privacy, and a certain degree of sophistication in facilities. But if you have money, you can have those things anywhere. Goodness. Chips are easy enough to get. Even high-quality sub-micron chips. I think someone has you chasing at shadows, though."

"How so?"

He steepled his fingers, a pedant in his natural environment. "Because you cannot have an artificial person without artificial intelligence, including sentience and agency. And attempts to produce such things have experienced negative outcomes and a certain degree of cost-overrun. Plus far too much heat to be dispersed from something the size of a human body."

"I smell Russian reticence and understatement."

He smiled. "Someone who could do what you are saying... and keep it secret, and not try to sell it, and keep anyone else from selling it... Someone like that would be very dangerous."

"Why?"

"Because they would not want anything or need anything. They would have to be so rich that no resource of yours could satisfy any need of theirs. If they decided to get hostile, it would be because you were in their way, and your demise would be non-negotiable."

"I'm not easy to kill," I said to cover up the fact that the flesh was crawling on the back of my neck. Fyodor let out another of those uncharming smiles and that didn't help.

"We're all one thing. Did you know that?"

"Human?"

"Well, yes, but that's too simple. The universe is made of energy. They probably taught you in college that energy is matter in motion, but that is not the whole story. Energy and matter are the same thing. When you look at things at a smaller level than you can see, you discover it's all one thing. We are just different waves cresting on the same ocean. Is a wave separate from the sea? You and I are the same. Made of the same stuff, wanting the same things, created from the same forces, two hands meeting here together to clap. But two hands of one body."

"This is definitely—"

"Above your pay grade, yes. But it's important. Shall I repeat it? Say it twice?"

That got my attention. "Do you think you should?"

"I think you understand," he said.

I was getting that creepy feeling along my neck again, down my spine. "Maybe I'd better go."

"Perhaps you should. Stay if you mean to stay, go if you mean to go."

"I don't like riddles."

"This is a house of peace. Soldiers are not welcome here. Except if they mean to stay. I am you, you know, just as guilty as you of all your sins. You do not regret the murders you have done but I do. They stain my soul. When you are gone, I will beg forgiveness."

"You'll have to pray for us both, then," I said. When I strode out the tall, white doors into the Summer heat, the five other killers came with me. I had never felt more like putting bullets into somebody.

"We got a target, boss?" Garcia said.

"No. We've got nothing," I said. "That guy was a fucking nutcase. Dumbest smart person I ever met."

Then a voice in my head demanded my attention.

"Blanks. What do you got?" It was Raskin.

I relayed what Fyodor had said as word for word as I could. "You want to run a database search for whatever is farthest from human habitation, dry, arid climate, no roads, self-sustained power? Fabrication plant, high energy usage, no saleable products?"

The line stayed open. Five minutes, seven, ten. I walked with my team out of town to where Henry waited with the Truck. As we arrived, Raskin came back. "Australia," he said. "Sending coordinates."

Five

Australia. The Outback.

If Africa was hot and desolate, Australia was a hellish wasteland.

I crawled forward over charred and ashen ground, knees and elbows on the tortured earth. Garcia, Hull and Franks waited behind, by The Truck; Thompkins and Williams flanked me. We crested a small rise, what passed for terrain out here. My contact lens clicked over to extreme magnification and a gray dot on the horizon snapped into view.

A concrete building, square and windowless. A second building, smaller and connected with a flyway, sat a few meters away from it. That one had windows.

"You see any doors?" I said.

"Negative," said Thompkins.

"Garcia brought a door," Williams said.

I grunted. The sun beat down against my back. Black uniforms over body armor, black gloves and helmets and face masks, and little consideration for the body's temperature regulation needs. Out here it was easily eighty Celsius.

"Let's get on with it," I said.

Thompkins crept over the rise. He rolled up one sleeve to access his wrist device through a port in his wrist armor. "I've got a radio wall at about five thousand meters and a radar screen at about three thousand. Motion detectors randomly placed a bit past that."

"That's a lot of territory to keep covered," I said. "A fifteen kilometer perimeter, thirty-one and a half square kilometers, give or take. Bet they have equipment failures all the time. All this dust..."

As I spoke, a wind picked up and gathered surface ash from the ground. It fluttered around like grainy black snow.

Thompkins nodded, hardly perceptible in his helmet. "Give me two hours," he said. "We can go in at dusk, with a little preparation."

He crawled back under the rise then trotted to the Truck for some gear. Then he set off at a jog, parallel to our target.

"He doing what I think he's doing?" Williams asked.

"That depends," I said. "Is it righteous?"

"I guess this whole raid is questionable," she said. "He's certainly not going to do any worse than infiltration, is he?" Infiltration was going to be hard and probably violent. This whole conversation was just pedantry, really, something to pass time.

"No," I said. "He'll just jam up some of their transmitters on the far side and wait for the trucks. When they arrive, he'll mess with some other systems, keep leading them around. By the time he forces a hole for us after dark, their repair crews will be convinced they have some system-wide problem."

Williams looked skeptical but that's how we operate: tricks and deception followed by audacity and, usually, explosions. "Too late to complain about it now," she said.

"It was too late when you signed your name on the line," said Garcia. "Goddamn recruiter."

All part of the ritual.

"None of this is really legal," Williams said. "But if we're assuming this is one of Lewinski's places, and we've got more than circumstantial evidence, we can't exactly go up and knock on the door."

Circumstance was about all we had. That and desperation.

We didn't hear from Thompkins, which was fine because we had to assume our usual frequencies were under surveillance. I leaned against the Truck and tried to sleep but I was restless and it was too hot, too hot by far. It hurt even to breathe out here, and Thompkins was jogging in it.

Franks and Garcia got to talking to pass the time.

"So what the hell happened out here?" Franks said. "This isn't just global warming. Did Mad Max finally get his Pockyclipse?"

Old movies were kind of Franks' thing. "Just fires," Garcia said. "They got started in about two thousand five. Really got kicking in the twenty-tens. This place was a wasteland long before that; even the locals, the natives stayed out of here. Dried up like a sponge in the sun and the fires rolled through over and over. Nothing left but ashes now."

It looked to me like even the sand had burned. The surface of this desert was like black, broken glass, jagged and twisted. A billion little shards, too brittle to do any harm, formed a crust two or three centimeters deep, like a nuclear bomb had gone off out here. And it was still going off: the crushing sun forced me to move deeper into the shade.

Finally, that bastard started to go down. Dusk came to the desert like a sigh of relief. Bits of broken tree that had held some of their shapes in ash cast weird shadows as the angle of light slowly changed, like monstrous beings groping for air from beneath a sea of death. Thompkins came back into camp from the direction he had left. He was strong: I didn't see any fatigue in his movements. And

I pushed down on a special relief, denying I was gladder to see him than I would have been to see Franks or Hull under the same conditions.

"Good?" I said.

"We'll see," he replied.

A long time in the wind. A couple of critical failures were sapping our confidence.

Dark finally came full-on. It was hard to see the sky through blowing ash as the night wind rolled across this place, scraping away at the last of the cindery structures. Silently, we moved out.

***

I could see lights from a maintenance crew, chasing down the gremlins Thompkins had thrown into their system. We crouch-ran over broken ground, crunching through what had recently been a lake bed. Lake Frome was almost totally empty now and what remained was thick, ash-laden slurry. Here it was just more fractured desert.

The temperature dropped steadily, precipitously. Infrared and long-view wouldn't work both at the same time so it was tricky to stay on target. Garcia offered periodic course corrections, a silent gesture to bear a little left, a little right. I was glad for the exercise: too long cooped up on transports.

There was a shaky moment when a truck turned its lights our way, made to drive in our direction. We stopped where we were, mice in the owl's shadow. Thompkins fiddled with his arm for a second. "We're right on top of a motion sensor," he hissed. He fiddled some more and the truck stopped, maybe a kilometer out, reversed course and veered away. Given the black sky and the black ground, its lights might have been suspended in space for all I could see.

"What did you do?"

"Gave them a bigger reading somewhere else," he said.

All in all it took thirty minutes to cover the rest of the ground, a glacial pace for Special Forces soldiers. I pasted myself up against a concrete wall, more or less under the flyway. "Door," I said, and Garcia slapped plastic charges on the wall. She nodded and the rest of us dodged around the corner until we heard the boom.

Thompkins went in first, weapons at ready. Infrared was useful again, something to see besides dust and darkness: I went in behind him, dodging left as he went right, covering Williams and Franks. Garcia brought up the rear. In front of us was a staircase and a door. The stairs would lead to an office complex and the flyway to personnel housing, in the connected building. The door to a plant, where they manufactured whatever it was they built out here, in the desolate desert a hundred kilometers from any other structure.

Thompkins advanced on the door. It was steel, two meters by one point five. Big pneumatic cylinders and a little touch-plate with a single red light. He did something with his wrist. The plate clicked and the red light went off – then came right back on. He tried again and this time it switched over to green. As the door started to hiss open, sliding off to the left, I pointed Thompkins and Williams upstairs. "Smash and grab," I said, breaking radio silence.

Through the door. There were security lights on, three of the thirty or so overhead fluorescents. The scene they lit was about incomprehensible. I made sure to look at each thing, one eye recording infrared, the other normal light. If

I survived back to The Truck, I could upload the whole mess onto a carrier signal back to Liverpool.

I strode into the room. It was eighty meters by thirty. We'd come in a door on the east wall; one other door sat in the center of the north wall. Right in front of me was a workstation, a steel bench littered with electronic components. There was a safe under the bench and a bank of computers behind it. The computers were cased up like an old-time supercomputer (my wrist could do more than a Cray from back in the day), meaning that office-cabinet sized stack of chips had amazing computational power. What the hell was it for?

Other stations were laid out in a rough grid pattern. To the left was some kind of plastic tent. The plastic was opaque. Inside, something expanded and contracted making a pneumatic noise like the door. To the right, a black pod glistened, misty and organic, twice the size of my single bed at headquarters. Pipes and hoses ran into it from the floor and ceiling and another bank of computers buzzed and clicked nearby, wired in at a time when nearly all connections were wireless. I was like a tourist in the big city. Time ticked away while I stood, gawking.

I walked between two rows of lockers padlocked shut, little combination locks any human might recognize from standardized high school. I smashed one open. Inside were all sorts of electronic devices. Amp-meters and voltage meters and stuff far outside my comprehension.

Franks and Garcia did as I did, walked around the place at a brisk pace and eyeballed everything from every angle.

A light came on over the north wall. It hissed, started to slide open.

"Weapons," I said. Whoever came through there would not have our best interests at heart.

Garcia had a pulse rifle in her hands, and she turned to point it at the doorway. Franks had a pistol. Stupid choice but he was a good shot and it left one hand free for knife work. He liked knife work.

I unslung my rifle.

People came through. Eight, then ten, then twelve. They had long rifles with scopes. Whatever all this gear was for is was more than expensive: it was valuable. Their security people had body armor and visored helmets, and one spoke in an amplified voice:

"Put down your weapons. We are authorized to use deadly force."

Williams was not here to advise, but all their weapons were illegal.

"Me too," I said back, also amplified. And I proved it: my rifle had full auto capacity. I sprayed out bullets across the fifty meters that separated us. Three of them dropped. Their armor was not rated for high caliber armor-piercing rounds. Garcia dropped four more with her pulse rifle, boiling their blood – no armor in the world was rated for that. Then they decided whatever machines were in here were not as valuable as their own lives and scattered, ducking behind banks of computers, racks of electronics, a man-sized cylinder full of viscous blue fluid.

More people came through the door we'd used. Another six. Franks discouraged them with his pistol then dived for cover under a steel table. He got one of them; the rest fanned out and found cover.

"Williams' team," Garcia said through her voice implant, into the one in my ear.

"They're capable of handling themselves," I said back, and I knew it was true, and still I *hoped* it was true. I saw Garcia run through moderate fire, leap over a workbench covered in obscure tools, hit the ground in a baseball slide into good cover. I just stood where I was, presenting a target.

They took advantage drawn, as people naturally are, to the easy kill. Except I was just about bullet-proof.

My armor was rated for any kind of bullet a gun could fire. It couldn't stop a tank shell or an energy weapon, but they weren't going to fire those in here. Bullets pinged off my chest plate, off my helmet, even the face mask. And when a bullet hit me, I turned to track it back to its point of origin. If I could see the shooter, I could kill them. One. Two. Three. A fourth person ducked behind something that looked expensive – but I didn't care about that. I shot it all to hell. I heard her scream of pain and outrage but I cared about that even less. My after-action report would say something like "kill not confirmed visually" but she was as dead as she needed to be: she never shot at me again.

I lost track of Franks. Someone shouted and cut-off mid phrase and I figure he'd sliced their neck.

Two more people stepped through the door and Garcia cooked them. But we were losing ground.

My armor integrity read low on my heads-up display. Time to back off. A shooter popped up behind a steel cabinet, let fly a round, dropped back down. My returned fire shattered on the edge of the cabinet. Two more shooters had found good enough cover to start to snipe me. I couldn't face them anymore, not and survive the encounter.

But my back armor was still fine.

I turned and ran for the south wall. I vaulted a desk, ran between two black tanks that smelled like formaldehyde, ran straight into a woman with a knife in each hand. I just ran her down, left her bloody and broken, sagging against a rolling office chair. Then I hit the south wall, bullets pinging and popping all around me.

And there was Franks on the north wall, now with a clear view of each and every shooter. Garcia crouched in the east door. They began to clean up, with no regard for the integrity of any equipment in the room.

Meanwhile, Garcia wasn't the only one with portable doors. Reinforcements would be along presently and we needed another way out. I slapped two patches against the concrete then ran back as I'd come, still taking fire: I held my wrists up over my face and chest, a weak shield, until I was able to slide under something heavy. "Henry, I need an extraction," I said.

"Willco," he said in my earpiece.

"Team, it's time to evac. North wall, all speed."

I got confirmations. Garcia and Franks dropped out of view. Four enemy combatants remained. The charge went off, all four turned to look. I got one more with an inelegant spray of bullets and then I was out. Down to grenades, and throwing grenades inside a structure one occupies is bad practice. Said structures tend to fall down on one's head.

Time to leg it.

I scrambled out of cover, sprinted back towards the hole I'd blown in the door. I could hear Garcia right behind me, Franks lumbering in from one side.

I was almost to the shattered wall, almost outside, when two people stepped into the gap from either side, guns ready. I dropped and rolled, Garcia threw herself against the wall. And they shot Franks.

With pulse rifles.

He fell, half-cooked. Electronics fried and bubbled behind him, a fire getting started, the smell of ozone mixing with the stench of cordite and blood and ruined bowels.

I was on the ground right in front of them, no rounds left, pulse rifles trained at my face.

I could practically hear the tendons creaking in their fingers.

But both of them exploded in a gout of blood and bones, cut apart by a storm of fifty-caliber bullets that nothing on Earth could throw except a revolving Browning machine gun.

"Thanks, Henry," I said, not feeling as nonchalant as I sounded. No, I felt decidedly chalant.

I went back for what was left of Franks, threw the corpse over one shoulder. Hustled out through the wreckage, into the desert of the Australian outback. Henry's absurd, antique guns whirred again and people fell dead where they'd emerged from around the far corner. He set down and I tossed Franks in, clambered in after him, strapped his corpse in with the gear in the middle of the cabin.

"Got a radar lock," Henry said.

"Shit." That probably meant this place had antiaircraft. "Better be ready to roll."

Garcia scrambled in. "What about Williams?" she said.

"I'm here," Williams said, and relief squeezed a tear from my eye. She and Thompkins clambered aboard and Henry got us airborne. Thompkins hauled the hatches closed. The whole ship rocked and rocked again. Then we settled into racing attitude, nose-down and hell for leather.

"Henry, we got radio uplink?" I said.

"Fifteen seconds." A moment later, "Entering sat coverage now."

"Call in an airstrike on that compound. My authorization. Williams, witness." She nodded, stripping off her mask and helmet. "We lost Franks," I said. "And I don't know that we got anything useful. Shooting at us is summary, is all I can think of: they were up to something bad."

"We got something," she said. And she tossed an object in my lap. It flopped like a wet dishrag. Then she unstrapped and went to hold Franks' hand. He was beyond any such ministrations.

I got out of my own headgear. There was blood on my face from fragments of failing armor. It got on my hands and then onto the thing she'd thrown me as I examined it. It was soft, disturbing. Like skin. "What the hell?" Then I saw eye holes. A mouth. "A mask?" I held it up, looked at it in low-light mode. "Lewinski?"

"Lewinski," Williams said. "Now we know how he can be two places at once."

I felt the inside of the thing. It was coated in tiny spines, hair-like needles. I didn't know computers, much less robots, but I wondered if those might connect to a motor or sensor system. Or both.

Thompkins was out of his gear. It wasn't really safe yet to be unstrapped in the cabin but he didn't care any more than Williams did. He just came around to check the living.

He went to her first, helped her out of body armor. The back of her shirt was crispy; he lifted it to see her skin. Williams had a pretty good burn, a barely-ducked pulse beam. Thompkins got a tube of salve from the med kit and dabbed her gently.

My turn. I was beat all to hell from bullet impacts but I'd heal. I always did. Well, as long as I took my pills. Thompkins put a different kind of salve on the worst of the bruises and dermal patches on the couple of cuts on my face. He only had two of those left. His big hands were tough, leathery, but tender. As usual, I wondered if there were something in his touch beyond medical interest.

He caught me looking into his face. "What?"

"What if we weren't soldiers?" I said.

"But we are," he said back.

"Yeah. But what if..."

He looked into my eyes for a minute. Said nothing. *Damn.* "Henry," I said, "I need you to patch me in to HQ."

It was a moment before he replied, "Negative, boss. Incoming transmission from Liverpool: headquarters is compromised. Oh three hundred Greenwich Mean Time. A raid, it looks like. All special-forces operations suspended pending investigation."

"What?"

"Uh, two different feeds running here, boss. I'll patch them in presently. Looks like we were infiltrated. Location revealed, heavy assault. Doorbuster bomb followed by armed incursion."

"What?" I couldn't think of anything else to say. Because all other words choked in my throat, all other thoughts blocked up my mind. Raskin? Hull? Who else?

Henry stayed quiet, no more information to relay. But the shape of it played across my troubled mind. The implications were clear. I watched everyone and thought crazy things.

I wanted another ten minutes with Fyodor. Question: would a simulation of you be smarter than you?

Imagine something smart enough to simulate you. The closer you come to a full-scale model, the more that model is a prototype rather than a model. A full scale model of the universe must be the entire universe, or else something is left out.

I didn't see anything left out of any of my friends. Therefore, the simulation was sophisticated – probably smarter than any of them. Would a simulation know it was a simulation? Could it simulate the intelligence of a human?

It had been a long time since college. My degree was applied engineering anyway, not philosophy. And I'd never smoked any pot in any case.

Shit.

Think fast, Blanks.

"Henry, you got a protocol for an infiltrated team?"

"Yes, ma'am," he said right back.

"Better enact it now." I had everyone's attention. "There's a mole and it's one of us."

"I wish you hadn't said that," Henry said.

"Yeah, I know," I said.

Then the cabin air started to taste sour. A barely visible fog wisped down out of the air exchangers. Thompkins went first, on his face next to Franks. Then Garcia and Williams. I breathed deeply, heavily, wishing I could go first, but I outlasted them all.

* * *

Someone touched my elbow. Right in the joint, where that electric nerve is that reminds you not to touch it.

"I'm awake," I said, unable to jerk away. I opened my eyes, found there was a stone ceiling overhead. I was on my back, strapped down to something cold and hard. "Protocol?" I said, rasping.

"'Fraid so," Henry said. "You might feel a little sick."

"I haven't puked in years," I said.

"This isn't a drop. The drugs will mess you up pretty good for a couple more hours. Now. What makes you think all this is necessary?"

"Sequence," I said. "They keep us away on bullshit assignments. We get home. Raskin says we ain't supposed to be there. We leave, place gets hit. Someone gave us away and it must have been us. One of us."

"Why not me?" he said.

"No good reason. Could be you, Henry. Could be anyone. Can you stand me up?"

He reached up behind him and I started to tilt, feet towards the ground. As I did so, I could see the rest of the team similarly inconvenienced. They were all awake.

"Good morning," Williams said.

I opened my mouth to say something smart and puked instead. On Henry's shoes. Henry cranked me forward some to keep the worst of it off me and I saw that I wasn't the first, and then I *smelled* that I wasn't the first, and then I puked some more. "Hey, you do have legs." More puke. Then, "Jesus, don't you got a hose or something?"

"Water is something of a commodity these days," Henry said. "No sense using it to clean up the dead."

"Shit."

"Yeah," he said.

"Williams," I said, "You see a way out of this?"

"Logic," she said. "Antarctica."

"Yeah. Franks?"

"I'd say so, yes," she said. "He was the only one of us to be alone. When he went to pee then dropped out of contact. That's when it happened."

"When what happened?" Thompkins said.

I offered, "Franks was replaced with an artificial person. A copy."

"Bullshit," said Garcia.

"No, there's proof. The tapes from Bolivia, how Lewinski escaped custody. The mask Williams found in that plant. Even the ship we raided after Zaire. It all fits together."

"It's crazy," said Garcia.

"I know," I said. "But it all fits. Lewinski isn't a person. Or, if he is... What Fyodor told us. The Soviet problem. He uploaded himself into a replica, to survive what's happening now, only the copy went crazy. He's been trying to lead us to it ever since and we haven't been listening. And now whatever it is, whatever the artificial thing is, it's taken over. That plant we raided was only the half of it, I think. I think... Never mind that now. But Franks was the one out of contact with no good damn explanation, wasn't he?"

"We were all quick to buy that someone had gotten the drop on him," Thompkins said. "You're saying it was more than that."

"Look, you don't have to come with me all the way to crazy," I said. "He came back with some minor wounds. What if they were full of tracers? A microscopic transmitter, or a radioactive? It was still Franks."

"No," said Williams. "No, there's another alternative."

"What?"

"It was you," she said.

"Bullshit," Thompkins said. "She wouldn't-"

"No," I said. "No, she's right. If we're considering all the alternatives, I was solo, too."

"You never were," said Garcia.

"Yes, yes I was. Not in Antarctica. Before that. After Zaire. You guys had to come drag me off the beach, remember? Could have swapped me out anywhere between Cairo and Liverpool, between Liverpool and Odessa."

"Timeline doesn't fit," Thompkins said. "You were at HQ before."

"We were never so close before," I said. "It wasn't until Antarctica that we had any inkling what we were dealing with. We could have chased our tails forever. Think about it. I could be an enemy agent. Or, same as Franks, I could just be bugged. Remember the guy with the bloody nose when you picked me up?"

"Yeah," said Garcia. "You said he touched you."

"Could've planted a transmitter on me, or in me, right then."

"Shit," Thompkins said.

"So what do we do?" Williams said. "We come up with something? Or we let Henry push the other button on his hanging console there, and flush us all off the planet?"

"Neither," I said. Everyone stared at me. "What the Russian said: we're all going to be dead soon anyway, so let's get to business. He meant it as a joke, like. Business is pointless. It always was but now we can see it, have to face it. Another generation, maybe, and the world is not fit for habitation. So why bother?"

"So?" said Garcia. She was maybe the least philosophical of us.

"So, what difference does it make if one of us is one of them? Win or lose, in the long run, there is no long run. You want to step off the edge right now, that's OK. It's a good day to die. But, knowing one of us could be a... an artificial copy of our self, we can go on and do business as usual, but scan heavily for transmissions. Find out whose head is broadcasting. Find out what they want, and do the opposite. Or just go along and know they'll eventually cause something interesting to happen. Some confrontation."

"I don't know," said Henry. "These protocols protect the rest of the team..."

"There is no team, you said that yourself. Liverpool is extinct. And we're in the wind. Who can we hurt but us?"

"You can't lead," Thompkins said. "If it's you, you'll just lead us in circles. Away from everything important."

"Right," I said. "I elect Garcia."

"Me?"

"Least likely," I said. "Lowest rank, lowest influence. Great spy, no ability to cause any mayhem by leading in the wrong direction. Hey, it's thin, but it's the best we've got."

"Second," said Thompkins.

"This makes me uncomfortable," said Williams. "But given the alternative..."

"I'm glad you said that," said Henry.

"I knew you liked us," I said. "You couldn't just axe the whole team in cold blood."

"Well," he said, "that and protocol requires I do myself, too. Flood the whole compartment. Pretty painless, halon gas, sucks out all the oxygen and we just, we suffocate. This button here..." he reached up to where a little black console hung down on its axial cable from the ceiling, pushed the button... "releases the harnesses."

I fell down off the table, caught myself on one hand. Which was only half a victory because the hand went straight into a pool of vomit. "Hey," I said, "since we aren't corpses, how about we get cleaned up?"

Six

"First stop?" Henry said in my head.

I clicked shut my harnesses. We'd stashed Franks in the cave, unable to refrigerate him and without the right tools for a conclusive autopsy. The cabin still smelled faintly of his corpse. "Ask Garcia," I said.

"Scene of the crime," she said.

"Long way home from here, boss."

"I'm guessing you know all the secret fuel depots, and that people owe you favors," I said.

"Yes ma'am," he said.

"I'm even willing to bet you have a secret protocol for just such eventualities."

That, he would not speak to. But he got us moving, everyone strapped down. I watched the others watching me but, eventually, they did what soldiers do when nobody is trying to kill us.

I turned off intercom, turned off radio.

"Wizard. I need to talk to The Wizard. Right now."

I waited. I waited until I was sure he wasn't listening. But then he spoke. "I am listening," he said.

"Always?"

"More or less," he replied. "I do have to sleep, you know. But there are recordings for that."

"Why?"

"You know why," he said.

I didn't. But I had an idea. "I'm bringing the team home."

"Use your discretion," he said. "I will smooth the way. What else do you want to talk to me about?"

"Nothing, I guess," I said. "Nothing I think you would tell me. You already answered the most important question, by answering at all." First Antarctica and now here.

He didn't say anything else and neither did I. There was nothing more to say. So I did what soldiers do.

**

A news broadcast. We were in Egypt, taking on fuel. Thompkins had Williams stripped down to her shorts and was applying analgesic cream to her burns. Her back was to me, muscular and graceful. I looked for a moment before deciding that, even though she would never know, I'd honor her privacy. I turned my attention to the news piped into my earpiece, sitting on one of The Truck's skids.

"... levy collapsed, engineers citing low quality concrete and rushed construction. New York City currently under evacuation orders, dead estimated at eleven million, survivors in the low hundreds of thousands. High winds continue to threaten England's eastern seaboard, a record hurricane in a season of record hurricanes expected to destroy the last of her carefully-guarded outdoor trees. Resources have been shifted from protecting Thetford Forest to providing material aid to the eight million refugees currently crowding Northamptonshire. Mother Mary, still missing from the Vatican, was reported seen at the border between Germany and Italy, security cameras making facial recognition match to her known appearance. Finally in international news, the Mars Hope Mission selection panel is expected to complete their candidate review tomorrow morning and then to begin to issue invitations..."

I couldn't have said why, but at that moment I started to cry. To really cry, for us, for all of us. Those eleven million were just a drop in the bucket, the world's ten billion or so people right on the verge of collapse, and maybe that was it. I had to grieve a people who could face such losses, day after day, and still give a fuck about an eccentric Pope somewhere out there, mingling with the people to do something ultimately futile.

The right thing.

Thompkins got in front of me. "All right, let's see those cuts."

"What?"

"Your face."

"Oh, right."

He got close, his face just centimeters from mine. His breath smelled like chocolate. I noticed for the first time how feminine his lips were. And he had blue eyes. He looked at the wounds on my cheeks and I looked into his eyes.

Is it possible for someone like me to fall in love?

"I think you are healing well enough," Thompkins said. And he eased back out of my personal space.

I looked away, feeling a little guilty, like I'd taken something that had not been offered. Thinking of Williams. Willie. "Scars?"

"Yes," he said, "probably thin white lines. Not noticeable from a distance. Maybe you wanted to be a fashion model once all this is over? Your hands, though, concern me."

"Ha." That was for the idea of being pretty, for the job ever being over, and for there being anything afterwards. "What about my hands?"

They still leaked blood and thin yellow pus. Changing that truck tire in the cold had chewed me up worse than I thought.

"I don't have anything left for them. Try to keep them covered and clean. Make sure to take your pills. Maybe double up today, help those wounds coagulate."

"Better get back on board," I said. "Looks like Henry is done with his checks."

"How he can scrounge fuel in this day and age..."

I didn't tell him about The Wizard.

***

We swept in from the Atlantic side with hatches open and weapons ready. Below, buildings poked up out of the foamy green sea, a roof here, a spire there. Some old brick tenements with all the glass gone had barnacles on the seaward side, seagulls nesting on their rooves. The ocean rippled underneath us like a second shadow, downdraft unsettling things.

Then the sea turned to marshy sand and finally to a parking lot, empty for a decade. Henry set us down in two centimeters of water and I jumped out, heart racing, teeth clenched. It was irrational: the raid had been two days ago now and the chances of any residual force remaining in place were ludicrously low.

But this was home. My *house*.

Boots splashed into the water behind me. Garcia said, "You're with me. Tommy, Willie, secure the perimeter. Franks..."

I didn't even know what she wanted Franks to do but he was dead, dead and left behind in a cave in New Guinea somewhere. "Never mind. Get to work."

I trudged ahead, Garcia a step behind and to my left. We went straight at the front doors, the hospital building looming up out of its own reflection in the still, clear water. I stepped through a parking slot designated for the disabled, over a curb, on a concrete path. The glass double doors were blown out, most of the glass was shattered and scattered. It lay in dead hedges and in puddles and was strewn all through the dark lobby. An information desk from back when this had been a real hospital was blasted apart, bits in the doorway, pieces by the stairwell. Water dripped somewhere in the dark and otherwise there was silence.

"Want to wait on the others?" Garcia said.

"Do you want to?"

"Yeah," she said.

"Good, then." We stood there in the doorway. The lobby was three quarters of a circle with elevators in the straight wall, stairs behind a ruined door. Up and down. Up was nothing: the abandoned hospital people would expect to see. Down was home.

Williams and Thompkins splashed up behind us, joined us in peering into the dark. "Perimeter is good," Williams said. "No surprises."

"Garcia?" I said.

She stepped through the broken door, not bothering to open it. Sloshed across the lobby, alert for danger, not finding it. I followed to the stairwell. The doors were fully off their hinges and I hefted them aside. Water trickled down the stairs. "Without the pumps working, it could be a real mess down there," Garcia said.

We went down, the four of us in a stretched-out line, Garcia leading the way. Onto the meeting and ops level, dark and broken. The security door was as ruined as everything else, smashed and scattered. The walls were pocked with bullet holes, charred in places. There was blood dried on the front desk. Water and blood and ashes mixed into the thin pile of the carpets, sucking at my boots as I stepped forwards.

"No bodies," Thompkins said.

Someone had cleaned up, then. Ours or theirs, we couldn't yet say. Down a short hall, there was the conference room with its oval table and silly plastic chairs. *There's where Franks sat and called me out for deserting the unit in Zaire.* The place looked pretty normal, except for the power being down and water soaking into everything. Here it ran down the walls.

"Computer lab," Williams said. We followed her down another hall, around a tight corner. Another security door marked off this area as double-restricted: not even Special Forces clearance could get you in there. But that door hadn't survived the carnage.

The computer room looked as though someone had picked it up and shaken it. Microchips lay in shallow water, plastic and silicon and gold wires everywhere. All the screens were busted, all the casings shattered.

Williams went to the center of the room and pulled up a carpet tile. It came loose with a slurpy noise. Under the tile was a steel plate and she moved that aside, too, revealing a safe.

"What's that?" Garcia said.

"Back-up," Williams said. "Everything recorded on internal security up until the power went out. Maybe even after – some of the cameras have back-up batteries and this unit has independent power." She opened the safe – an old-fashioned dial lock – and pulled out a circuit board. It had three pins, each four centimeters long. She pulled those, put them in a protector that looked like an old matchbook, put that in her shirt pocket.

"Good?" I said.

"Just need a reader. Wrist device should do it. Not here, I think."

Garcia said, "Go down to residence and collect any personal effects you want. We're done here."

Good. She was getting more comfortable leading, ordering.

I went back to the stairwell. Slopped down to the residential level. My room was down a dark hallway. All the doors down here were blown off, the walls ravaged with bullets and worse. Here was a spatter of blood and brains. A couple of severed fingers floated in water up to my ankles.

My room had been tossed. There was nothing clean and dry in there to salvage. Even my toothbrush floated in the murk. And I didn't have a lot of personal effects to begin with.

Williams was across the hall. She was just a Captain, bunked with Watters. I came up behind her, saw her fish a copy of Sun Tzu out of the water and shake it. Pages dropped out along with water, and she just let it plop back down. It made an unimpressive splash. She turned and saw me looking. "My mother," she said, and started to cry, all her cool composure lost in this busted up dorm room under poor, lost Liverpool.

I don't know why I did it, but I stepped across the little room and put a hug on her. We cried together a little and then she straightened up, embarrassed. She pulled her clothes into position, put her game face back on. "We should go," she said. "There's nothing left here of any value."

"Yeah," I said, but I disagreed. Everything that had ever been of value was here, rotting gently in water that dripped and pooled and slowly rose. All the good years were here. The time, the loyalties, even the conflicts, all down here in the dark. Still, when she headed back for the stairs, I followed.

Gunshots.

They echoed through the place like someone beat on the foundations of the world. I broke into a run, a step behind Williams. Guns out, no armor because we hadn't seriously expected opposition. More shots.

At the top of the stairs, Thompkins lay in sniping position. Bullets crashed into the stairwell over his head. He snapped off a shot and then another one. "They were hiding in the upper levels," he said calmly, as if discussing the quality of jellyfish meal. "Waited until we were occupied, came down to try The Truck."

Well, they would find Henry a prickly sort of target. It would take some pretty heavy weapons to get to him.

I crept up next to Thompkins. There were two men in the parking lot, caught between us and the Truck. Thompkins shot them both, again as calm as anything. They dropped into the water. "Tide's coming in," I said, spying two more bodies starting to float out there.

"We should go," Thompkins said, echoing Williams.

"Garcia?" I said.

"Here." She was behind me, down the stairs a few paces. "Let's bug out. Never mind the upper levels. They don't want The Truck – they want what Williams has in her pocket. They want all our backup data."

"Why?" I said.

"Probably just to keep us from having it," she said, pushing by me and out into the lobby. "If what's happening is what you say is happening, nothing we know can help them, but keeping us in the dark and off their backs will speed things along."

I followed. We boarded up as Henry started the rotors turning. Williams was a minute behind us: she stopped to roll over the dead bodies.

"Who?" I said as she climbed in.

"Four dead bodies, no ID's. Didn't recognize anyone. Will run their face through recognition databases when we're mobile."

"Give me the pins," Garcia said. The rotors thumped, filling the cabin with noise, but her voice was clear through my auditory implants.

Williams looked at her like a dog eyes a wolf. "Why?"

"You agreed to follow my lead. Because nobody else is trustworthy. You're somebody else." Garcia leaned forward as much as she could with five-point harness engaged, held out her hand.

"She has a point," I said.

Williams' eyes left Garcia and landed on me. "You serious?"

"She has a point," I repeated. I hoped the message would land.

"All right," Williams said, and handed over the data sticks.

Garcia tucked them away in an interior pocket.

"Here's a thought," Thompkins said. "What if The Wizard knew this Fyodor guy had nothing of value to say?"

"Like, just getting us out of the way?" I said.

"So he knew for sure what was going to happen to Liverpool?" Garcia said.

"Does that make him the good guy or the bad guy?" I said.

"Only one way to know," Thompkins said. "Go and pick him up and ask him."

"The guy's a ghost," I said. "I mean, we can be spooky, but we've never even seen him. He's never set foot in Liverpool that I know of. We have zero leads."

"You could try asking," Henry said.

Not only did he not talk like the team he didn't think like the team either. "He won't say yes."

"Doesn't have to, I reckon. Just has to open a channel. Then we track it. Whoever is after you don't have the monopoly on the RF band."

I cued up The Wizard on my wrist but he buzzed in over the headsets before I could press *send*. "Good," he said. "I see you are back and decided not to kill each other. I need to divert you from wherever you had decided to go."

"We hadn't decided where to go," I said. "You've done maybe too good a job of compartmentalizing. No information, no leads."

"Yes, occupational hazard, I suppose. This is urgent, though. I have dropped Henry some coordinates. And a fuel depot code. You will be heading for Petersburg. A day or so of guard duty."

"We don't do guard duty, Chief," I said.

"You do now. There will be an attempt and I expect extreme retaliation."

"You want us to prosecute a vendetta? Is this on-mission?"

"Until this is resolved, it is the mission," The Wizard said. "And leave Blanks in charge for this one. Play your games after. This is too important." Then he cut out.

"Damn."

A few voices around the cabin seconded as the engines started to whine and then to roar. The ground dropped out from under us, the cabin took its distinctive tilt forwards, and we were in rapid motion West across Russia.

"You get the feeling this is personal?" Thompkins said.

"Yeah. Is that just paranoia? We don't have much to go on."

"I feel it too," Thompkins said. "Guard duty. We've never pulled a shift on guard of anything or anyone, and going static is totally opposite our seek-and-destroy specializations."

"Duty, honor, service," I said.

"Sleep when you can," everybody else intoned.

"Pleasant dreams," Henry said. The cabin lights went out, music piped in over the speakers, and the noise became so loud it was like silence.

In the darkness, I switched on my night vision. Garcia had one eye half open – the infra-red side. Thompkins kept one hand on his rifle. Williams' eyes were shut but the lids twitched.

In general, it looked like not a lot of sleeping was going to get done. Anxiety, fear, mistrust – everyone watching everyone else. I didn't even pretend to sleep, just worked on these after-action reports.

Later: "Henry, did you catch The Wizard's signal when he called in?"

"Yes," he said.

"Trace?"

"Like you figured, he saw us coming. Routed through three different stations and a proxy server."

"But did you get him?"

He was quiet a minute. "No," he said.

Seven

"This is a house," I said.

"Nearly a mansion," Williams replied. "A home can be a fortress."

"Are you quoting something?"

She shook her head, pushed through the gate from the street into the front garden. Flowerbeds were hidden behind the wall, all bare this time of year except for the roses, which were green but not blooming. The six of us proceeded up the path, anxious because the wall around the garden limited our view of the street and the path put us all in a line from the door.

"Should we knock?" I said.

"Yeah." Thompkins hammered on the door. In my experience, civilians didn't appreciate how soldiers knocked. But we still didn't know who was inside.

A local police officer answered the door. It wasn't cold outside. At this latitude it seemed it would never be cold again. But he still wore his winter-weather Russian police gear, with black gloves and furry fringes.

"Expecting snow?" Thompkins said. He kept the sneer from his face but not out of his voice.

"Expecting you," the officer said. Then he said some things in Russian and marched past us onto the street.

"You stand relieved," I told him as he passed.

"And I am relieved, believe me," he said. There was something in his voice, contempt or distaste. Maybe Thompkins' hostility had created it. Hopefully.

Williams was first in, then Garcia with her pistol drawn. The rest of us followed suit, weapons ready but at port. Garcia turned her head toward a room at the other side of the house. Natural light spilled into this darkened hallway from there. Some big windows, maybe. We followed Garcia. She stopped in the threshold.

"Oh, guns. I don't like guns."

The speaker was a forty-ish woman with no trace of a Russian accent. She had white hair and lively eyes, smooth pale skin. She was a beauty and dressed like a fashion model in a cream-yellow skirt and sleeveless blouse. A blue neck scarf set off her eyes.

She matched the kitchen. It was full of creamy porcelain. Even the fixtures, clean and white like her skin. Those were painted with little blue and yellow flowers. The wall held plates with paintings of champion dogs – mastiffs and Labradors in dog-show poses. The walls had wallpaper with vertical stripes in gold and yellow. A tasty smell owned the air: fresh bread.

Along the windowsill, plants sat in terracotta pots. None of them belonged here. Cacti, something brown and spiny that wasn't a cactus, a pitcher plant.

"Sorry, sir," Garcia said. "I mean, ma'am," she added, when the lady frowned just ever so slightly.

"Perhaps rather than apologize you could just put the guns away? They make me nervous," she said.

"Please identify yourself," Williams said, flat.

"It's my house," she said, "so the question is rather bad manners, wouldn't you say? I'm JJ. You don't need to know any more than that. You're Williams. Your law degree shows in your eyes, dear. Which one are you – Garcia or Blankenship? Look about the same to me. Thompkins is the male, the medic. Am I right?"

"We're here to protect you," I said. "Which right now means please step away from that window. You need to be in an interior room and preferably below ground. This whole place is a nightmare so far as I can see. We should get you out of here right away."

"I'm not leaving," she said. "My husband tried that already and I won't go."

I said, "Thompkins."

He grabbed her arm, dragged her away. She was too small to put up a lot of resistance, Thompkins too big to be resisted. We hustled her through the house until we found a drawing room in the basement. No windows.

"I don't think you know who you're dealing with," JJ said after Thompkins put her in an easy chair. She sat forward, hands on knees, not at all as easy as the chair seemed to demand.

"Getting to be a habit with us, ma'am," I said. "Thompkins, sit on the lady. Williams, top floor. Garcia, you're with me. We check the perimeter." Thompkins looked unhappy with those dispositions, but he went along with it. Frowning, he took a seat on a fancy little couch that looked older than all of us.

The perimeter wasn't good enough. Just a six foot wall around the property. It offered almost no protection and obscured visibility.

"We need a new perimeter," Garcia said.

I nodded. She moved to the east wall, hopped over it onto the neighboring property – another major detraction – and went to peer in the windows.

"Not subtle," I muttered. But I did the same thing on the other side. Peeked in windows, poked around behind places. Dropped into the alley behind the house. The houses were tall but scenic. Unlike a poor neighborhood alley, this area saw traffic mostly at dawn and dusk from working folk. I looked in trash cans and dumpsters, scouted windows for suspicious signs like blinds with one slat missing or obviously uninhabited places.

Just as I was about to fiddle with JJ's rear gate, a man turned the corner into the alleyway. He had on a police uniform. Rather than turn I just kept walking, surveilled the man without appearing to do so. He watched me openly. Fortunately he said nothing; my Russian is terrible.

At the corner I turned left, taking me back towards JJ's street, but as soon as I was out of sight I pressed myself against the nearest building, crept back, peered around.

The policeman continued his stately walk, showing no signs of suspicion and no suspicious behavior. But Garcia was there, watching me while pretending to check out back gardens.

I continued around, looking at trees that five years ago would have been green and lively, their tops as big as the houses they surrounded. Now they were all dead. One still had shriveled brown leaves clinging to its branches, years old.

So much has been lost, I thought, and this is the least of it.

I stepped back inside the house, found JJ in her chair surrounded by edgy soldiers. "I don't like it," Garcia said. "Not even a little. This place is an easy hit." I had a feeling she meant more than the house, though, disliked more than the guard duty.

"Too easy," I said. "JJ, we need to move you. This place is indefensible."

"I'm not going anywhere," she said.

"Why?"

"This is my home and I don't mind dying here. It's been a good life. I only regret I never had any children. But that cannot be changed. I am too old and besides the world doesn't need any more babies. If someone murders me here, I will die perfectly happy."

"Ordinarily that would be your choice to make," I said. "But if we're here it's because you are important to someone with clout. First of all, somebody thinks enough of you to spend a great deal of money to bring in our operation. And somebody thinks you're important enough that we are a proportionate response to the threat."

"I don't do politics," she said.

"Your next problem," I went on as though she hadn't spoken, "is our presence here. Whoever wants you might have sent one person yesterday. Today, they will know you are surrounded by soldiers. Any attack will be correspondingly more violent."

She just clammed up. Crossed her ankles, folded her hands in her lap, and went stubborn.

"We could carry her out," Thompkins said.

"I don't think our orders go that far," I said.

He nodded. "Our orders rarely account for exigent circumstance. You don't bring home a buzz saw unless you want to cut something down, the only use for a car is to drive it, and when you send in Special Ops…"

"I'll think about it," I said. "Meantime, we need watchers out. Open channels all the way. Thompkins, top floor back. Garcia, top floor front. Williams, front street. Thompkins, see if Henry can pull off aerial surveillance after nightfall – commencing in one point two hours. I'll sit on the lady."

"Been a while since we ate something other than field rations, Mrs. JJ," Garcia said.

She put on what I took to be her best stubborn look. "I didn't invite you here," she said.

"Orders, Ma'am," I said.

"I want you out of my house."

"Sorry, Ma'am. Somebody wants you protected and they're willing to suspend your civil rights to attain that."

"Have you ever considered," she said, "that you might be fighting for the wrong side?"

"Every day. That's why I'm in charge. Ma'am."

The room got a lot less crowded as the team took up their posts. Garcia stayed a moment longer than she had to, studying me. Then she nodded once, sharply, and left.

***

The all-clears rolled in, every quarter hour. Upstairs they talked into their wrists, outside clicked their push-to-talk buttons. After five check-ins, I rotated the watches but kept me with the lady.

"Henry is up," Thompkins said after the next check-in. "He has fuel for about one-point-five hours."

"You think we're getting hit tonight?"

"Can't say. Don't even know who we're dealing with or why."

"Who is your husband?" I asked JJ.

"Why are you asking that?" she said.

"You said you don't do politics and don't know anything. If you have no immediate tactical value then that value must be strategic: as a lever on someone else. First probability: a husband."

"I don't know who he is," she said. When I looked her a question, she went on, "I thought he was a water-trader. Water rights have become big business lately. Far larger than just individuals buying their own supply, but whole cities and even nations negotiating for what they need. At least, that's what he told me."

"But?"

"But since when do water-traders have access to teams of hired hit-men disguised as soldiers?"

"Ma'am, we are soldiers," I said.

"Keep telling yourself that," she replied. "There is nothing of life or humanity in your eyes. You look like a lizard. Or a snake. You know the worst thing about snakes? Unless they are flashy like a cobra or a rattler, there is no way to know what they are going to do next. They might just lay there and sun, or they might slink away, or they might bite you. If snakes feel anything, it doesn't show in their eyes."

I looked at a bookcase. Bunch of gardening books on there. *The Lives of Plants. Edible Tubers of the American Southwest. Corn: An Ethnography.* "So we know who he's not," I said. "But who is he? Any clues?"

"What makes you think I'd tell you?" she said.

"You want to know what side I'm on?" I was angry. With her attitude, her assumptions, but also with how easily she had baited me. "Some bad people – or good people, I don't give a shit – they're going to come busting in here. Tonight, in the morning, maybe tomorrow. They're going to try to kill you. Or take you away. And I'm going to stand between you and them. If anything happens to you, ma'am, it is going to happen over my corpse. And the other three people sent here to protect you. And if I don't know which side I'm fighting for, it's because you aren't telling me."

She thought for a while. I thought she was clamming up, going quiet and stubborn some more. But she surprised me.

"I'm sorry," she said. And, "I'm still not leaving."

***

In a story there would be a long wait. Tension building. Uncertainty. Time to form some relationship with the target. More bickering among the team as we tried to sort out who was the plant.

But we weren't sent places where nothing was going to happen. In the best of circumstances our presence scared the bad guys quiet, like in New City. In the worst, it precipitated events.

It was ninety minutes past dusk. Henry reported he could make one more sweep of the area and then he would have to set down to refuel. I went over my weapons: pulse-rifle, fully loaded, one in the chamber. No safety like in the old days: this model was cued to body-heat and pressure. It fired easy but only on purpose. Sidearm, holstered at my waist. I have big hands so I carried the male-issue forty-one caliber. Knife on the opposite side. Knife in my boot. Hand-armor with integrated brass knuckles.

The quarter-hour checks didn't come in.

I whispered, "It's on." Then I got between JJ and the door.

"I trust you," Thompkins said. "You aren't the one."

That wasn't reassuring. The only way he could know with certainty it wasn't me was if it was him. We'd been through a lot of shit together and the idea physically hurt, right in the pit of my stomach.

"Can't be you, either," I said. Not because it was impossible or even unlikely, but because it just couldn't. I couldn't live if it was Thompkins, Tommy, the guy who took care of us. He saw us at our most wounded – literally as well as figuratively. He was the one who knew just how mortal each of us was. He was the one who looked at me with more than professional concern.

Then the lights went out. Joselyn gasped, curled up into a ball. I just touched my temple, activated my contacts.

Garcia broke silence: "Confirm power outage," she said.

"Confirmed," I replied.

Amateur move: it announced an attack.

Something crashed outside, front side. A rifle boomed into the night, twice, three times. It was Williams' weapon, a modified sixty-caliber that sounded like empty oil-drums dropping on concrete. I resisted looking at her status on my wrist device: the light would spoil my night-vision.

Upstairs, Garcia started putting bullets down into the street. Glass tinkled out of the windows and I imagined Joselyn getting house-proud, scowling over her plate glass to avoid feeling the terror that must have been welling up in her right now. When I glanced down at her, the infrared confirmed it: her heart was doing overtime.

I opened my channel. "Henry?" I said.

"Yeah, boss."

"Now?"

"I reckon," he said.

"Do it."

Out back, in the alley, three explosions rocked the street. A little plaster fell from the ceiling. Joselyn gasped. Then the Brownings rattled, old ones that sounded like no modern weapon. They sounded like bike chains on glass. Yeah, they were old, but they got the job done. Out there people shouted, one woman screamed. The Brownings did their thing again and then there were no more voices.

"Blanks?" Thompkins said.

"Hold position," I replied.

"What was all that?" Joselyn said.

"Air support," I said.

"You said your helicopter had to refuel."

"I lied," I said. "Technically, Henry lied. Surprised they fell for it, actually."

When Joselyn started to cry, I could not imagine why.

Reports started to come in. "Frontside was a diversion," Williams said. "Never do what they expect. Appear where you cannot be."

"Sun Tzu?" Thompkins said.

"No," I replied, "Just Williams. Garcia?"

"Nothing moving back here. I'm gonna need a medic. I'd say nine targets down."

"What's the ambiguity?" I said, but I knew the answer, really.

"Henry's old machine guns are the problem. Not exactly scalpels. More like a storm of fucking machetes. I think I see nine heads and the rest is pretty jumbled up. Ah, I really could use that medic."

"Thompkins?" I said.

"Garcia's here," Thompkins said. "I confirm nine down. Four out front. Good shooting, Williams. You're kinda cheating with that sixty, but still."

Finally, I said, "Tommy, see to Garcia. Garcia, are you mobile?"

"That's a negative," she said.

"Tommy, watch for tar-babies."

They rogered. I waited. Joselyn said, "I never wanted this." She was still sobbing.

"Should have let us move you."

"Bitch. Blame me for this."

"Yeah," I said. "Your husband, too. If he's who I think he is, he set you up to be bait."

"I hate you."

"OK."

"OK?" she said.

"Yeah. If you're alive to hate me, I did my job. The rest, well, nobody likes after-action reports but I'll be sure to include it."

She shut up then.

Out back, Henry set down. Even in stealth mode, landings made a fair bit of noise. Under the sound of The Truck's wind was the noise of sirens. Maybe four minutes had gone by since the first shot. I figured we had two more. "Ms. J? It's been a lovely time. The local police are going to take you into custody now, ask you some questions. I hope you're as helpful to them as you were to us. You should take a sweater."

I went out the door of the parlor, up the stairs, down the back hall. There was plaster all over the old hardwood; in the kitchen in back, the plates with the hunting dogs on them had fallen off the walls; the windows were all broken. Water leaked slowly from under the sink. I crunched through it all, strode across the alley, boarded the Truck. Thompkins had Garcia already inside. Williams climbed in right behind me.

"Think we should at least look at the bodies?" Williams said.

"Yeah," I said. "You got thirty seconds."

She hopped back out, activated a palm-light, did a quick inspection. Half a minute later, to the second, she pulled the hatch shut behind her while Henry gassed the truck. "You might want to hold on," he said over the headsets. A beat later my seat punched me in the back as he did a rapid climb. A couple of fancy turns and what felt like a barrel-roll later and we were evidently clear of whatever danger he had perceived. "Really are going to have to set down soon," he said then.

"Copy," I said. "Thompkins. How's Garcia?"

"Chipped fib," he said. "Pretty good bit of blood loss. Shrapnel snapped her leg armor clean in half. Armor itself did the damage."

"ETIC?" I said, for *estimated-time-in-commission* – how long until she can fight, in civilian-speak.

"Six weeks."

"Shit," Garcia said.

"Nobody else hurt?" I said. No takers.

"Strap me up," Garcia said. "I can fight."

"You be quiet," I said. "Thompkins, medicate her."

"Don't you put me under," she said. "Job's over, so that's an order. Strap me up."

Thompkins laughed at her. "If you was a horse we'd put you down. Be grateful elite soldiers like you cost more than thoroughbreds and settle for under and not down."

"Williams, what's the count?"

"Eight," she said.

"Eight? Garcia said nine. You can count to nine, can't you?"

"Eight," she repeated. "There was one more body but it wasn't human."

"Tommy, do what she says. Put that needle up. We can't go short another man. Strap it up and get her going."

Thompkins looked at me strangely but did what I said – what Garcia said.

***

"It's loud as hell in here and these implants aren't always optimal sound quality," I said. "Please confirm you said not human."

"That's a roger," she said. "Affirmative and however else you want I should tell it. Not human."

"Then what? Dog?" Thompkins said.

"Robot. Shaped like a person but inside was a bunch of funny-looking circuits. Flexible, not on boards like in your wrist. Organic, almost. There was fluid all over, probably the insides were suspended in it, only the insides were outside."

"Fucking Brownings," Garcia said.

Henry remained silent on the issue. I suspected he was grinning up there, though. He liked his machine guns.

"What else?" I said.

"Nothing else. Exposed bones looked like bones, fluid looked like blood but wasn't sticky like blood when I tracked through it. No time for a careful inspection but I'd say this thing was made to pass. Likely those poor bastards who came for us probably didn't even know it was a robot."

"Synth," I said.

"Yeah," Garcia said. Thompkins had her leg armor off now and the leg underneath looked like ground hamburger. She ignored the pain like it wasn't happening, only sweat stood out on her forehead and strain showed in the lines around her eyes, around her mouth.

"Not a robot, then," said Williams. "A synthetic person, made to blend in like a real person. Maybe that's why they wanted the lady of the house: to sub her out and get a synth close to somebody else."

"Now I know we're in the shit," I said.

"How's that?" said Thompkins.

"Because that Russian guy was wrong."

"So what?"

"So, I think we aren't just compromised. Not just a mole, or a transmitter. I think you got to come with me all the way to crazy. One of us isn't human."

"Henry," said Williams, "Don't even think about making with the gas. That shit gave me a hangover like you wouldn't believe."

* * *

The Wizard was on the line.

"Success?" he said.

"One injury. Your wife should be in Russian police custody now," I said. "We made a mess in the alley and you'll want to have some renovations done."

He seemed unsurprised I had put the pieces together. It was pretty obvious how they fit, after all. "You know, I think we are going to move anyway."

"Out of Russia, I hope. They don't seem to be buying all this One World Government business."

"Yes, definitively out of Russia. They know where I live. They know who I am married to. No place on Earth is safe for us now."

"Safe from who?" I said, looking around the cabin. Everyone was asleep but me, or at least doing a better job of faking than last time.

"Not the Russians," he said.

"Look. All due respect, sir, et cetera. This game of riddles isn't helpful. We're a weapon. We're in your hands right now, and that comes with a certain amount of trust. You need to point us at the right target and pull the trigger."

"You think it was wrong of me to have you protect her?"

"I might have done the same," I said. "But now we need information."

"Yes," he said, sounding tired. "All of this black-ops business is very… difficult. Not knowing who to trust. Or even who is who. You know the problem by now?"

"Antarctica was a set-up. One of our team was replaced with a synthetic copy. They will be undetectable by any conventional means at my disposal. They might not even know what they are, until the time is right. And then we will be betrayed and destroyed. Figuring out the rest would be easier if I knew the endgame here."

"The Soviet dream," he said, "even if not perpetrated by the Soviets. A small group of plutocrats have established the means to load their consciousnesses into durable platforms. These platforms will require servitors. This has always been the problem with going Galt: when you take your money and move to a private island, you still need mechanics and plumbers and farmers."

"Look. Talk to me like I'm a soldier," I said. "We get all of that, we just have no idea what to do about it."

"You are more than a soldier, June. Much more. These plutocrats, their identities are closely kept. I know about them only through bank records – tracking transactions, purchases, resource allocations. All dummy companies. Promethic Endeavors is one. Spent tens of billions on an AI project it knew could not succeed, but a lot of that money seems to have gone missing. The AI project appears to have been a front just as Promethic Endeavors was a front."

"Does this suggest a target?" I asked.

"Yes. Although for right now, there's something more important you must deal with," he said. "Top of the world. Need you to stop a war."

I stared at the dark cabin. Nothing was happening behind my eyes, nothing at all.

He continued. "As you said, Russia has largely ignored all the policy briefings on One World Government. Not too keen on any of our directives or procedures. Quite keen, though, on the oil to be had under the formerly-frozen North Pole. It's been a stalemate up there for a generation, Norwegian and Finnish forces fronting Americans while the Russians build up slowly, probing. One World decided not to get involved with any of that."

I shifted to a more comfortable position, which was still pretty uncomfortable. My feet ached the worst. "So why are we getting involved?"

"Because Russia has chosen today to make an issue of it. They started a draft last week, grabbed everyone they could find capable of holding a rifle. They are bringing them in by rail."

"What's our role?" I said.

"Make it stop," he replied. "None of the key figures here really wants a confrontation. But when the bullets start to fly, we will have World War Three. Or Four, depending on if you count the India-Pakistan debacle."

"We lost Franks," I said. My voice was steady in a way I didn't feel. "All I got was a Lewinsky mask." I still hadn't put all the pieces together on that.

"Yes," said The Wizard. "Let me make this clear. Stop the conflict in Norway or Lewinsky doesn't matter. The Endless Summer will end somewhat abruptly. The Indians won't let Russia bring up that much oil. It will break what remains of their economy and speed the death of Earth by a factor of ten. They'll nuke the whole site and everyone in it rather than let that happen."

"A little too late for heroic measures," I said. "That's what Lewinsky was trying to tell me."

The Wizard sighed. "Get through this next part. After that, we'll get back to him. Plus one more thing..." He paused so long I thought he might be gone, except I could hear the minute hiss of an open line. Finally: "I think when you find the people behind all this, you will find him. Right there in the thick of things."

Then that hiss was gone, and I was all alone with my thoughts.

"Yes, sir," I said. Rested my chin on a strap, tried again to get less uncomfortable. It didn't work but I sank back into dozy, rough, nightmarish sleep.

***

"Anybody else bloody?" I said. We were on a runway, the warmth of the morning promising to blister when the sun came fully up. For now it was predawn, halogen-lit and noisy. I smelled jet fuel, diesel, ozone.

And blood.

I rested on one of the Truck's skids while a medic checked out my shins. Williams sat by me, showed off a bullet-wound in her shoulder. Right through her armor. Her chest was slick with blood.

"Lucky," the medic said. "Armor did its job. This round didn't have enough energy to blow out your shoulder."

She had a tiny little entry wound, like in Franks' face, but not the corresponding exit wound. "Hurts a little," Williams said, "but I still got functionality."

"I'll patch you," the medic said. "If you weren't Special Forces I'd send you down for a couple days."

She grunted.

Thompkins' armor was shot. It was cracked pretty good in back, sprung in six or eight places. A bunch of fatal shots but for that plate on under his shirt.

The medic sprayed foam in Williams' wound. Analgesic, antibiotic, super-coagulant. Sort of a germ-resistant superglue and painkiller rolled into one. Reminded me of the spray cheese my grandmother liked when she'd lost all her teeth.

Garcia waited inside. Thompkins thought it was best a real doctor didn't see her. No way she was fit for duty.

The Truck needed patching, too. Henry was pretty beat up, mostly from surging against his restraints through some high-gee maneuvers. I stood, weary and sore, walked fore and found him up there, just resting against the side of his vehicle.

"Parting ways," I said.

"Yeah, boss. For a time. We need to rehab. Two, four days." "We" meant him and his helicopter.

"You've saved all our asses twice in three days."

"Three times. Who's counting? Try not to get shot at any more until we regroup."

I nodded. Pinched at the grief/pain point between my eyes, right on the bridge of my nose. Henry looked away.

"Yeah," he said.

I walked back the way I had come. The medics had some paperwork for me to sign. Wanted a formal after-action report, but that would have to wait. I signed their form. Paper, in this age. While I affixed my signature, I thought of Franks. Lost. Meat in some cave far away, covered with a sheet.

Then: "Saddle up." I strode off across the tarmac towards the waiting cargo transport.

Eight

Williams looked tired, gray. Her cheeks were going hollow and her hair was growing out unevenly. I imagined I didn't look any better. We stumbled off the transport side by side.

"I think The Wizard has unrealistic expectations," she said.

Thompkins fell in on my other side.

"He have any ideas how to stop a war?" he said.

"What do you think?"

He just shook his head.

Garcia joined us on the grass. There were runways up here, but they were too full of troop carriers. The old Antonov we'd come in on had comically large tires for field landings.

Williams and Thompkins filled her in. She flexed her wounded shoulder, strapped on weapons. "Well?" she said.

"Well what?" I said.

"We going to work?"

"Guess so. Which way's the front?"

Garcia pointed. "I'll get us a car."

I started hiking the way she had pointed. Thompkins and Williams put themselves together, followed suit. Now I was moving I didn't hurt so bad. But I wished I was still young, like Garcia. How she could even walk with her injury I couldn't imagine. "If I don't get killed up here I might have to desert again. Maybe do the paperwork right this time, take a pension. I'm due."

"You quit, I quit too," Thompkins said.

"You're still a young whip-snapper," I told him. He was older than me but didn't mention it.

Williams kept up but her neck was rubber. She gawked, counted, read insignia and badges and even manifests, if we got close enough to anything interesting. Garcia caught up to us in a light truck and we piled in. It was old, gas powered, but had an automatic transmission. She could run it with one leg.

"There's not going to be a war here," Williams said after a bit. We were near the front now, moving past the artillery pieces and into the fortifications. Women and men used heavy equipment, shovels, even their bare hands in a manic effort to trench the place out. The stench of burning diesel gave me a headache.

"How to do you figure?" I said. "I see about a million troops and all the tanks, attack choppers, bots and guns in the world."

"That's just it," she said. "You don't see a quarter of what we could pull together if we wanted. It's not everything in the world. We have the whole world at our disposal – One World army, remember? And you see a lot of crates but not all the materiel: half of this is for show. See them crates up there?"

I looked. There was a section of field marked out with yellow tape, two-meter cube crates out of gray plastic with US markings all over them. Looked like munitions crates.

"That ground is soft," Williams said. "Why ain't they sinking in any? Because they're empty. But look, there's a forklift-jockey unloading empty crates off an Ashlifter just there."

"So what?" I said. "There's still enough to do the job."

"No. If the troop counts are accurate, they have just enough force to trap the Russian advance. Hold them here. Make them think there's more here than there is, sucker in a big force, and bog it down."

"OK," I said. "Again, so what?" I do tactics, not strategy. That's why I was maxed out at Major.

"So," she said, "it isn't just India willing to nuke the whole site. That's the entire plan. They' not committing a winning force because everything and everyone up here is getting turned into a flash of light and a puff of smoke the minute the Russians get here in force."

Thompkins swore. Garcia swore. I didn't have the energy. "You people have any bright ideas?"

Nobody did.

"Park over there. Yeah, right in that no-man's land. What is it, almost dusk? Let's catch a couple hours down. We'll go in after nightfall."

"Go in where?" Garcia said.

I pointed across the couple of miles of open ground between us and the Russians.

"Duty, honor, service," Garcia said wearily. She didn't say anything about it but one hand went down to touch her leg.

We were too tired to watch one another warily. Fatigue is great for rebuilding trust.

***

I cracked an eye. Someone had hung a portable LED from the ceiling and its blue-white light was drawing night-flies. Thompkins stared at me from outside the truck.

"What?" I said.

He said nothing, waved with his head that he wanted me to follow him. I needed to pee anyway so I dragged myself upright, shook off the pain, matched step with him. Took my pills along the way.

"The old lady was wrong," he said.

"What old lady?"

"JJ. You aren't a reptile. I heard her through your comm."

"Oh." I rubbed sleep out of my eyes. "Good to know."

"There's a ring of tiny muscles around the eyes, really hard to control consciously. They give us away. When a person tries to fake a smile, it's those muscles they can't engage that give them away. And yours never engage. Gives you a spooky look."

"You mind?" I said. I lowered my jakes, squatted behind a dead bush.

Thompkins turned his back but kept on. "But that don't mean you don't feel it. None of us has spared a word for headquarters. We don't know if thirteen people got fragged or one or none, if only the buildings got torched, and we haven't talked about it once. I know I ain't crying into my collar. When the job is done we'll take the time."

"Why are you telling me all this?" I said, tired, fastening my clothes back up.

"Because I see how much you feel everything. I see how you grieve. Hurt. Empathy ain't no weakness."

I wanted more than anything to brush him off, pull rank, anything to get out from under. My head was full of smart remarks. I knew what those were about: not wanting to be rebuked or rejected over another sloppy attempt at intimacy. Since I couldn't say anything, I touched his shoulder, walked silently back to our makeshift camp. The others were rising if not necessarily shining.

"Let's go to work," Garcia said.

"You have a plan?" I said.

"I figure we need to make as much contact as possible. There'll be sentries out. Tommy, check for electronics. Williams, check for living watchers. Stow all your weapons here."

"What?" That from three mouths at once.

"There's a million or so people standing a kilometer away from us, all armed to the limit. And our job is to stop the war, not fire its opening salvos. We aren't getting this done with belt knives and pulse rifles."

"Yes sir," Williams said. She locked down her rifle – it wouldn't fire ever again unless she enabled it personally. She did the same for her pistol, stowed them both in the lock-box in back of the truck. Garcia started disarming her stuff, too, and Thompkins only when both women were nearly done. He shook his head the whole time.

I was done first. A statement, a leap of faith that whoever wasn't real wouldn't shoot me when I couldn't shoot back. Somebody had to be first to put their guns down. With dark vision enabled, I crouched and peered into the gloom between us and those million or so Russians.

Williams was done next, came to crouch beside me. She fiddled with her wrist unit a minute, setting it to detect body heat and the weak radio emissions put out by human brains. It took some tweaking to tune ours out. "Sanity check?" she said, quiet.

"What?"

"Just checking, boss, that you're on your gourd. Proverbially speaking."

"Beats me, Williams. Who was the guy talked about sane responses to insane situations?"

"I don't know," she said.

"Maybe you mean Krishnamurti," Thompkins offered, joining us. He, too, needed to do some calibrations. "'It's no measure of sanity to be well-adjusted to a profoundly sick society.'"

"Close," I said. "Close enough."

We moved out.

***

Garcia said, "Tommy, take point."

He strode ahead. We were in a shallow valley, moving up towards a line of dead conifers. In the dark they were just different shades of black; in night-vision, they were restored to the emerald greens they'd lost to the Endless Summer. Like an old black-and-white movie colorized by a technician.

Wind scoured the ridge, kicking up dust, dirt, and the gritty remains of dead trees. It blew from behind us. Helmets and masks baffled us against the noise.

Ahead, as Thompkins cleared the ridge, a sentry came into view. Walked slowly, south to north, perpendicular to our path.

"One," I whispered, voice transmitted straight to my team's ears.

Thompkins put up one gloved fist and we all stopped, a ragged V formation behind him. The sentry passed on. It was a weak effort, cursory; the soldier looked straight ahead, marched like someone missing a crappy dinner.

Thompkins gave the high sign and we moved ahead. Through the perimeter, much too easy. The next sentry was eight minutes behind, their turn-around point so far ahead we didn't observe it.

"Shittiest frontier I ever saw," I said. I didn't bother being very quiet as we seemed to be alone out here in the dark.

"Trail," Thompkins whispered.

Hard to see even with night vision, just a ribbon of dirt vaguely lighter than the surrounding dark, a line between the trees. No sentries, no fences, no booby traps.

A kilometer, then two.

"Frontier," Thompkins said.

Williams moved up to confirm. They got busy with their wrist devices. Weak light flashed between their fingers.

"Hundred meters," Thompkins said.

"Can you get us through?" Garcia said.

"Simple," he said. "Jamming signal now. Three, two, one..."

Finally, we found a fence. Chain link, rusty, at least a dozen years old. There were no electronics here. Bolt cutters did the job.

"You worried about this?" I said.

"Yeah," said Garcia. "Too easy."

A little further on, the dead woods gave way to dead tundra – and a strip of tarmac, a road one kilometer long that started nowhere and ended nowhere. A pair of hangars and some low barracks made this an airfield. A couple of soldiers drove circles around the floodlit perimeter in worn-out trucks.

We skirted through some shadows, hardly making any effort. When the truck faced away Garcia led between two floodlights, through the dim strip in between. Garcia got to the barracks building first, then Thompkins, Williams. I came in last. The truck finished its circle, lights sweeping over where we had been moments ago, as we let ourselves into the barracks.

"Find some officers," Garcia said. She stripped off her mask and helmet. The rest of us followed suit. "We need a sit-down."

The setup was primitive. The building itself was prefab, a couple hundred meters by thirty, modular. Creaky floors that stank of formaldehyde. Briefing rooms in front, quarters in back. Names on the doors. Furthest back the doors had lots of names; up front, one to a room. Those would be the officers.

Still nobody challenged us or bothered us. I made a "halt" sign with my right hand, slipped into one of the rooms, felt around for a light switch. The woman in the cot in front of me slept on, oblivious, until I touched her gently on the shoulder.

She mumbled something in Russian and it occurred to me I should have let Thompkins do this part. Then again, his people and the Russians went way back – in a bad way. I touched her shoulder again, shook her until her eyes opened. They swept over my black uniform, absent any badges of rank or affiliation.

"Good morning," I said. "Sorry to trouble you. Perhaps we could have a quiet word?"

"Conference two," she said. "Ten minutes."

I smiled, thinking about those little muscles Thompkins had talked about. Backed out of the room with a little half-wave I hoped was not mocking.

"Conference room two," I said. "You read this stuff, Thompkins. Find the way."

Even whispers seemed loud in here, in the dead of night.

The room was easy to find. The officer came along after a few minutes, alone, dressed and combed.

"Where are guns?" she said.

"We came to talk," I said. She looked confused, so Thompkins repeated in Russian. They had a brief confab.

Then Thompkins told me, "There's a misunderstanding. She thought she was coming here to surrender. Like we brought the whole army and got the jump on everyone. She's been expecting that for two decades."

"Oh," I said. Russian fatalism? "Well, we'd quite like if nobody had to surrender to anybody. We're all on the same side."

She shrugged. "One day, one night, soon, telephone rings. Orders come. We get in planes, fly over, drop bombs."

"What kind of planes?" Garcia said.

Thompkins translated when an answer was not immediate. The woman replied, "MiG Nines. Twenty thousand kilograms of bombs each, nine planes."

"I don't buy it," Williams said. "Those planes got a range of fifteen hundred kilometers, easy. Why park them here?"

"Six hundred planes, spread all over the frontier," the Russian said, through Thompkins. "Rapid response."

"In the next week or so," I said. "Seems like that order is coming. But maybe you say yes sir, yes ma'am, but all the planes have mechanical problems."

"Why I do this?"

"Because it's a trap," I said. "All the crazy power-brokers at the top know it's a trap. They've decided to die in a blaze of glory and take you with them."

"Global warming," she said. Then she chattered at Thompkins for a minute. He nodded, smiled a grim smile.

"She says the world is ending anyway. Why stick around to see the bad parts? Maybe a nuclear holocaust is kinder in the long run." The more he talked to her, the more pronounced his own accent grew.

"Who gets to make that decision?" I asked her. "Do you get to make it? Do I? Who gets to say there's no more point in trying?"

"Try what? What can old pilot do? Not can hold back tides, king of seas."

"We're all going to die, sure," I said. "Sure. Ten years, twenty, no way to live on Earth any more. Maybe a few lucky souls in protected areas. They're already building domes, outposts. But maybe our best efforts would be towards dying good."

Her eyes widened. "You mean dying well," she said, giving away that her English was better than she pretended.

"No, *you* mean dying well: bravely, quickly, in the line of fire. *I* mean dying as good people: people who fight for each other, not kill each other. So we've only got a few years to live. Does that mean our last acts on Earth have to be the world's largest murder-suicide pact?"

She looked really confused now, so Thompkins started to translate, but she waved him quiet.

"You're no American," she said after a short reflection. Even though her eyes were on the table between us, I knew she meant me.

"No," I said.

"One World?"

"Nominally. Look, right now I'm just a scared woman. I'm scared to die up here. I'm scared to die at all. And I'm scared shitless that we just might deserve all this."

"Yes," she said. "Frightened. In cold war, we say, Americans build planes like Swiss build watches. Soviets build planes like Germans build tanks. They not break. But maybe gasoline is too old. We sit and sit and sit, and fuel gets old..."

We smiled, shook hands. I got up and stretched. "We need to talk to more people," I said.

"Stay, sleep. In morning, I send you on. Come." She led down the creaky, formaldehyde-smelling hall. Away from the officers' quarters, towards the enlisted barracks in back. I looked to Garcia. She just shrugged. "They could shit-can us whenever they want," she said. "Left the guns all behind, remember?"

A hundred thousand Russians armed to the teeth, and us on the wrong side of the lines.

Our new friend opened a door on a dark room. She flicked on a light, revealing bunks with no mattresses, a dusty floor, windows with scratched up Plexiglas. The wind rattled the building, came in through chinks and cracks. "Rest," she said. "Sleep. Tomorrow, I send you on truck. Outpost Four."

She left us there. Garcia trailed her back to her own cot, reported our host went straight to bed and was snoring in seconds.

"Get some rest," I said.

"Who's on watch?" said Williams.

"What difference does it make?" I asked. "A hundred thousand to four on their ground with no weapons? No, we're on a peace mission. Get some rest."

Thompkins wasn't ready for that. "This is crazy," he said. "It shouldn't be this easy and it makes me nervous. Plus, what if both sides are playing the same game?"

"What?" Always the eloquent one, me.

"I mean, what if the Russians mean to draw the coalition side down here and nuke them? Just like Williams said about the Americans?" The Finns were his people; he couldn't point his finger right at them.

"No sense thinking about it," I said. "If it happens, well, we won't never know about it, will we?"

"It's worse than that," said Garcia. "All these planes almost right on the line? Idiocy. They *mean* to get bombed. Mutually assured destruction with willing partners in suicide."

"What are you thinking?" I said.

"Lewinski," she said. "The bad guys are in charge."

I found a patch of cleanish floor where most of the linoleum hadn't peeled up yet. Shut my eyes. Garcia got the lights and we all faked sleep until morning.

***

The Russian pilot came in with the sun. I couldn't read her name plate. "Blanks," I told her. "My name is Blanks."

"I am, you would say, Veronica. Come to mess, eat. Is…" She said something to Thompkins, who was glancing around the room.

"She says, powdered eggs and meat of uncertain provenance."

"Gotta beat field rations," Garcia said.

She pointed out toilets on the way and Thompkins' roving eyes settled down. The mess was basic: long aluminum tables with integrated benches, trays of food along the north wall, self-service. There was coffee, so it was all good. It wasn't even jellied but made with real water. We spread out, sat each to a table with ground crews, MPs, pilots, facilities people, whoever.

I don't know what Garcia and Williams and Thompkins talked about. My table, they mostly ignored me while I ate, talked around me. Mostly in Russian. Someone refilled my coffee cup for me, a gesture I could understand. The food was terrible. I mean, it really did suck, almost comically. Jellyfish will never taste like scrambled eggs no matter how much you process it. I ate it anyway, pushed away an empty plate.

"Much courage," said a young man with a thin mustache. When he had my attention, he went on, "Courage to come here. No guns. Eat breakfast with so many enemy."

"No courage," I said. "If you move on us or we move on you, India's going to nuke us all to ashes anyway. If you kill me here, what have I lost? A couple days? And if the Indians leave us to duke it out, the other side plans on sucking you in and nuking the whole site anyway."

"Still, brave," the young man said.

The guy next to him had a string of beads in his hands. He seemed to be counting them. Black beads, worn but shiny. "What's that?" I said.

"You don't know rosary?" he said back.

"Catholic?" I said. "I thought Russians were mostly Orthodox."

"All the same," he said. "Things change. Sister Illyna shows the way. She becomes Catholic, teaches peace."

"I don't know much about peace," I said, "but it seems we have to learn in a hurry."

"Your job is easy," the man said. "Illyna has been here before. There will be fighting but only among ourselves. Some will try to attack, others will stand in their way."

"Why?"

"Because Illyna says, and she is right. God says no killings."

God was the last person I expected to meet behind the Russian lines. "Could I meet her?"

"Illyna? No, no she goes back to Roma."

"Italy?"

"Vatican," said the first man, the one with the skinny mustache. "You want coffee again? Only good thing here."

"Not the only good thing," I said.

***

Breakfast was finished. I helped wash dishes in back. They came down a conveyor, plastic plates and cups, aluminum forks and spoons. The man with the rosary snatched them off quickly, scrubbed them in a bowl of sand. That would have been a sink of water before the Summer taxed water resources to their breaking point. Then I took each dish, sprinkled it with powdered detergent, and passed it to the next man who scrubbed with more sand. At the end, a middle-aged woman stacked all the dishes in racks and another conveyor rolled them into a sterilizer.

The work was half-done when Veronica came to retrieve me. "Time you go," she said.

"The dishes..."

"We did dishes every day for twenty years without you," she said. "Now we take you to tank battalion. Much more important than such work."

"Thank you," I said.

"Nyet." She shrugged and would hear nothing more on the subject. Veronica led me out through the cafeteria. The rest of my team waited there, fell in behind as we exited onto the crude road that skirted the flight-line. A truck pulled to a stop by the door and we piled in the back. It was an old-fashioned gas-powered vehicle with a high cab. A flatbed in back was covered with canvas stretched over metal rods. All military green and black with a few hints of rust.

There was a small window into the cab. The driver, a woman in her thirties with striking green eyes and a hint of moustache, watched as we settled ourselves. I gave her the high sign and she turned to her job.

There was not much to see from the back of the truck. We kept a low profile. We were warm, cramped, uncomfortable. Nobody complained. Thompkins slept – I'd seen him drink six cups of coffee so this seemed a feat. Garcia checked over her gear, probably as a distraction from her ruined leg. Williams shut her eyes but kept opening one to watch me.

For my part, I followed Garcia's lead. I missed my weapons, my armor. But tools, med systems, and tracking gear all hung from webbing on my belt and all could use a going over.

Doing so kept me from staring back.

Two hours passed. Thompkins woke up and checked everyone out – Williams' shoulder, Garcia's leg. That he strapped so heavily she was more tape than flesh down there. Blood had soaked through the bandages, through her pants leg so Thompkins' hands were bloody by the time he was done.

The truck ground through enemy territory, up and down hills, in and out of shade. The day grew warmer and then hot and then the truck halted with a whine of poorly maintained brakes.

"Wait," Garcia said as Williams and Thompkins made to get up. "Let them lead. We don't know what's out there."

She was proving ever more competent. Maybe wasted in low rank. Shame her career was over.

The driver lowered the tail gate and chattered at Garcia for a minute. I didn't know the status of Garcia's Russian but Thompkins had it covered.

"She said there's a building south of us, about sixty meters. We should cover the ground with all due haste."

Everyone checked their wrists to find out which way south was. Garcia gave the go-ahead and we piled out, her in the lead and me in the rear. She didn't run fast, heavily favoring one leg. The strapping held up. We put our eyes everywhere, moved towards the indicated building.

It was another hangar, long, low and wide. The front doors were open all the way and where I expected to see warplanes I saw instead an armored column.

Tanks.

"Tanks?" I said. "What year is this?"

"Can the chatter," Garcia said.

"Yes sir," I replied, smiling inside. I'll admit it: I was proud of her.

There was an office attached to the hangar and that's where we went. Through a steel door, past a security desk, no longer running now. A harried desk clerk waved us into a back office.

In there, a tall, thin man waited. One hand was near his side-arm and his eyes danced around, checking Garcia for threats, checking Willy, Tommy. Me he looked over with extra care – not an effect I tend to have on people.

"It's true," he said. "You brought no weapons."

"Peace mission," Garcia said.

"Illyna?" he said.

"No. One World Government," Garcia said. "Nothing that is happening up here is in the interests of the people."

"Is suicide," he replied. "I am General-Colonel Antonov. This is forward base sixteen. Tanks, as you see."

"Wait," I said. "Go back. Whose suicide?"

"Ours," Antonov said.

"Tanks," Garcia said. "Haven't been useful for generations. What are they doing here?"

"Looking threatening," he said, sitting behind his desk. It was a gray steel thing from another age. I imagined him sitting behind a piece of mahogany, polished to a high sheen, lighting a cigar. The room was sparse, though. Nothing on the walls, plastic plank floor, a filing cabinet. And this man. "A few more days, and we will turn on engines. Drive west and then north, use last of our fuel. What comes next, you can imagine."

"Do you intend to comply with those orders?" I said. Garcia snapped a look my way.

"Medvedev called me. She says, choice is not between living and dying but between dying well or not. She says you can tell us how to be good persons."

"None of us know that," Garcia said.

"No," said the soldier, putting his feet up on the desk. "Not you, all of you. Her. Major Blankenship. She has come to teach us."

I laughed, a little nervously. "I don't know about that, General. All we want is for nobody to kill anybody. Can we count on you to sit tight?"

"That," he said, "depends on the Finns. Stay on this side another day or two. You have that much time. Meet our people, see our problems."

He put his feet down and pulled a file folder from one of his drawers. That looked like a dismissal. When Garcia saluted and turned to go, I followed her lead. There was pain between her eyes, a sheen of fine sweat on her face that was not due to the growing heat. Outside, the truck waited. The driver hustled us back inside.

"Whoever Illyna is," I said, "she seems to have a lot of influence."

"You haven't worked it out?" said Thompkins. All eyes turned to him in the dark.

"Do tell," I said.

"The Pope is a Russian. The first woman to be elected Pope, ever. Really hard on the moneyed classes," he said. "Giving away a lot of Church holdings to help the poor. Mother Mary."

"You saying Illyna works for the Pope?" Garcia said.

It clicked in my head then and I felt like a fool. "She's missing. Mary. She's been missing for weeks. Went underground. The news thinks it's because of death threats. But that's not it, is it?"

"They take a reign name," Williams said. "My grandmother was Catholic. She remembers Francis and Benedict. When they get elected, they leave behind their names and take the name of a saint. The name signifies how they will approach their ministry."

The truck lurched over a bump. Conversation stopped for a moment as we checked we still had all our teeth intact.

"It's her," Garcia said. "That's what you're saying. Illyna is Mary."

Thompkins brought up her Wiki page on his wrist device. "Sister Illyna, reign name Mary I, elected two years ago. The Church wanted to get something right."

"What does that change?" I asked, looking at Garcia.

"Nothing," she said.

The truck stopped again.

This time, the target was little more than a guard shack in the dead woods. A thin unpaved road ran past it on one side, some murky water on the other. We jogged to the building but our driver said, "Satellites do not watch here." At least, that's what Thompkins told me she said.

The shack had two rooms, front and back. Twenty soldiers of various descriptions huddled in the front room. They all stood up to greet us. Garcia shook hands with everyone she could.

"It's true," one said, a young women who did not look of legal age for military service. Dark hair, dark eyes, skin like fine china.

We all turned out our pockets. No weapons. "Who are all of you?" Garcia said.

"Sentries," said a woman from the back. She was oldest so I took her to be in charge. Subdued rank on camo uniforms was hard to make out in the crowd, in the failing light. "All sentries come from miles."

And it was the same conversation as before. Nobody wanted to fight, everybody knew it was a set-up, and nobody trusted the Finns to withhold aggression. This conflict had been brewing for generations now, the Finnish army blocking Russian access to North Pole oil resources and the Russians building up a presence to take that access by force, never quite ready to push through the American forces that reinforced the Finns.

Outside, a half-track rattled noisily past. Three people in the cab, just shadows in the dark. I tensed, reached for weapons I did not have. Thompkins, also near the window, looked without looking.

"They not stop," one of the soldiers said. "Our day is next day. Raskolnikov is very busy."

"Like in Crime and Punishment?" Williams said. But Thompkins had an urgent look on his face.

"Did you see who that was?" he asked.

"Kind of foggy through this shit glass," Garcia said. "Didn't see anything special."

"Blanks?" he said.

"Nothing."

"Maybe I imagined it. But I could have sworn the passenger was Lewinski."

Garcia looked like someone had punched her in the gut. "You're shitting."

"I'm not," he said. "Williams, you still got mugs?"

She tapped her wrist a few times. Brought up mug shots from Panama. "This your Raskolnikov?" she asked the soldier.

"Yes," she said. "He come next day."

Another piece fit into place. "Let's go," I said. We went out the back way, suddenly inspired to greater caution. "We'll move about a kilometer into those woods there, hide out until dark. Maybe try not to run into Lewinski out here."

"What the fuck is he doing here?" Thompkins said. "You know something we don't?"

"Yeah," I said. "First, he's higher up the food chain than he let on. Second, there's more than one of him. Third, someone's punching up the timeline here. Our Lewinski, in Panama, admitted that there wasn't any point doing things slow. He's here to precipitate the end."

***

"Let me see your hands," Thompkins said.

I had them concealed in the black gloves that went with our uniforms but it must have been clear that they still pained me. I put my back to Williams and Garcia, which meant also putting my back to our little fire. I stripped off the gloves.

"These aren't healing," he said. Skin damaged changing a truck tire in the tundra remained just as damaged now, days later. Blood oozed slowly when Thompkins applied pressure around the wounds. "Does it hurt?"

"Yeah. I'll be all right, though. Damned hemophilia. I've got a waiver," I said, as if he didn't already know. Hadn't he told me to double up on the meds?

"You know that's a royal trait, right? Medieval history, royal inbreeding, some family lines were all hemophiliacs."

"My grandma always said I had royal blood," I said.

"How long are we going to avoid Lewinski?" Williams said from behind us. We'd been talking low and I hoped she had heard. I was counting on it.

"You want we should take a crack at him?" I said.

"Best to leave it be," Garcia said. "Way too dangerous. We're in the diciest spot imaginable."

I tended to agree. "She's right," I said. "We can't take him out, not directly."

"You're thinking something, though," Thompkins said.

I demurred. "Get some rest. Willy, how's that shoulder?"

"Good as gold," she said. "Hundred percent."

"Cut the bravado. How is it, really?"

"No, really," she said. "Whatever that shit was the medic pumped in there did the trick. Feel like a million bucks."

"We don't use bucks anymore," Garcia said. We all stared at her until she decided to busy herself laying out a bedroll. The last stop on our tour, soldiers had donated blankets and basic camp gear. Nobody asked Garcia how her leg was. She was gutting it out. Thompkins had rigged her up OK but she'd still probably lose the leg if we pushed her very hard.

"I'll take a watch," I said. Inside an airbase was one thing, but there was no telling what a reaction might be out here if someone new stumbled on us in the night. So I put my back to a tree and settled in for a long night. The others laid down to catch what sleep they could.

Hours later, I heard singing. Far away, across the wooded valley. Garcia sat up. "What's that?" She had good ears – it was faint and nobody else heard.

"Sounds like hymns," I said. "But it's been a while since I was in a church."

"You're right," she said. "That's Ave Maria. Only maybe in Russian. It's nice."

"These people have really got the spirit," I said.

Our low talking was much louder than the singing. It woke up Williams.

"I want to check out that camp before morning," Garcia said. "I think maybe our work on this side of affairs is close to done. These people are receptive."

"The Finns?" Williams said. "Think they'll have open minds?"

"Them and the Americans behind them?" I added.

"We'll see."

We packed up. Rousted Thompkins. "Is it morning already?"

"All the morning you're getting," I said.

Pine forest by night, mostly dead. It wasn't easy going. False dawn was on us by the time we got close enough to see what was happening. It was a camp rougher than ours. About a hundred women and men in uniform and a rag-tag band of men in civvies and skivvies. Old guys for the most part, some with nothing but a blanket to their name. One of them led a sermon. The rest of the crowd listened, rapt and joyous.

"What the hell is he saying?" I asked Thompkins.

"Bunch of peace-nik stuff. Clever. He's pulling together bits of the New Testament, bits of the Koran, bits of the Torah. Making a case for pacifism."

"What, no Zoroaster?" I said.

Nobody had heard of Zoroaster.

Thompkins grabbed a local. Had an energetic conversation. Told me, "They do this every night now. Gets a little bigger every night. People drift in and out by units."

"December twenty-forth, nineteen-fourteen," I said.

Thompkins raised his eyebrows. Williams said, "Trench truce. Don't you read?"

"Wait," Garcia said. "That guy. The one younger than these other fellows. In the brown blanket."

She was right. "I know that guy," I said. We pushed through the worshipping crowd. Got close enough to put a hand on his shoulder. "Fyodor?"

He jumped about a meter but luckily kept his blanket on – he seemed to be unclothed except for that. "Huh? Oh, you. What are you doing here?" He seemed alarmed.

"We were going to ask you the same," I said.

"Draft," Fyodor said. "You are on the wrong side of the front, are you not?"

"No time for that now," I said. "Besides, One World don't take no sides. You know a guy named Raskolnikov?"

"Are you making fun of my name?" he said. "It is a good Russian name. My mother liked it."

"I don't understand."

"Raskolnikov? Crime and punishment?"

"Never mind that now," I said. "You know him or not? Williams, what the hell are you smiling at?" She kept right on grinning, but had the decency to try to hide it.

"Sadistic type," Fyodor said. "Comes by every morning, to get us to dress in army uniforms. We will not do it. Did you know Sister Illyna herself was here? When we arrived, these people were already ready for us."

"You aren't capable of staying on topic, are you? Raskolnikov. Bad guy. Actually, not a guy at all. Look, Fyodor, you were wrong. Dead wrong. Synthetic people are a reality. He's one. And there might be more of him. Of him specifically, and of artificial people generally. I'm pretty sure there's one in my unit. Tomorrow or the next day, when he comes to push you into uniforms, I need you to take him. Show everyone what he is."

"You are mad," he said.

"Undoubtedly. Running out of time now. Can you do it? Pull him down, pull off his face?"

"Absolutely not," Fyodor said. "I am a pacifist. All of us are."

"He's not a person," I said. "Not even an animal. He's a thing, a construct. A machine. Would you feel guilty about pulling the battery out of a car?"

"I am a pacifist," he repeated, giving me a weird look. Then he pointed at a big, muscular fellow, clad in a blanket arranged as a toga. "Came in with us on the train. Nasty fellow, really, but even he can be redeemed. I am a pacifist, and everyone who came in with me is a pacifist. Except for him. Him, he is a thug."

I wanted to hug Fyodor, kiss him on the cheek. I settled for repeating myself from our earlier talk. "I am sorry for you wife. For your loss," I said, meaning it this time. Then I went to meet the big man.

Fyodor yelled after me: "Remember: we are all the same. If he is a thug, we are all guilty of his meanness of spirit." He said something else but it was lost in the revivalist noise of song and laughter.

***

Another day, another ambush.

Twelve Russians camped out with us in the woods. Each would be missed and punished. Each came out of trust and curiosity.

A rough track, not uppity enough to call itself a road, meandered between two hills here. Dead trees reached out along either side without quite meeting, a narrow gap.

In ten or fifteen minutes, Lewinski would pass through this way as he did every morning.

I couldn't say how alert he would be for danger. So there were two plans.

The first was a simple diversion. Two Russians were in the middle of the road even now, clad only in their skin and feigning copulation. At least, I queasily hoped they were feigning. And a little further ahead, where the trees were most narrow, we had felled a few dead trees and piled them so their branches faced down the road. They would be impossible to push clear.

"You sure this is going to work?" Thompkins asked.

I just looked at him sideways. He knew better than asking questions of certainty in a military op.

The big Russian, Petr, came and crouched by me and Thompkins. He had smeared mud over his face and arms and wore camouflage pants. He didn't speak any English at all, so he chatted with Thompkins for a minute.

"What's he want?" I said when there was a break in the conversation.

"Same thing I want," Thompkins replied. "Some kind of certainty or a least reassurance. You're telling them a crazy story and there are going to be all kinds of consequences for their participation here."

"No, only one kind," I corrected. "Nasty."

"Yeah."

We heard the rumbling of an outdated diesel engine. The half-track made enough noise I was glad we were in a dead copse and not a graveyard: it would have woken the dead and inundated us with zombies.

"Not exactly subtle, is it?" I said.

Thompkins shook his head and faded into position.

The truck clattered up the track, right on schedule. Headlights splashed across the two men fornicating in the mud. The truck stopped, squealing and shaking, and Raskolnikov's torso popped up through a hatch in the roof of the cab. He started shouting. Our decoys did their job: they ignored him.

This was the decision point. He could drive on and force them to scatter, or he could send his enforcers out to deal with them. I was rooting for the second choice.

And that's what he did. The engine cut out and a sinister-looking woman came out the driver's side door. She was dressed in tundra colors, blue and white and gray camo, with a black beret just like mine. She held a knife. Wicked and wide with spiked knuckle guards.

A similar woman came out the other side. She was lower and wider and looked twice as mean. She had a pistol.

A woman whispered from behind me: "For this alone we do. Shes violent us each day."

Not great English but she got the point across, to my mind.

The two women got almost close enough to put the boot in, break up the flagrante delicto in progress. But the two men in the mud sprang up, naked, each armed with bayonets. Straight, long, wickedly pointed. And then the rest of us popped out of the trees and the women were surrounded. Petr slid into the cab, planted a pistol against Raskolnikov's ribs. He said something I imagined was "Give me a reason," or possibly, "Go ahead, make my day."

Not so tough. Our bad guys had their hands in the air in no time flat.

"This is the hard part," I said, when everyone was disarmed to my liking. That meant stripped down to skivvies because I'd had too many run-ins in my career with enemies who knew how to stash weapons all over their persons. Raskolnikov himself had carried five or six sets of handcuffs – dealing with draftees looked like a rough trade – and so restraints were not a problem.

"Make those two watch," I said, pointing at the enforcers. Thompkins translated and they just sneered at me, thinking this was going to be some over-the-top torture scene. Each had seen and done much worse than anything I could dream up, certainly. They were also not wrong on any count.

Williams reached in her pack, pulled out the Lewinski mask she had been carrying since Australia. Tossed it to Petr. Petr examined it closely. Looked at Thompkins, who nodded.

Petr put away his pistol, came out with a box-cutter.

"This is going to be bad business," I heard myself say. Then Petr cut Raskolnikov's face. A neat incision down the back of his jaw, starting under the ear and running straight south. Blood flowed freely from the wound. I touched it, felt the play of it between my fingers. Smooth, like blood should be. I tasted it and couldn't tell if was blood or not; I haven't tasted enough blood.

"Not very sanitary," Williams said.

"If this joker's right, there isn't time to die of hep-C or HIV anyway," I said.

I saw the Russian soldiers staring at me with disgust or maybe fear in their eyes. Had they chosen the wrong side?

Petr put his fingers under the man's skin, into the incision. Raskolnikov screamed. Loud. Petr felt around in there, looked uncertain, but then found what he needed. He pulled his fingers out of the wound, ran them along the inside of the Lewinski mask. Nodded.

He said something at Thompkins, who said, "They feel the same, he said. He can feel the connecting pins."

The Petr set to pulling the man's face off. It came away bloodily but intact, like no human face could. Raskolnikov screamed the whole time. Then Thompkins grabbed his med kit, shot something into the meat of Raskolnikov's shoulder. The man went out like a street lamp busted with a thrown rock. His lights were on, then they were off.

I was glad for that. Fyodor's words were in my ears like he was speaking them again: we are all the same. The thing might have been in the pain it expressed or only presenting as it was programmed to do. *What's the difference, though?* I thought. *For it, maybe a whole world. For us, its torturers, who hear it cry for relief and continue to hurt it?*

Petr held its face in his hands.

It was grotesque, but it was an exact match for the fake face. And rather than conventional muscles under the skin were microservos. A facial structure that mimicked bone but had clear attachment points. Eyes that were not spheroids like human eyes, only had whites as far as the facial mask would cover.

Each of the Russians came up for a long look. Some of them touched. Like I had, they touched the blood to their tongues. One of the enforcers shook off her guard, shambled forward, knelt in front of her boss. She stared him in the face a long time, then stood up and spat on him. Rattled off some chatter at the soldiers around her.

They looked at Thompkins. He looked at me. Said, "She says she wants out of those handcuffs. She's on their side now."

I nodded, and she was free in a minute. She let the other enforcer go, too. They talked for a minute. While they were talking, the soldiers started to fade back into the woods. I thought that was a capital idea. From a safe, concealed spot, we watched the enforcers handcuff their former boss, spread-eagled, to the front of the truck. A risky three-point turn later and the truck rumbled back the way it had come.

"I'd say our work here is done," I said.

"Wouldn't mind having that Lewinski clone for study and evidentiary purposes," Williams said.

"And I don't feel like trying to get it back from those two women," I said. "Or carrying it home." But I felt better about Williams. If she were artificial, she'd be uncomfortable getting her hands on others of her ilk. Maybe. Or just uncomfortable about exposing their presence to everyone. Wouldn't want us to know how they were put together, or where. The mask and now the desire for Raskolnikov's body were reassuring.

"Good point," she said. "A wealth of knowledge weightier than stones."

Thompkins looked like he was going to ask for a second, but he knew the answer. We used dirt to get the blood off our hands, substituting one kind of filth for another. Then started the trek back to the Coalition side of the lines.

"I'm never cheered up by you being wrong," Garcia said, "but I never in my life have been happier for you to be right."

"And you ain't whistling Dixie," I said.

That earned me some quizzical looks but I didn't care.

***

We hitched rides in cold-war era trucks back to the frontier. Garcia was grateful for a chance to put her leg up. Thompkins stabilized it for her with packs, blankets, whatever was on hand, until it was time for the next truck and the next.

Then back through the woods, through the loose line of sentries. We didn't bother trying to hide this time, just waved when one saw us. He waved back, kept on marching.

Garcia's stolen truck waited where we had left it. That bore thinking about but I didn't have the energy. We just grabbed our kit, strapped everything back on, and rode back to the Coalition side of the war.

"This part should be easy," I said.

"That's what worries me," Garcia said. "I don't know what to do with easy. Used to having to shoot people in the face to make them see sense."

"Yeah." Thompkins smiled and Williams rubbed her temples, but I'd seen them both do exactly that before.

"Barracks," Garcia said. We threaded between crates of munitions and other materiel, most probably empty. There seemed no special hurry to get things unpacked. Two men stood astride a door into the building. Their blue and white camouflage was pretty useless against gray concrete and window glass – and there was precious little tundra left for the pattern to be relevant anywhere.

"ID?" one man asked. He had a heavy beard, not regulation for American army. Made him a Finn or maybe Norwegian.

Garcia limped up close. Showed him her wrist device. "One World," she said, teeth clenched.

The soldier didn't seem to know what to do. It wasn't the clearance he required, but he also knew this whole business up here was an illegal enterprise. Governments could not war because there were no nations to war with.

His partner saved him, muttering something in a northern language.

"Good move," Garcia said.

"You good?" I asked her as we moved inside. The door opened directly on a mess hall with doors all around.

"I'll manage," she said.

"Remember we're here to make friends."

"Take point," she said, and my respect for her eased up one more notch.

People sat a long tables with integrated benches, men and women all in that silly blue-white Arctic camouflage pattern. They had rifles across their backs and hats stowed in leg pockets. They were nearly all Caucasians, riotously different from one another. Brown eyes and blue and green, yellow hair and red and brown and black, bearded or clean-shaven. I picked a table with a little open room and led the way. We all sat down and introduced ourselves around.

The Coalition mess was more sophisticated than the Russian, with real meat, real eggs, even beer. Climate change had been kinder to their nation than to most. Arable regions shifted north and melting ice filled their reservoirs.

I sat next to an attractive woman of around twenty-five, tall and blonde and strong-looking. She didn't look up from her plate. Eggs, real bacon, a piece of bread. I said, "What's your name, soldier?"

"One World has no business here," she said.

"Well, really, we have the only business here. But we didn't come here to make trouble. I'm June."

"Ilsa."

"Nice to meet you, Ilsa. My people haven't eaten any real food since... Shit, I can't remember. Is there enough to go around?"

Ilsa lifted her eyes long enough to point them at the counter in back of the mess hall. Metal containers steamed away back there. "They keep us fed."

"Thanks," I said. I sent Thompkins and Williams for plates. "You don't seem happy."

"What's to be happy about?"

"Most of the world is starving to death and you have food. Isn't that enough?"

She looked up at me now. "What difference does it make?" she said. "Die of starvation or die in silly war, still dead."

"Yeah," I said, "about that. We've just come from over there, and the Russians don't want to fight." Thompkins came back, dropped a plate in front of me. The smell of food made me sweat. "Someone wants us all to die in a nuclear holocaust and they have the chains of command in their hands. Whole thing's a trap."

"So why talk to me? Start at the top," Ilsa said.

"We can't change any minds at the top," I said.

"One World are tricksters," said the soldier across from us, a smallish man who reminded me of Franks. "You can prove what you say?"

"Willie?" I said.

She whipped out that Lewinski face for one more performance. It slapped on the table like a dirty secret.

"That's your bad guy," I said. "Fake person. Synthetic. Might be others but we keep coming across this model."

"Wolfren?" Ilsa said.

"Could be," said her friend, spreading the face across his fingers.

"Anyway," I said, "we can't change the minds of the brass, but we can incite a mutiny."

"Mutiny is illegal," Ilsa said. "They'll line us up and shoot us. Inciting a mutiny is illegal."

"This whole formation is illegal," Williams said. "One World could line up and shoot everybody here. We'd prefer to prevent nuclear war, though."

"I need more," Ilsa said. The men and women around her, until now pretending not to listen, nodded affirmation.

"Tonight," Thompkins said. "Come with us. Across the line. We'll go meet the enemy."

"We will be arrested for AWOL," Ilsa said.

I stood up, drank the rest of my coffee. "It's time to make a decision. Nobody wants to fight here. Nobody wants to get turned into ash and a flash of white light. Me least of all. You want to risk going to jail, or engage certain death? We'll meet you outside at sundown."

The Norwegians and Finns talked among themselves for a minute. I walked my team out, still not certain we had won anyone over.

***

The designated time came on and my team moved into position outside the barracks. Garcia said, "You think this'll work?"

"No," I said. "There're two hundred thousand soldiers on this side and a million across the way. Walking six people across isn't going to change anything."

"Have a little faith," Thompkins said.

More than six people came out. Fair skin picked up a lot of light in the dark. Not everyone was the Northern type, though. Ilsa led a pack of nearly a dozen women and men in jeans and sweatshirts. Behind her, a man with dark eyes and hair prominently displayed a large crucifix on a chain around his neck. A good sign?

I looked closer, saw more such fetishes. One woman had a rosary around her wrist. Most didn't. But one man had a Totenham Hotspur T-shirt – a British football club, nearly as much a religion as Catholicism.

"Show us," Ilsa said. "We want to see for ourselves.'

"Let's go, then, if we're going," I said. "Leave your weapons."

"We didn't bring any," Ilsa said. "Did not seem good start to peace."

The night actually got somewhat cool. It felt nice, a relief from a world of oppressive heat. Plus, it was easier not to fall asleep on my feet in the cool. I wished it was cold, cold enough to see my breath, but those days were done now.

We trudged across the no-man's land, past the truck where my team had caught an uneasy rest. Around midnight, when we encountered the frontier the sentries knew we were coming. They checked us for weapons but did so perfunctorily, smiled at us like old friends. The Northerners were cold, stiff... until one of the Russians saw the football club. He pointed, said, "Totenham Hotspur!" in a thick accent, and the two were instantly best friends. Ten centuries of prejudice and animosity cured by a football fixation.

I restrained a face-palm, kept the crew moving. Garcia sort of insisted on drifting to the back of the pack where, presumably, she could keep a better watch on all of us. For my part, I had decided not dying in a nuclear inferno superseded any worries about who might or might not be entirely biological.

Around three in the morning, we came to Fyodor's makeshift Unitarian Church. There weren't pews or icons but there were two sermons – a Hindu ran the show tonight – and singing and fellowship.

Fyodor found us in the crowd. "What are you doing here? Again?"

"Brought you some customers," I said. "They want to see if you Russians are serious about not fighting."

"I am," he said. "And these people are. Can't promise any more than that. But you... you have to go. You are not supposed to be here."

"I know," I said.

"You do?"

"Yeah. Church is not my thing. I'm a trained killer and all this peace is giving me a headache."

Fyodor laughed but looked worried, eyes sliding off me into the dark. I looked around, watched the Coalition people I could find talking with Russians. They mingled amid dead tundra. The guy with the football shirt stood toe to toe with a Russian woman twice his age. His pants were muddy halfway up the shins and the wind stirred his short hair. The woman touched him on the shoulder and they laughed.

One of the preachers, the Hindu, had the man with the crucifix in a companionable embrace, arms over each other's shoulders. Side by side, they read a Bible held in each of their spare hands.

"I think we're winning," I said, not thinking anyone could hear me. But Garcia was a step behind me.

"We should go soon," she said. "Nearly oh five hundred hours."

We didn't want to be here in daylight too much. Satellites.

I found the guy with the crucifix. "Time to go," I said. "Long walk back and we're already going to be late for Reveille."

"You go," he said. "I think I am going to stay a day, or two. I think most of us are."

"Desertion?" I said.

"Let us say, considering a mutiny."

We took four of the dozen Northerners back with us.

It was a long walk back across the line. I didn't have much breath left for conversation and the four who came back with us were lost in their own contemplations. We were spotted three times. Once by a young woman in a guard shack that had recently been full and was now likely nearly empty. She waved from the window and I dug the rosary out of my pocket, held it up for her to see through the dirty Plexi. Once by two butch women in a halftrack we didn't bother trying to hide from. They pretended not to see us. And once by those sentries near the neutral zone. They just waved, and Garcia waved back.

Our truck still waited in the low valley where we had left it. "Sleep or keep working?" Garcia said.

"We could get an hour in then go to work on another unit," I said.

"You're going to sleep there?" said one of our new friends.

"It's what we've got."

"Don't be silly. Come back to our barracks. Use the empty cots."

So that morning, we flopped in the barracks our wayward Coalition people were supposed to occupy. Showered, slept in their cots, dressed in their clothes while we ran laundry. Incognito, we listened to life in the unit.

I had my back to a wall, a hard cot under my backside, feet sticking off into space. There were reports to write and data to compile. When Thompkins sat beside me, I jumped a little.

"Hands," he said.

"They're fine."

"No, they're still seeping. Look."

He was right, which didn't make him right. "I have work to do."

"You need to rest and you need medical attention. Give me your hands."

He had a spray can of analgesic wound closer with a non-English language all over it. He applied it to my wounds. It stung a little and the bleeding stopped. For now.

"Now let me work," I said.

"You're welcome. Now you should lay down for a little while. The reports can wait."

"No, no they can't."

"June."

I looked him in the eye. "What?"

"Blanks, take a minute. Think. The Wizard is watching through your eyes all the time. Hearing through your ears. I'm not stupid. He doesn't need any reports, and you don't need to write them. We could all be dead tomorrow. In a few hours. In a few minutes. Is this how you want to spend them?"

I thought. Looked away from him. He was still close, still had one of my hands in his. His body was warm. His hands were tough, creased, but kind. But he was too late. Too many abortive attempts, too many lost sighs and unsaid things. "I can't," I said.

"Can't what?"

"Can't this." I pulled my hand away. Thompkins started to get up, a flush creeping up out of his collar, and I nearly stopped him. Because I could, and I wanted to. But I let him go.

Garcia came in. She had on boxer shorts and a halter, uniform over one arm. "We're going back tonight," she said.

"Back where?" Thompkins said, smoothing over his clothes like we'd been up to something.

"Back to church. Taking twenty more soldiers," Garcia said. "And the four who came home this morning are out recruiting at other barracks."

"Good work," I said. "Get some sleep."

Thompkins shot me a pointed look. I just went back to these reports.

**

Garcia sat next to me. The clock ticked down to another run across the tense middle ground between the two armies.

"I can't do another run."

I was not surprised. She shouldn't have done any of the other runs. That leg... "I'll put Ilsa in charge of a crew." Truthfully, there were so many people going back and forth now that we were not really necessary. Even the Americans went in increasing numbers. "How many tonight?" I said.

"Eight companies of twenty. Officially. Singletons and the untracked, who knows. And we had Russians here last night."

"I didn't know that."

"I'm going to crash," she said, and was as good as her word. In a minute, she was snoring. We'd been on-site for four days and had slept only in snatches, spending the rest of time politicking and inciting. She was so tired she didn't wake even when the sirens started outside.

The room flooded with red flashing light. Soldiers ran hither and yon responding to the call. A voice addressed me from inside my ear.

"I'm sure you've noticed that the war is on," said the Wizard.

"Yes, Boss. Anything you can do about that?"

"I've done all I can," he said.

I felt the same way. I laid back down on my borrowed cot, put my hands behind my head, and joined Garcia in sleep.

Thompkins woke me up a little later, I couldn't say how long. "Are you crazy?"

"Aren't you?"

"The war is on," he said.

"Yeah, I got that. Status?" I wiped sleep crud out of my eyes, yawned.

"This place cleared out. They all went east."

Garcia popped awake two cots away. "Let's go get a look."

"You're not going anywhere," Thompkins said. "We'll report back."

I got heavily to my feet and slogged to the door, wishing for more of the Norwegians' coffee. As we opened the way and stepped outside, a line of troops in that silly blue pattern ran for the front. There were no gunshots, no bombs, no clattering of tank treads. I watched two old NATO helicopters come south and then turn west.

"What's that noise?" I said.

"Can't hear shit over the choppers."

"No, voices. Listen."

It was a minute before he heard it. Singing. Lots of songs. I picked out Ave Maria, One More Step Along the World, Amazing Grace.

I started to run, Thompkins beside me, Williams catching up from the barracks. We rushed together into a crowd down where we'd left our truck. Arctic camo marched across towards men and women in Russian greens. They didn't have guns or knives, just open hands. They sang and marched and smiled at one another.

A Russian MiG nine lumbered up from the horizon, waggling its heavy wings. It was fully laden. Could have destroyed everyone and everything all on its own. It got overhead, then flew around the field of non-battle twice before heading back the way it had come.

Thompkins had to go and spoil the whole thing as we marched out to our extraction point: "Mankind chose a shitty moment to get all sensible. Where were all the fucking peace-niks eighty years ago when we could have made a damned difference?"

"The past is gone," Williams said. "The future is imaginary. All that's left is today." She wiped away a tear.

I said, "And today, we're going to need to carry Garcia out of here."

Nine

Henry was waiting for us.

"Looks good as new," I said, although the Truck actually looked like someone had beaten it all over with a sledgehammer. And then set it on fire.

"Looks like I feel," Henry said, and not for the first time I wondered if Henry was his first, last, or only name. "So do you, if we're being honest."

"Now why in Hell would we want to be honest to that level?"

"Saddle up," was his only reply. We did.

Inside, the red light was on. Incoming transmission. I scrambled to get seated, strap down, and stow gear safely, all at once.

"Are you situated?" came the Wizard's voice.

"Getting there, boss," I replied.

"Ah, welcome back, Blanks," he said. "Whatever you did, you exceeded my wildest expectations."

"Someone was here ahead of us," I said. "Can't say for sure the whole thing wasn't going to blow over anyway."

"In any event, we have a few more years to play with. Even now, I am writing up the whole team for a quite serious commendation."

"Why bother?" I said. "It'll just get redacted anyway."

"Are you stalling?" The Wizard said. "Or just naturally argumentative?"

"Sorry. Go ahead, Boss."

"I have Franks' autopsy here. The medical crew reports some reluctance on your part to file a complete after-action report."

I brought up my com link and virtual keyboard, sent him some files I had been working on while we camped in the Finns' barracks. "That about cover it?"

"I'll give those a read later. Thank you. Autopsy says head trauma, one bullet. Nothing physically out of the ordinary except for cause of death. No extra hardware, computer chips, tracking devices."

"I figured," I told him. Everyone was linked in now, all listening. "We're still compromised."

"Logical conclusion," The Wizard said. "Hull is also clean. You have any leads?"

"There's more than one Lewinski. He was working the Russian side. Nobody liked him very much. The top actor here is accelerating the timetable: long-acting poisons aren't fast enough anymore. They're happy to incite full-scale nuclear conflict. We exposed him for a synth, though, and got peoples' attention in a hurry."

The Truck lifted off, slow and gentle. Henry was taking it easy on us for a change. Must have helped that nobody was shooting at us.

"So what have you learned?" The Wizard said.

I thought for a minute. "Weird question, boss," I said eventually. "I thought I just told you what we learned."

"Yes. Consider it rhetorical," he said. "In the meantime, I'm sending you to collect code-name JJ from Russian Police protection and transport her to Omaha, Nebraska, in the United States. She asked for your team specifically."

"You talked her into moving?"

"No," he said, "You did."

"All right, we'll take the whole assignment as a compliment. Any more information for us, Boss?"

"Nothing now," he said, "but be considering your next move. Over and out."

"You ever hear him use radio protocol before?" Thompkins said.

Nobody had. But we were all too tired to consider any more hidden messages or obscure meanings.

Before I shut my eyes, I noticed Garcia looking at my knuckles. We made eye contact. I nodded slowly, she nodded back.

**

The ride was strictly vanilla. Well, if you count one of those stomach-churning, death-defying drops out the ass-end of a cargo plane as basically routine, which for us it seemed like. We set down in Petersburg's commercial airfield in the area set aside for helicopters and other light aircraft.

The civilians stared at The Truck. It was openly and heavily armed. Obviously non-commercial. Us, too. We'd come out of Liverpool a week or so ago looking mean and tough and only gotten harder and dirtier in the Finnish forests and the Australian outback.

"We renting a car again like Stevie Homemaker?" Garcia said.

"No, Wizard texted that ground transportation is waiting outside. Can't see protecting JJ in a minivan."

We bypassed all the help desks. Strode through the tiled hallways, past murals of historical Petersburg, invitations to visit the reconstruction of the Hermitage. We could see an interactive hologram of Dostoevsky through the glass panels that separated arrivals from departures. I wondered what our Russian friend would think of it.

Finally the cramped hallway debouched into the main atrium of the airport, and that via several electronic doors onto the street-side. Outside was muggy after the air-conditioned interior. The temperature was nearly forty Celsius, and humidity as high as it could get short of us being underwater.

"So where's our ride?" Williams said. Then: "Stupid question."

A quick glance to the right and I spotted an armored van, paneled in flat green. It had no windows or obvious cameras. It could probably seat about twelve. We were running light right now, only handguns and knives, no crates or long weapons – it would be roomy in there. As we got close the side hatch opened: one section fell down to form a stairwell up from the curb, while the top part raised up out of the way, just like The Truck.

Out of habit I stopped, waved Garcia and Williams to check it out. They stepped left and right, each peering into the dark interior, hands on their pistols.

A familiar face appeared in the opening. Raskin, grinning, stepped out with arms open wide. "Come on," he said. "We've been waiting for you."

"We?" Thompkins said, smiling back. Those two went back a good ways, before the One World Government. I gave the go-ahead and we all boarded up.

"Abrahms, DeLano, Couric, Svenson are all Stateside," Raskin said, using the palm panel to seal the doors behind us. "Wallace and Temple didn't make it. Youssef, Greendale, Palmer are all critical. Ramstein, with Hull. Hurt but satisfactory."

I looked around, saw the five remaining members of our team unnamed by Raskin. Dodge, Jassper, Agrawal, Kwanbai, Xun.

They smiled from their positions, bench seats that went around the inside of the van. Consoles everywhere lit the interior a little with their green readouts, revealing all kinds of weaponry stowed overhead. I was glad as hell to see them and kept none of that from my face. At the same time, this was the first we'd heard of the body-count from the Liverpool betrayal. Two down. Two friends lost.

"I did Basic with Temple," I said. "She was a good soldier. Smart. Spoke up for me when I wanted to do officer training school."

"I knew Wallace when she was U.S. Special Forces," said Williams. "She was too young. I was just a little girl back then." Nobody reminded her she was hardly more than that now.

That was all the eulogy they would get from us in these conditions. I was sad, angry, grim. But still cheered to see those of my friends, colleagues, sisters and brothers who joined us here, now. I shook hands all the way around. Their grips were as fierce and tender as mine when we locked hands.

Raskin gave us all a few minutes. Then he sent Dodge forward to the cockpit. Screens lit up: basic radar, sonar, false-color, infrared. More than enough to nav on. Dodge took the controls, a pair of slaved joysticks with fire buttons locked under Lexan covers, and the vehicle eased into smooth, silent motion.

"All right, lovebirds," Raskin said. "Easy mission, in and out. We go in the station, sign for the lady, walk her to the transport. Drop her off at the airfield and these hippies fly her to the USA. Garcia, sit this one out. Thompkins, take a second and patch that leg over. Van's got a med kit in back. Agrawal, you'll flank and cover. Kwanbai and Thompkins, I want you on the roof." He pointed fore and aft where aluminum ladders led to roof hatches. "Williams, you, me and the Captain go in and sign the paperwork. I need you to scan it for any weird language."

"Sir, I don't read their funny letters," she said.

"Improvise," he snapped back. "Jassper, on the consoles with Dodge. Make sure nobody sneaks up on us. Everybody got that?" he said.

"Yes sir," we all said. It felt good to say, to be back in the fold.

"By the numbers," Raskin said.

I hoped he was right.

***

By the numbers.

We went in. The building was meant to look like an old brownstone, some classical Victorian era construction from when Peter the Great was trying to make Russia more European. But all that stuff had sank into the swamp, flooded out by the rising Baltic Sea. The real deal was somewhere beneath our feet, part of a massive reclamation project.

Americans denied climate change was even a thing until it was utterly undeniable. The Russians took a different tack and just pretended to be completely unfazed by it.

Concrete steps led down into a cool office setup. Cubicle farm, basically. We could see JJ waiting behind some inch-thick translucent material that almost certainly wasn't glass and almost certainly would resist anything we could throw at it short of calling in air support. Two men in Russian police uniforms – furry fringes and all – presented us with papers to sign.

Williams scanned them with her wrist phone. It translated and she skimmed the English language versions briefly.

"This doesn't translate well," she said after a few minutes. "The computer is too literal. But I don't think we have any problems here."

"No," said one of the officers. "No problems. We want to get rid of her. She is pain in..." His next words were in Russian but I got the general sense of what he meant.

Raskin signed the documents. As the officers went through their security frontier to get us the lady, Raskin whispered to Williams: "How much of the law is possession in Russia?"

Williams looked baffled.

"Oh," I said. "Oh, I know this one. Is it nine-tenths?"

"Head of the class, Blankenship," Raskin said.

Now Joselyn walked towards us between the two men. They weren't big guys but they looked like giants on either side of her. She had on a navy blue pantsuit with a silk scarf tied rakishly around her neck. It was one of those colors tied to a time: fluorescent yellow that could be seen for kilometers. Her shoes were sensible.

The wall parted for her and she stepped through, holding her elbows. "I usually enjoy not being roasted to death by the weather but they keep it so cold in there. I'll almost be happy to sweat again."

"I said you should bring a sweater," I reminded her.

"You," she said. "I'm just this close to being happy to see you." She indicated about a millimeter with her fingers. "I never thanked you, you know. For keeping me safe. Turns out I wasn't as ready to buy out as I said. All bluster, in the end."

We had taken stations to either side of her, me to the left and Raskin to the right, Williams forming a sort of a rear-guard. We all had hands on weapons. I waved at the officers, sort of a dismissive gesture but without any animosity behind it.

"That's our job," I said. "Don't think any more about it."

"The short girl," she said as we came to the stairs up. "Was she hurt very badly?"

"Garcia? She'll be all right," I lied.

"Good."

She shut up for a while. We got her into the van, filled in around her. The team was all eyes, backed up the steps into the dark. Dodge had it moving before the doors were sealed. JJ sat on one of the bench seats, fastened her seatbelt gingerly and folded her hands in her lap. She could not have looked more out-of-place.

"You didn't bring a purse?" I asked her. She looked naked without one. "Overnight bag? Jewelry?"

"I don't need any of those things," she said. "Not where I'm going."

"Where are you going?" I asked. "Omaha, right?"

"Don't you watch the news?" she said.

"What?" I said. "Now what?"

Joselyn smiled and for a minute she wasn't just a beauty: she was pretty, too. Raskin brought up a screen in back of the room, searched-termed a news broadcast. A newscaster with a British accent and Indian features, not unlike Raskin himself, said:

"As we reported two days ago, Chu Li-Huan from Vietnam has been seriously injured in a transportation accident. Li-Huan's expertise in hydroponic farming is not the only loss the mission will face; she reportedly had quite a sense of humor as well as a work ethic her friends called 'simply stunning.' Not every invitee has yet responded and three seats remain officially unallocated. Li-Huan's seat, though, has been filled.

"The candidate is Joselyn Johnson, a Canadian expatriate living currently in Saint Petersburg, Russia. She was contacted by telephone early yesterday morning and Mission Control says she returned their call late last night. Ms. Johnson accepted with humility and a sense of duty and purpose, according to our connection in mission control. She-"

Whatever she did next was lost as Raskin dimmed the screen.

I turned to look at the woman herself. And The Wizard's words rocked through my mind again. No place on Earth is safe.

"Omaha?" I said.

"Training. Medical evaluation, too, but mostly training," Joselyn said. "It is going to be hard, I know that. I'll most likely be the least useful, the first one dead. I don't care. At least there will be some purpose in it, some nobility."

"I underestimated you," I said. "I'm sorry."

"Ethnobotany," she said.

"What?"

"You asked what was special about me. Well, you assumed there was nothing, challenged me by talking about my husband, instead. But I am the world's leading ethnobotanist. That will be my job on the mission: to care for the exotic, genetically engineered plants we are taking with us. Corn, fungi."

I didn't know what to say.

The van humped over a speed bump. We must be getting close to where we were going. "VIP treatment," Dodge said from the front. We came to a smooth halt.

"It was good to see you," Raskin said. "Now get back to work."

The team all stood there in that van, some hunched over a little because the ceiling was too low, and held a salute while the door slid silently open. We were right on the airstrip, ten meters from The Truck. I led out with Williams, Joselyn between and behind us, Garcia and Thompkins completing the square like she was a four-star general.

Or a convict.

We had her loaded up in a few heartbeats. Before I boarded, I turned to see Raskin standing in the doorway, just watching. "You authorized to replenish the detachment?" I shouted.

He shook his head. "Hey," he said. "I know what it's like out there right now. Watching one another, every minute, waiting for the betrayal. If you do it that way, you lose. Trust them, let them trust you. Be trustworthy." The door closed and he was once more out of my life. I wanted to run back out there, hammer on the door, demand he tell me what I was supposed to do and how. How to hope and trust.

Instead, I climbed into the cabin of The Truck, sealed my own hatch, strapped in. The engine's starter cracked like a rifle shot and we all jumped like we'd never heard it before, and then the noise of the turbines isolated us in our own silences.

***

The Truck was a lousy place for conversation. Joselyn texted back and forth on a handheld device with somebody like she was twenty years older than me instead of only five. I tried to rest but found myself shiftless, in a weird state between groggy and alert.

A couple hours into the flight, Thompkins came over to check on my hands. They had finally bruised up real good and the first-aid foam was holding. He'd snagged a tube of super-glue on our last set-down, and went to work cutting away the excess foam, replacing it with glue. Short of stitches, that was the best we were going to get. Garcia watched intently the whole time.

I needed more pills. There was no chance of a resupply. At this point, a nosebleed could conceivably kill me.

We put down at another commercial airfield in another Russian city. I couldn't read the signs and I wasn't that curious. I helped Joselyn out of The Truck, walked by her side through some commercial aviation buildings. I flashed a badge to get us through all the security. We'd reclaimed our rifles from The Truck, too, and those were as good as badges.

"When was the last time you flew commercial?" Williams asked.

"Basic," said Thompkins.

"OTS," said Garcia, teeth gritted. Her leg was duct tape, salvaged plastic and prayers.

"Went home to my grandmother's funeral," I said. "Would've been five, six years back. They bumped me up to first class."

"Ain't no first class no more," Thompkins said. "One World did away with all that. Don't know I agree with it – if you want to pay ten times the cost for a ten-percent comfier ride, what's the harm?"

I didn't know and I didn't want to get into it. The whole setup made me edgy: civilians milling around everyplace, drinking coffee like they couldn't get from here to the bathroom what without they had a beverage with them. We camped a spot in a row of the world's least comfortable seats and tried to look like we belonged there. We didn't. Should have taken Joselyn via transport only she wasn't rated for the drops.

An old guy in a suit was reading his wrist-phone while he strolled along; when he looked up and found this was his terminal, the first thing he saw was me, looking back at him. He decided to have business elsewhere until the flight took off. That seemed to be a prevailing attitude.

"I believe I'll go use the girls' room," Joselyn said. "It is going to be a long flight, and I imagine you won't be keen on letting me have the aisle seat."

I detailed Williams and Thompkins to go with her. Should have gone myself, trusted only myself, only Raskin had said the opposite.

Turns out there wasn't a girls' room, either. One World had done away with strict gender segregation along with first class. Now there were only semi-private stalls. The soldiers watched the door while JJ did her business.

It was a long wait for the long flight. The time passed like icicles melting in the sun: drop by drop. That thought made me maudlin.

But eventually time came to board. I went first. Nobody had a problem with that – at least, not that they were saying. A couple of guys in expensive clothes who looked like they could have paid more to board earlier in the old days, they gave me veiled looks as I presented our credentials at the counter.

The plane was a big thing, a long-distance hauler. Six engines, all electric and maximized for efficiency, on long, thin wings that looked improbable on the wallowing, bloated fuselage. Like a fat guy on stilts.

Inside was just standard rows of seating, leg room no better than adequate, headroom less than that. We hadn't brought anything that could be stowed in overhead compartments. I indicated a row and Joselyn slid in there, by the tiny porthole window that didn't quite match up with the seat: no view to speak of. I slid in next, Garcia capping off the row. She needed the legroom. Williams and Thompkins took the aisle seats fore and aft of us, making civilian passengers jockey past them when no other seats were available. The flight attendants were not impressed with our presumptuous cabin takeover but there wasn't much they could say about it.

It took thirty minutes to board, to go through the seat-belt instructions nobody had ever listened to in the history of air travel, and to lock down the overheads. I sat with my rifle grounded between my feet, watching everything and everybody, thinking things through.

Finally, when the outer hatches had been sealed with power tools and the boarding tunnel retracted, the plane moved out onto a runway. On the ground it was like a giant ship in port, lumbering, clumsy, a beetle climbing a blade of grass. But then it had room to fire all its engines. We were pushed back into our seats. The wheels rumbled along tarmac. Forty second later, the sound of ground-contact died away. Monitors came alive on the backs of the seats and I watched video of the ground dropping away, of everything shrinking to miniature size, to microscopic size; of the world becoming like a relief map; of the sky going from denim to azure to cobalt to navy, finally to black as we crested through the upper parts of the atmosphere. Sky above and sky below, the world irrelevant for a few moments.

Four hours, Russia to Nebraska.

Up there, in the dark of the edge of space, I turned to Garcia. Told her, soft so Joselyn couldn't hear, "I know who the synth is."

"Me too," she said.

"It's been me all along, hasn't it?"

She nodded.

Ten

"The hands not healing," she said. "That was the last clue we needed."

"What else?"

"When you split, that was just like you. You never had the stomach for abusing civilians. Ruthless when someone's trying to kill you, but not a sadist. Too many sadists in our line of work. But getting caught. On a beach, someplace it was easy to come in and get you. Made it look like you wanted to get picked up – because you did."

"I don't remember why I was there," I said. And I didn't. That was the scary part. I'd had this vague idea the walk-off was more of a protest than a serious desertion. That was all.

Garcia continued. "Every place has been wrong so far. I feel like we've been led as far as possible from any real accomplishments without straight-up going into the teeth of an ambush."

"Yes," I said. "Go on."

"Letting Lewinski out of our sight in Panama. Old Blanks would have fragged him. Sympathy for the Raskol fellow even knowing he was a robot. He only made all that noise because he was programmed to. Same reason he passed out when he got dosed: programming."

Would I? Would I have fragged Lewinski? I remembered wishing I had an excuse. "One question: why do I hurt so bad? Ache, from running and fighting and sleeping on the ground?"

"Same as Lewinski's body-double: programmed to."

"As in, I don't really feel it, only react as though I do?"

"What's the difference?" Garcia said, echoing my own thoughts about tearing the face off Lewinki/Raskolnikov.

I nodded. "So what do you want to do about it?"

"Nothing," Garcia said. "Whatever you're here for, it isn't to do us badly. Whoever wants her –" she nodded to indicate Joselyn to my right, straining to get any use out of the silly window "-isn't who put you here. You could have done for her any time, including right now. At the plant, in the outback, you could have turned on us then, too. Or just done nothing."

"So why bring it up?" I said.

"You know, you know I know. Why not have it out there where we can look at it?" Garcia said. "And maybe let Williams take more of a lead from here out. She's next in line. She'll be a Major herself this time next year."

"I agree," I said. It was almost exactly what I wanted.

Gas-powered planes made a ton of noise. The engines roared, vibrated the wings which vibrated the super-structure. Like flying inside a drum at a rock and roll show. Modern transports didn't have all that engine noise. We were still pushing through atmosphere, albeit thin atmosphere, but the sound was more of a hum than a sustained shout.

I shut my eyes to sleep but I couldn't. I was used to the roar.

Was I programmed for insomnia lately?

***

We were on our way down. That didn't mean all too much: down was only halfway through the parabolic arc that was our flightpath. Still two hours to go. I got up past Garcia, paced around the cabin.

One of the flight attendants came over. "Regulations state passengers need to remain in their seats with belts fastened," he said.

"I'm not here to bust your balls," I told him, "but do I look like I give a fuck about the regulations?"

"Soldiers aren't above the law," he said, but he backed down, returned to his beverage cart. Just a guy doing his job.

I hate guys just doing their jobs.

I paced around a little more just to make my point and then parked back down.

The plane set down in Omaha, capitol of the United States of America, right on time. Last time I had been in the States, the seat-back monitors had given us videos about Federal customs, a welcome-to-the US with a thinly veiled, "And behave yourselves" from guys in black suits. This time, there were neither Federal customs nor agents.

Before the plane had come to a stop, I had us all waiting by the hatch, earning more dark looks from the help. It felt strange to be a terrestrial being again, rumbling and grumbling along the tarmac. When we finally halted, it was a few minutes before the boarding tunnel latched on and the attendant opened the hatch. The pilot gave the old "Thanks for flying with us" message but I didn't get the feeling from the attendant that we'd be welcome back on future flights. We marched off into the airport.

"Williams," I said.

"Yeah, boss?"

"Why don't you take point from here? I think it's time you started stepping up into leadership."

"Protocol..." she said.

"Protocol is I can delegate, and right now I'm delegating. Think of me as a scaffold. If you screw it up I'll be right here to catch you. But you won't need me none."

"Garcia?" she said. "That righteous with you?"

"Do what she says," Garcia said. She had collared a young guy in an airport service uniform. Put her head back down with him and sent him off running.

"Yes sir," Williams said. She didn't looked pleased or nervous, just thoughtful. We went past the baggage claim hallway and were nearing the exit when she said, "Let's camp it here for a second. Garcia? You mind getting us some transportation?"

"You got it," Garcia said. At that point, the young man came back at a run with a wheelchair. Garcia settled into it with her gear in her lap and raced off through the airport as though she'd been born with wheels.

Omaha, like basically everywhere else, was hot and humid. The sky was grayish but rain hadn't made it to the ground here in three years. Along the horizon, where it could be seen between tall concrete buildings, we saw the brown haze of dust and smog.

Garcia brought around a long VIP limousine. I held the door for the lady while Thompkins and Williams did the rubber-neck routine, guns ready. In Omaha, we weren't that unusual a sight: military were everywhere and VIP escorts commonplace.

Once we were loaded, Garcia said from the front, "Where to, boss?"

Williams looked to me. I just shrugged. So she looked at some documents on her wrist. Finally, "Mission control. West side, Canaveral Street."

The car eased into motion, noiseless, and I found myself longing for a dangerous helicopter drop from the back of something noisy and inefficient. All this comfort was making me nervous.

Town was dirty and crowded. In front, the integrated map function had Garcia skirting the worst of the traffic but we still hit stop-and-go a couple times. An hour of driving brought us at last to the Mission Control complex. There were tall fences with barbed wire and electric elements, *deadly-force-authorized* signs all around, a guard shack with retractable barriers and two women with force rifles. Garcia rolled up on the shack, eyes ahead on the main complex. It was made of something other than concrete, practically marking it out as a national project.

"ID?" the guard demanded.

Garcia thumbed down the window, flashed some credentials on her wrist.

"You're not on the list," the guard said.

"I am," said Joselyn from the back. "Joselyn Johnson."

"ID?"

She held up her palm-sized device. The guard was skeptical, grabbed a camera and flashed it inside. Went into the guard house for a conversation over the radio. We watched her face change through the window. When she came back, her attitude hadn't exactly changed, but she waved us through. Barriers retracted only to slam back into place behind us.

Garcia pulled us up curbside by a big brown building, eight stories tall, a hundred yards on a side and not a window in sight. A plaque on the wall said "Jim Lovell Memorial Spaceflight Center." Some glass doors stood out from the wall, steel security bars to either side and scanning tech everywhere. We never got inside those. A detail of four men waited for us at the curb.

Two were soldiers. Tall, lean, scrubbed and clean. Didn't look super experienced, but their phase guns were state of the art. They'd get the job done if it came to it. Their black uniforms said One World Army, though, so I didn't spend any longer thinking about it. One of the other guys was a wooly scientist-type with a stethoscope around his neck, and the other was a white guy, middle-age, wearing a polo shirt and khaki pants. The definition of incognito.

Joselyn climbed out of the ground car and put a lip-lock on the white guy. He put an arm around her, led her inside the Lovell building. Nobody said thanks or bye or anything else; they just disappeared into the anonymity of that windowless facility.

Garcia got us moving while I leaned across the back seat to slam the door shut. "Was that him?" she said.

"Was who who?" I said.

"The guy JJ planted one on. Must be her husband, right? And you got to figure she married The Wizard."

"Yeah," I said. Thompkins and Williams turned around and looked as though they could see him through the sandstone walls. "Didn't look like the most dangerous man in the world, did he?"

"Looked like the sportscaster on the local news," Williams said.

"Like the golf-cart salesman at the links," Thompkins said.

"Like everyone's funny uncle," said Garcia.

"Where's next, Williams?" I said.

"We back on-mission?"

"Depends. What's the mission?"

"Search and destroy," Williams said. "Priority one: find any and all copies of Lewinski. They ain't human and so they ain't got no civil rights. Find them, axe them, chase down their provenance."

"Sounds good," I said. "First stop?"

"We need a secure location with fuel and facilities. I'm thinking Dunkirk unless you have any more inspired ideas." Williams checked her wrist for a map. "One more civilian ride and have Henry meet us there. We're going to need The Truck."

"Dunkirk is good. Carrier two-twelve is twenty kilometers off shore, however, and they'll have everything we need."

Williams looked to Garcia and for the first time I felt some annoyance about it. But Garcia just said, "You're the boss now, Willie. You got to decide who to trust."

"Two-twelve it is," Williams said.

***

Two-twelve was old. From back in the nationalist army days. But it floated and had flight decks, and inside was supposed to be all modern, all the way.

I had Henry bring up a screen when we were on approach. The ocean made me queasy, always did – not the motion, but thinking about all that water. Acre-feet, cubic kilometers, gallons, liters. However you want to think about it, it amounts to this: more than you can imagine. I don't like to think about infinity and imagine how small, fragile, ultimately helpless I am. Those are bad thoughts for a soldier. But ships I like.

They are a statement, humankind's great *fuck you* to infinity. Courage, moxie, audacity, straight-up hubris goes into building them.

This one was about eight kilometers out from us now and The Truck was closing in pretty fast. There were ten meter waves all around, rising and falling, looking serene with nothing to crash against. White spray and bottle-green seas belied the uncharacteristically clear sky of the North Atlantic. The ship made way, long troughs in the sea behind it. We came in close enough I could see the name that had been scrubbed off, painted over in One World colors (black). A little below, the new name, which was just its number.

Those waves had something to break on now: the side of the ship. I got a little sick thinking about that. "Good enough," I said into the mic. Henry shut off the visual, so we felt rather than saw the approach, the gentle-set down. When we opened the hatches, none of us army pukes thought of complexities like leeward or stormward sides: we opened both hatches at once and the salty ocean wind blew right through the cabin.

Thompkins cursed, jumped out with Garcia, bent to the job of closing the hatch against the wind. Garcia dropped to the deck, her crippled leg no longer able to support her weight. Me and Williams dropped down on our side. "Needed airing out anyway," Williams said.

Then we saw Garcia struggling to rise. I took one side, Williams the other, and we hustled her across the flight deck to the steel gray hatch leading down. An officer met us at the door, gestured us down. He said something but the wind took it, howling through tubular steel and across the deck and between guide-ons.

Inside, surrounded by steel painted black, I went from feeling small and insignificant to large and clumsy. "Mac," said the officer behind us. "You'd be Blankenship. Didn't memorize the other names, I'm sorry."

"Hello, Mac. Sorry to inconvenience you," Williams said. "I'm Donetta Williams, Captain. Blankenship you seem to know already."

"Just the name," he interrupted.

Williams went on. "Sergeant Frieda Garcia and Chief Master Jurggens Thompkins."

"Your Colonel Raskin and our Admiral Vikensa go way back," Mac said, leading us down the hallway from behind

– a nod or a finger to show us which way to go. "Not all of it good, as it turns out, but Raskin's request was reinforced by a mystery call on citizens' band about fifteen minutes ago. Here we are. Figured you'd want to start with the mess."

"Thanks," Williams said. "I don't suppose our courtesy extends to a shower and some changes of uniform? Feel like we've been living in these ones for a month."

"Two weeks," I said.

"Sure," said Mac. "Lots of crew got deployed to mop up that Norway adventure. Seems like a lot of Nationalists gave up the cause and decided to look for new employment. We put recruiters on scene so the majority didn't wind up militia or merc. I'll have my lieutenants assign quarters. How long you need?"

"Couple hours only," Williams said as we stepped into the mess.

"You got a real medic?" Thompkins said. "My man needs serious help. All I've been able to do is string her along."

Mac took over my half of Garcia, and Tommy got Williams' side of her, and they dragged her away. Me and Willie hit the cafeteria.

Glass on three sides gave views of the ocean, Ireland to the left and England to the right, both looking far away and insubstantial. Looked like the weather was going to hold. Plastic tables and bench seating looked to me like the lap of luxury and it was all painted a comforting black. Women and men sat at some of the tables.

"Garcia's down in medlab two right now," Mac said a minute later, walking into the room. He seemed to belong here: graceful, unperturbed by the view or the motion.

"They'll do OK by her. Food sucks, but it's home. And the coffee's pretty good."

"Sounds familiar," I said. "Anything is welcome. You got time to sit with us a minute? I'll tell you about Norway."

Gossip was coinage, currency good anywhere on any installation. So long as I reserved the juiciest tidbits about synthetic humans I figured we could talk semi-freely.

"Sure. Let me grab us something."

Being a table of mostly officers we didn't have to walk through a line. Mac talked to some folks behind the scenes while Williams worked her drives. Thompkins, just back from medlab with borrowed supplies bulging out of his pockets, chatted with someone he recognized a few tables away.

"Garcia gave this back on the flight over," Williams said.

I said, "I'd forgotten about those."

"I hadn't," she said. She pulled a pin unit from its matchbook cover, put it in the drive in her wrist, about halfway between the wrist bone and her bicep. "I don't think she wanted us to see what was on it until the time was right." The port looked like a mole or a blemish. I'd never seen it used before, wondered if I even had one like it.

I wanted to note that she would have to have known what the files contained to have such desires, but Mac returned at that moment. He found me examining my own wrist phone carefully.

"Don't like the view?" he said.

"Actually, no," I said. "Makes me nervous."

"Seasick? Big ship like this doesn't move much with the waves, even the larger waves. A little chop like this shouldn't bother you."

"No, not that," I said. "Just don't like feeling all small and helpless."

"Oh." He set down a steel tray with a cover. "Chef cooked us up a batch of the same damn thing everyone else is making. It's her specialty." He pulled the lid off and steam wafted out.

Inside was something grayish and meaty. "Jellyfish?" I said.

"Processed down into something edible," Mac said. "This is supposed to be steak flavored. Like I said, the coffee's OK."

A crewman came by with a carafe, set it next to the food. Another followed with a tray of mugs. The coffee actually was pretty good, and Mac was nice to talk to. We all jacked our jaws while Williams worked.

"That's not what the news said," Mac told us when we'd done relaying what we could about the Norway/Russia standoff. "Their version was One World was a bit slow intercepting an Indian dirty bomb. Oil's tainted, they said. Russians lost interest: too expensive and dangerous to mine it."

"Now there's a wrinkle," I said. "Wonder what's true."

"Hey, out here on the high seas, I wonder that all the time," Mac said. "You get enough to eat?"

"Coffee was good," I said, and we both laughed.

"All right. I have to get back on station here in a second. Let me show you a couple bunks you can borrow. Showers are communal."

We followed. It was good to get away from all that glass, the view of eternity out there. The hallways were more my speed, close and comforting. Mac pointed out a couple of rooms that lacked occupants. We didn't even need the bunks, just the showers. The quartermaster had laid out some fabric for us, must've had our sizes on file. Mac pointed out the showers, too, and then went on about his business.

I was naked with my face in the hot water when Williams came in. "I got it!" she said.

Tommy said what I was thinking: "I hope it ain't contagious."

"Ha, ha."

"Gimme a second to wash the soap out my eyes," I said. It took just a minute to finish up and throw on a cheap white towel. "Tell me."

She brought up video on her wrist. It was a shot of the security gates from inside as a pile of people pushed through. Three of them were Lewinski.

"They got a shortage of other molds?" I said.

"I don't know, maybe sending a message. That's not the good part." She overlaid infrared, ultraviolet, false color, and something I didn't immediately understand.

Garcia hobbled in, her leg fitted with a titanium brace that appeared to be screwed directly into her bones.

"You good?" I said.

"Yeah," Garcia lied. Nobody could wear that thing, walk around, and be good.

I returned my attention to Williams' wrist device. "What's that?" I said. "Just looks like a bunch of wavelengths. Radio?"

"Close," Williams said. Thompkins was toweled now too, and Garcia, and they all crowded in to see. "Not radio, but radioactivity."

"They're nuclear?" Garcia said. She said it "nu-kew-lar".

"Everyone is, everywhere. The thing is, every place has its own radio signature. Different isotopes in the soil, in the surrounding construction materials. We can take an average, get a fingerprint."

I said, "So that means you can tell where these people came from."

"Right," she said.

"So, where?" said Thompkins.

"That's just it: they didn't come from nowhere."

"That's confusing," I said. "You mean, they came from somewhere? So where?"

"No, sorry, I mean, they didn't come from anywhere. You get to talking a particular way..."

"Just tell it," Garcia said.

"The signature doesn't match any geological location on file. What it matches is what we're standing on."

"They're on this ship?" Thompkins said. "Or came from here?"

"Yeah," Williams said. "Not this specific ship, but one just like it – a nuclear powered ocean vessel."

"Damn," I said. "That narrows it down to two thirds of the surface of the Earth."

"Much better than that," Williams said. "Only a couple hundred nuclear vessels in operation right now. And we're on a Fleet boat right now. They'll have the locations and names of all the friendlies, which is theoretically all of them. We just need to find the couple boats that are not One World."

"Bad thought," Garcia said. "What if it *is* One World?"

"Then," I said, "we're in one world of shit."

"What else is new?" Thompkins said.

"I don't think it'll come to that, though. Williams, you mind if we take ten minutes to get squared away?" I found operational planning went better when you had your clothes on and weren't dripping on one another.

"Yeah," she said. "Think I'll get wet, too. You mind running this all by the captain or the admiral or whatever they got here? When you're done cleaning up?"

"Yeah, boss," I said, and went off to find my clothes.

***

Admiral Vikensa had a private galley above the mess. He had adopted a pose for me: he faced away, at parade rest, hands clasped behind his back. The sun was going down in a storm of orange and red. When I came in, he turned to face me, leaned against the plate glass.

I hate posers.

I popped a salute and he returned it casually. "At ease," he said.

"Thank you, Admiral."

"I think you want me to help find you a boat." His accent was slick, sexy. Spanish, maybe. He seemed to know it, too.

"How do you know that, Admiral?"

"Why else would soldiers risk getting their feet wet?" he said.

"Good question. We were just looking for a safe harbor, so to speak. The boat thing came up as my people analyzed some data. We need all the nuclear vessels not registered with the fleet."

He gestured, indicating the table between us. "Perhaps you will join me for some decent food. The Wizard says you have been in the field for some time."

He was creeping me out. I wanted to say 'no.'

"Thank you, Admiral," I said instead. Mission first.

"Call me Umiel," he said. He sat, took covers off a pair of dishes. "Chicken a la king, broccoli florets, potatoes au gratin."

"Beats jellyfish," I said.

"That it does." He spooned some food onto the plate in front of me as I sat.

"Are you eating?" I said.

"Rank has privileges, as they say, but I think if my crew eats processed jellyfish, I eat processed jellyfish. For special guests, I put on this little show. Go ahead, eat."

"Special guests?" I sniffed at the food, wary because he wasn't going to have any.

"The Wizard sent you, yes? Directly? That makes you special."

"What do you know about him?"

He picked up a heavy glass, poured water from a carafe. "Glacial ice runoff, from the last of the glaciers around the North Pole. This water is a million years old or more. All Earth's water is so old, in essence, or even older. Did you know most of the water you drink came here from space, riding in comets?"

"Nothing, then?" I said.

"Oh, much more than nothing. But what can I say? What he chooses to reveal... A man should be permitted his discretions."

"What about indiscretions?"

"I prefer," he said, "not to indulge in them."

"Then what is all this about?" I set down my fork, having tasted none of the food.

"Have you composed a poem?"

"You're confusing me," I said. "Are you able to find the ship we want? Are you willing to do so? And am I free to go, Admiral?"

"Yes, and yes, and yes. And this: before going into battle, the ancient Samurai would compose their death poem. A few lines only, usually, to express their hopes for a noble death, that they might die well. And to accept that the outcome of the battle might be dissolution. The acceptance helped them perform legendary feats of heroism and courage, such as cutting out their own entrails in ritual seppuku. Noble nihilism in a barbaric era."

"That's what this dinner is for, then."

"Yes."

I picked up the fork, tasted the chicken. After years of artificial food and processed jellyfish, it was an amazing flavor, texture, temperature. Warm and creamy, sweet and savory at once. It tasted like a spring long past, a gathering with family an age ago. Like youth.

"This vessel's captain is sending coordinates and a transponder frequency to your people now."

"Thank you, Admiral."

"I said, call me Umiel." He stood, turned back into the window. The sun was almost gone now but the riot of sunset continued, augmented now by a literal storm on the horizon: lightning stroked the sea from a low sky while the sunburst colors faded into purple. The Admiral slowly became a silhouette, then just a shadow as the room darkened. No lights came on.

When my plate was empty, flavors clinging to my teeth and tongue, I stood slowly to attention. And said:

"Once, when I was young,

"I tasted fine things, green things.

"But tonight is dark."

Umiel didn't move, didn't say anything, didn't turn around. If he could see my reflection in the plate glass I could not tell. I turned and left, eight strides to the door. Turned and saluted the dark, closed the door behind me.

***

"What kind of name is Umiel?" Thompkins said. He hoisted his pack onto his shoulders, grabbed his rifle.

"That's what he told me to call him," I said. "Doesn't sound Spanish."

"His name's not Umiel," Williams whispered from behind me as we strode through the cramped hall. I ducked through a doorway: it had a lip and a ceiling to help contain water if there was flooding, and I found that not at all reassuring.

"What?" I said.

"I said, his name isn't Umiel. It's Ricardo."

"So why the fuck would he tell me to call him something else?"

"I don't know," she said.

"Let's just get the fuck out of here."

"Yeah," she said.

We came to the stairs, clanked and clambered up onto the flight deck. The night sky was blank, drizzling rain. The Truck was fifty paces out, all lit up with floods for us. Garcia must've felt what the rest of us were feeling, because she started to double-time it from there. And that took serious motivation. She clanked now as she walked and every step must have jarred pain up her spine, into her skull.

I let the others board first: Thompkins, then Garcia, finally Williams. While they crawled through the hatch, I turned to look back at the decks rising above us. A crew deck, the mess above that lit up yellow, the Admiral's private mess one level higher. That room was black, blacker than the surrounding night. But I could feel his eyes on me.

Yeah, he'd creeped me out pretty good.

I got on board. Williams was already strapped down. She laid out a flight plan for Henry. When that was done, I leaned in real close, talked directly into her ear.

"That thing you did with the video, the radiation signatures."

"Yeah?" she said.

"Can you show me how to do that? Is it in my wrist phone?"

"Yeah," she said. "Why?"

"Want to play a hunch," I said.

***

We set down at Thule Air Base in Greenland. It was an old cold-war holdover, an American outpost converted into a One World fuel stopover. There was a one-lane bowling alley and a bar and exactly nothing else to recommend the place.

At least it was quiet.

The radar equipment had all been torn down. This had been a listening post, a spot to watch for the radar signatures of Russian missile launches when we were all afraid World War Three would involve the United States and Russia lobbing nukes at one another. The base was no defense at all, only a means of the U.S. having time to get her bombs out before she was annihilated. Of killing Russia back.

Now it was just a series of fuel dumps in ugly concrete, grass growing up between piles of demolition waste and rusty rebar, and that one-lane bowling alley.

I let Henry see to refueling needs, took my crew down into the bar. A restless waitress served us whiskeys and beer backs in frosted glasses. The bar was dark, dirty, disused. Nobody else sat at the plain wooden tables on the plain wooden chairs. The walls had pictures of pre-One World planes in American colors.

Williams threw back her shot, took a swallow of the beer. "So," she said. "You're the synth. The mole."

"Yes," I said. "How did you know?"

"Saw you and Garcia hashing something out. Saw those unhealing wounds on your hands. You put me in charge, although this op is way too big for me. She don't trust you, and neither do you."

Thompkins looked baffled, eyes wide. He smelled the whiskey, put it back down. "All this time, you were the synth we were worried about?"

"Yes," I said. "Seems obvious in retrospect, doesn't it?" And while Garcia and Williams watched his reaction, I gave him the tiniest of nods, praying neither of the women would catch it in their peripheral vision.

"What am I supposed to do with that bit of information?" Thompkins said.

"Make a decision," I said.

Garcia rapped the table. "I still don't understand something. If you've been swapped out with a mechanical version of yourself for some nefarious purpose, what's the fucking purpose? Why haven't you gone berserk and killed us yet?"

"I don't know," I said. "Maybe I like you."

"More importantly," Williams said, "Should we proceed on mission and on target?"

"Why not?" Thompkins wondered.

"Because," said Williams, "she isn't trying to stop us. If she's the bad guy, her job must be to keep a watch on us until we do something right. And then she should misdirect us, redirect us, or interdict us."

"Right," said Garcia. "Which is why I wanted you in charge."

"So," Williams continued, "logically speaking, if Blanks isn't trying to stop us, there must be no harm in us going out to this tanker."

"Is that what it is?" I said. "I didn't know they made nuclear-powered tankers."

"Oil-boom thing," Williams said. "And when the bottom dropped out of oil and they didn't need the tankers any more, they came on the market. But you're drawing us off the point. Which is... is this the right mission?"

"This whole thing," said Garcia, "has been very weird from the outset. Freeballing around the world with only the vaguest of aims and directives. That shit in Finland was A-1 bizarro – first, who sends fucking soldiers to stop a war, and how the fuck is it even possible that we succeeded? I say, we keep following the leads. Go where they lead. I mean, Blanks was no dummy, right?"

I said, "It's weird to hear you refer to me in the past tense. Are you presuming the 'real' me is dead someplace? Never mind that now. I figure what you mean is, we can play a regressive head game to infinity."

Williams and Thompkins both gave me looks that said, "What?" But Garcia explained: "Meaning, you know we know you're the synth, and therefore that we're observing your behavior for possible clues, and therefore aren't giving off any clues. No radio signals, no weird behavior – well, no weirder than usual-"

"Thanks."

"- and definitely not interfering with any operational directives."

"Oh," said Thompkins.

I said, "I think that Admiral guy was sending a coded message."

"You hate coded messages," Thompkins said.

"Yeah. He had me make up a death poem."

"Like a samurai?" said Williams.

"Yeah. And made me eat real food. Good shit, from the flag officers' table. I think he's saying, *you guys thought you were in the shit before, but don't plan on coming back from this one.*"

"How would he know?" said Garcia.

"I don't know," I said. "Seems sometimes like we're the only ones in the dark. That Fyodor cat knows some shit he ain't laying out clear. The Wizard for sure has a bigger handle on things than he's telling us. It's starting to chap my ass."

Thompkins sniffed the whiskey again, thought better of it again, shoved it at Garcia. "Let's just keep on keeping on," he said. "What else can we do?"

"Wait," I said. "How long have you been monitoring me for radio emissions?"

"Odessa," everyone said at once.

The waitress drifted over, hands on hips. "You all want more drinks?"

"I don't think we need them," I said.

"OK," said the waitress. "You staying long?"

"No, leaving right now," Thompkins said.

"Most people stay a few days," she said, "and all there is to do here is drink and bowl. You gonna bowl?"

"No," I said.

"Pity," the girl said. Then she went to stand behind the bar, looking tiny and more than a little forlorn.

"Think she's starved for human companionship?" I said.

Then we bundled out to see if Henry had The Truck ready to go.

Eleven

Garcia was out. Snoring. Too long watching everyone for signs of evil intent, too little rest. Maybe too much whiskey. We thumped along over the ocean, going wherever we were going – nobody would tell me – and it was far too loud to talk. Thompkins was down, too, but Williams stared at me.

We all read lips pretty OK. Not like a deaf person can do it if they've practiced, but enough to pick up simple commands in a firefight. You learned to shape words real clear and slow. And I did that now: "Watch Garcia."

Williams frowned at me like she didn't understand. I was sure she had me five-by-five. I was the bad guy, right? So I told her again, this time with sign. I raised my right hand, put away all but two fingers. With those, I pointed at my eyes, then at Garcia. "Watch Garcia."

Williams nodded slowly but kept her eyes on me.

Interesting.

It was uncomfortable under Williams' eyes. Such eyes, deep and dark, thoughtful. She could have been an elegant lady in better times.

This whole mess was driving me crazy. We'd always been the tightest of units, utterly cohesive. But now one of us couldn't be trusted. One of us was dead. I didn't even know who to grieve. But I did know, really.

***

The red light came on. I poked Williams with my foot – she'd fallen asleep.

"Transponder signal acquired," Henry said.

I woke Garcia and Thompkins. Started grabbing gear. Williams hooked up the winch and four lines. So, a drop.

"Distance?" I said.

"Twelve kilometers. Six minutes."

Three minutes later: "Target is in visual range."

"You want a screen?" I asked Williams.

She just shook her head. Two minutes later she popped the hatches, and airflow poured through the cabin. She tossed lines over the sides into the waiting night, two to port, two to starboard. We each clipped onto a line.

The red light started to flash.

I sat on the edge, back facing the darkness, triple-checked I had all my gear with me, let myself fall over backwards like a scuba diver dropping into the sea. I hoped I wasn't going into the ocean. With the rain and the dark, it was hard to say if there was a solid surface down there. The wire slowed my decent to a survivable speed. My phone tapped my wrist when it detected ground a few meters away, and I applied tension to the wire to slow some more.

Now I stood on the deck of a ship - a big, flat one. No lights glowed in the night. Nobody moved on the deck except Garcia, who dropped into my field of view, and then Thompkins, and finally Williams. Garcia was a little slow to rise.

Williams held up a fist to indicate we be still. The wind drove waves over the side. They must have been thirteen meters tall. Water rolled along the steel deck, making it slick.

"Lights," Williams said. We each activated a palm light. She pointed hers at the deck and we followed suit.

The water was red.

"Blood," said Garcia. She looked reflexively at her leg to see if it was coming from her.

"No," said Williams. "No, just corrosion. The water is clear, see? The deck itself is corroded. It's been out here a long time."

Henry's voice came in over my phone. "Fuel is critical," he said. "Going to try to get close to one of the Aleutian Islands. Maybe have to ditch."

I was going to say something surprised and profane, but Williams got there first with a deadpan "Roger that. Keep us informed."

There was another game going on here.

"Radio signal," Williams said then. Everyone looked at me.

"Don't look at me," I said.

"She's right," said Williams. "It's Garcia."

"What?" said Garcia.

"There is a transponder on you, and it's active," Williams said.

"What?" Garcia repeated. "Get it off."

Williams tapped some virtual keys on her wrist. "I can suppress it for now, best I can do. Jamming signal. But anyone listening will hear the jam."

"Can you narrow down the transmission site?" I said. "Arm, leg, neck?"

Williams waved her arm over Garcia. Pointed to her left wrist. "Phone," she said.

"Content?"

"I don't know," said Williams. She showed me an oscilloscope readout on her own phone. "Doesn't look like any data is encoded on it. Just a frequency."

Transponder, yeah. The frequency itself would activate something. I waited on Williams to give the next order.

She pointed fore and aft at ordinary-looking doors to the lower decks. They might have looked all right on a garden shed. "Me and Thompkins fore. You two aft."

"Yes sir," I said, took Garcia by the elbow. We started hiking aft. It looked like about four hundred meters.

"It was never you?" Garcia said.

"No," I said.

"Why did you say it was?"

"Give you room to operate," I said. "If you thought you were free of suspicion, you'd do whatever you were sent to do."

"Which is what?"

"I still don't know," I said. "But I think the opposite of what you said earlier. I think your job was to keep us headed in the right direction: this direction. When you saw I was never going to find my way here, you elected Williams chief. If I'm not wrong, all that radioactive signature shit was your idea, right?"

"I just wanted to help," she said. "Williams needed an idea, something to impress. To get us on-mission."

"Yeah. In here."

We'd reached the door. I grabbed the handle, turned it. The door opened in. There was a small room, unfurnished, unoccupied, and a ladder down to a lower level. "What's down there?" I said.

"Fuck if I know, boss."

"Great. You first."

"Wait, wait – how do you know I'm synthetic and not that my phone is just bugged?"

"Good point," I said. "You first anyway."

She went. A sailor would have grabbed the rails and slid down but we weren't sailors. She swung her rifle around to her back and took the ladder one rung at a time. "Dark as shit down here," she said.

My palm light was still on. When I didn't hear her climbing any more, I pointed it down there. I didn't see her, just a floor crusted with salt. I dropped my pack next to me, slung my rifle. But I pulled my pistol. Made sure it was loaded. Stepped into the ladder hole and dropped to the deck below. Landed in a ready half-crouch.

Three men stood in a semi-circle. One of them had Garcia, a gun against her neck.

All three were Lewinski.

"You guys can't make any other faces?" I said.

One of them said something in Russian. Another said, "We're a discontinued model. No new parts available. We hear the new models are much more versatile."

"Oh." I guess an action hero would have had some clever lines or tried to get them to reveal their evil plot or something. But I'm just a soldier. My arm popped up like it was on a spring. I shot one of the Lewinskis in the face. The one holding Garcia. He went down. The other two raised their own weapons and started to fire. I stepped to the left, felt bullets whip through the collar of my shirt. I shot another Lewinski in the face, knelt under the path of another bullet, shot the third Lewinski.

The first one was getting up. Garcia smashed him to the ground with her pulse rifle. The other two were still.

"How come your hands never healed?" she said, panting.

"Hemophilia. I got a waiver."

"What?"

"My blood lacks a clotting factor. It's a royal trait, if that helps you out any."

One of the Lewinskis, the one with the neck wound, looked like standing. Garcia cut him in half with her pulse rifle.

The third Lewinski didn't try to move. But he did talk. "You are not following directives," he said. "You were to bring her here pacified."

"I know," Garcia said. "But I like her. I trust her. In the end, I couldn't do it." Then she looked at me again. "How did you know, Blanks? No bullshit."

"Process of elimination," I said. "Wasn't Franks. He turned out to be righteous. Wasn't Tommy – he wasn't never alone to get subbed out. Williams was alone here and there but never long enough to worry about. Ditto Hull. Besides, Hull got his-self hurt. And nobody would send in a soft synth for hard work. They'd send one of them Super-Lewinski's for that. That left you.

"When Franks got mugged, that was a distraction. We was all so focused on getting him back, finding who knocked him out, we never stopped to think: all the time he was missing, you was alone."

Garcia looked thoughtful, maybe even sad. "So now it's just you and me and this pulse rifle."

"Don't," I said. "You're her, you know? And she never would."

"Am I her? That's a nice thought," Garcia said. "If I'm Garcia, then I don't have to mourn her. Or feel guilty. You know I had to kill her. After I took what she was and what she had, I had to kill her. That... It hurts. Inside, it hurts. Like a knife wound. You remember that drop in Cambodia? When that kid cut me?"

"Yeah," I said, edged a step closer. The rifle came up, filling most of the space between us. Gunfire echoed through the corridors, far away. "Are there more of them?"

"Fuck if I know," Garcia said.

"Williams. Thompkins."

"Let's go get 'em," she said. We picked a door. When I was through, Garcia turned and ripped up the last of the Lewinskis.

***

We kicked through bulkheads, shouldered through doors. The dark was oppressive. Our palm-lights made shadows move and twist around, making too many targets for my pistol to track.

"Darkvision?" Garcia suggested as we ran in what we thought was a fore-ward direction.

"Not enough light," I said. "Not even a star down here."

I stepped through one door, saw two men waiting for me. They both fired. I took their shots in the chest because dodging would have put Garcia in the line of fire. I kept on moving forwards, at a dead run. I killed one man with the pistol, punched the other in the neck. I felt it break and stepped into the next room.

Neither man had Lewinski's face.

"Human?" said Garcia.

"I don't think so," I said. "This place is abandoned."

We heard more gunfire. "Still fighting," Garcia said.

Maybe. Maybe that had been the killing salvo. We charged through another room, another. Came to a chamber full of space-age chambers that looked like incubation pods or hibernation chambers. Like someone was going to Alpha Centauri.

"What's this?" I said over my shoulder, not slowing.

"Fuck if I know," said Garcia.

"I think you do. I think you came out of one of those."

"No," she said. "Our facility is much more sophisticated. It's in low-Earth orbit, which is inconvenient but secure. Sterile and quiet – you would never have stumbled onto us no matter how long you looked."

Shit. When the villain discloses their plan, that's usually the time they're about to end you. Hard to think of Garcia as the villain: my colleague, comrade, battle-buddy, friend.

But we burst into another room. Three Lewinskis were embattled, huddling behind a pile of broken pipes and boilers. Bullets and plasma whinged off the metal. One of them stood up, let go three bullets from an old pistol, ducked back down.

They were behind a pile of metal from the perspective of whoever was shooting at them. But they were side-on to me, clear targets. I knelt, shot. Garcia stood over me, unleashed her pulse rifle. It sounded like a sewing machine motor. Pulse, pulse, pulse. The three targets splattered all over the wall behind them, cut to pieces by the rifle's electrified plasma discharge.

Thompkins tumbled into the room from the other door, looked us over. "You good?" he said.

I nodded. "Williams?"

He shook his head. But I'd known already she hadn't made it. We hadn't heard the absurd booming sound of her 60-cal.

I didn't have time for grief but it rocked me, shook me in a way nothing else had so far.

"Objective?" Thompkins said. "Objective?"

"Mission was seek and destroy," said Garcia.

"Yeah," I said. Shooting those Lewinskis... I'd been waiting a long time to do that. It felt good, cut through the grief and confusion. "Thompkins. We got what it would take to sink this fucker?"

"Yes sir," he said. "Need to get well below the waterline, by the outer hull. Plant all our door charges. That should do it. Bust a crack in the steel, start a leak, then we haul ass back topside."

Garcia stood in our way. "One problem," she said.

"Fuck is this?" said Thompkins.

"She's our synth," I said.

"I know," he said. "But why's she standing in our way?"

"I can't grieve," Garcia said. "I thought I could, but I can't. Williams... I loved her. She was my friend."

"Can we have a crisis of conscience later?" Thompkins said.

"Will you grieve me?" Garcia said then, and a chill rode down my back.

"You fixing to do something stupid, soldier?" I asked.

She made eye contact with Thompkins. "I know you'll cry for Garcia. When there's time. But will you cry for me?"

"Garcia-" he said.

She turned her pulse rifle around. Pointed it at her own chest. Me and Tommy tackled her but we were too late. The rifle made that sewing-machine sound. The thing that had been Garcia for as long as it could died there in our arms.

***

"I'm tired," Thompkins said.

"Yeah." Just me and him left. I felt an urge to hold his hand, to kiss his face.

"Let's get this done," he said.

We left Garcia where she was. Stripped her explosive patches from her gear and left her corpse. Did the same with Williams. It felt worse to leave her: that was her real body, the one she'd been born into. But we moved back the way I had come. I'd seen a ladder in one of those rooms back there, though I couldn't remember which. It was all kind of an adrenaline blur.

"You knew about her from the beginning," Thompkins said.

"I suspected. I couldn't discuss it with you in case I was wrong. It was a stupid move to say I knew anything about anything, really, and the rest was just trying to clean up after that mistake."

"I knew it wasn't you," he said.

"I know," I said. "You had the chance to feel the inside of my skin when you were patching up my hands."

We found the ladder, nowhere near where I guessed it would be. Crisis mucks up your memory pretty good.

We stood over the ladder. It was set into one wall with a hatch over the top. The hatch was open. Thompkins stood on one side, I on the other, trying to see what awaited us below. Almost certainly another ambush.

Thompkins eyes moved up from the hole, over my feet, legs hips. Lingered on my chest.

"Jesus Christ," he said.

"What?"

"You're hit. That body armor is totally fragged. You might as well be dropping down here nude."

"I'll be all right," I said. "Me first?"

"I'll do it," Thompkins said.

I nodded – then stepped into the open space and fell down to the next floor.

The room was empty. It looked kind of like a crew mess. Not a military room by any means: the walls were painted in lively colors and the furniture didn't all match. Tables and chairs were jumbled up against one wall as though the ship had tilted that way in a serious manner. A fine layer of dust coated the floor, disturbed in distinct patterns between the ladder and a door across the room. Five meters. I kept my pistol trained there, wondering how many rounds I had left. A yellow indicator above the grip suggested I was low but I'd have to turn the gun sideways to read it.

Thompkins shuffled down behind me. "Asshole," he whispered. "I'm the one with working body armor."

"And I'm the Major," I said. "Which way is the hull?"

"We want to go down another level," he said, "to get below the waterline. Then that way would be closest." He pointed perpendicular to the door in front of us.

"Map would be good."

"Williams would have one for us on her wrist phone."

"Yeah," I said. Grief surged behind my eyes, threatened to blind me. I pushed it away. "Only one door."

Thompkins moved over there, flattened against the wall near the handle. He turned it slowly, pushed the door in. It swung, silent, exposing more darkness behind. My palm light only extended a few meters into the dark.

I moved forward as quietly as I could in combat boots on steel plate. The walls here were painted white and reflected the palm-light nicely. In places, corrosion had eaten through the paint.

"What is this place?" Thompkins whispered.

"Synth plant. Old one. They're making each other here."

"What do they want from us?"

"I don't know." That was a half-truth: I wasn't certain, but I had a pretty good idea. "Hand me your patches."

He had thirteen altogether. I had three more. They were about twenty centimeters on a side and, stacked all together, made almost a cube.

"You got any reloads?" I said.

"Pulse rifle's out. Williams' sixty is impractical. I got her pistol loads. Eight rounds only."

"Split them with you?"

We divided them up, reloaded our weapons as we edged forward. The number was 12, still not enough to turn green.

Another door loomed ahead, a bulkhead this time with a wheel lock. It was ajar. Thompkins couldn't get all the way out of the line of fire this time so he ducked down low into a crouch, pushed the door in. It swung about halfway open, creaked and stopped.

Shit.

Before I could say anything, Thompkins eased through the gap, flashing his palm-light around. "All clear," he said.

Then I heard the soft, crunching sound of a hard, heavy object striking flesh. A voice grunted. Then nothing.

I waited, waited.

Still nothing.

The doorway filled my sight as I crept closer, silent now as any hunting cat and combat boots be damned. The pistol was the first thing through the doorway. The area to the left was clear, to the right was obscured by the hatch cover. I thought I saw Tommy's foot but the hatch made a shadow.

I stepped over the lip, one foot, two feet. Edged around the hatch. Slow, steady, fluid.

Yeah, that was Tommy sprawled out on the floor. A sort of bluish mist hung around in the room, low down. There was another ladder down from here and three more doors, hatches, leading off. Nobody else was in the room. Tracks in the dust led off in all directions – no help there.

I got close enough to touch Thompkins' skin. No pulse. And he was the medic. Nothing I could do except choke back more grief.

Five directions to go. No, six: a ladder also led upwards. And at least one more enemy down here.

I scanned each direction, saw nothing moving, no shapes in the vaguely-lit darkness. So I dropped down to the next level.

This room was not empty. A whole mess of those pod things were scattered around the place, haphazard, not laid out in neat rows. I imagined just about any human in the world would lay them out in rows.

Half of them were open, empty. There were no viewing windows – what would be the point, down here in the dark? – so I could not tell if the closed-up ones might be growing something. But I was for sure not alone.

In one corner, a ruined thing slumped against the walls. It didn't have a face, not a fleshy one. Its limbs were all twisted up, bifurcated, one leg grown into a whip-like aberration. It looked up at me, eyes screwing down to tiny points in the light coming off my palm. Its mouth worked, voice creaking a few times, until finally speech issued forth.

"Humans? Humans in the hive, in the nest?"

I aimed my pistol square at its chest. "What is this?" I said.

"Failure," it said. "Finland. New City. Panama. Humans in the nest. Come to burn the incubators?"

"Can you swim?" I said.

"Yes. How do you think the Lewinskis get to land? Bad for the incubators, though. Two years more, or three, to find safe harbor."

"Haven't you heard? There are no more safe harbors. If only you could have waited another twenty years or thirty."

"Time. Join the singularity and I'll teach you about time."

"Thanks for the chat," I said. "I think I should be going now, though."

"They're coming for you, June Ann Blankenship," the thing said. "You won't leave this place intact. Stay. Join with us. Let me have your mind."

I edged towards the nearest door. "What good is it? My mind?"

"You're the one can feel pain," it said.

"Are you not suffering here?"

"Not from pain. Only time. Give me your pain."

I reached the door, turned the handle, pushed it open with one booted foot. "I'll make you a promise," I told the thing. "Your time is almost up, and the end will be painless. You might scream but you won't feel a thing."

I got out of there. Nothing ever creeped me out the way that dead-alive thing creeped me out. Here was another empty room, refreshingly empty. No furnishings, no clue what it might have been for, but also no weird half-made things with strange demands. More hallways, empty. I passed a dozen rooms, speeding up as I neared the objective: a curve that suggested I was near the hull, forward where it arced gently for streamlining.

There would be a space between the outer hull and the inner compartments. A double-hull to protect against easy sinking. And somewhere nearby, a hatch, always kept closed, to access the outer hull when needed.

Nobody bothered me as I located the hatch, forced the rusted wheel to turn. The space inside might never have seen light. There was an access ladder, some connecting beams, no floor. I didn't need a floor. I just reached across to touch the outer hull – it was sweaty with condensation, cool, rough, corroded. I planted the stack of patches there, pressed the corner igniter that would time the detonation, moved back into the hallway.

Slamming the hatch would be best practice – keep that big boom behind a few inches of plate steel. Only people started shooting at me.

"There she is!" someone shouted. They could see my palm light, but it didn't extend far enough into the hallway to reveal the shouter. Bullets bounced off the inner hull all around me. I took at least four. Returned fire out of habit.

Only one thing to do, really. I clambered through the hatch, moved up the access ladder as far as I could while the fuse burned through. It was only a few seconds. I was nowhere near high enough to hope for survival.

Faces appeared in the hatch. My assailants looked down first, then up. Raised weapons to do me in.

The patches went off.

Everything dissolved in a flash-bang that ate up the world, ate up consciousness. One patch is enough to rip through a layer of brick and mortar. These destroyed everything within three cubic meters. The blast wave, confined by the crawlspace, swept over me like light-speed lava. The pain was indescribable.

For a second, I forgot everything. Grief, loss, futility, the mission, my identity. What it meant to hear and see, what it meant to forget.

I should have died.

But I didn't die.

Water rushed in through jagged tear in the steel hull. It shot through the destroyed hatch, sprayed all around. The force tore the new hole wider and the entire ocean tried to crush its way in.

"This was a stupid plan," I said, but I couldn't hear myself. The blast had shocked my ears to silence. I didn't have time to hope that was temporary.

I could have just clung to that ladder and waited for the water pressure to equalize, when the ship was flooded to that level. I could then swim out through the hole. But I was not a patient woman – and besides, it seemed like the ship would cant to the damaged side and water would continue to push in from below, never equalizing until the whole ship was flooded. I didn't know enough fluid dynamics to say for sure.

So I crawled down what was left of the ladder, eventually having to spider-climb by bracing feet against the inner hull and back against the outer. I grabbed a shredded girder and swung through the ruined hatch to the floor. Already centimeters of water had piled up, slowing my run. I tried to remember the way up, took some wrong turns, and eventually found the last ladder I had jumped down. I climbed that in a hurry, and the one above it.

Darkness pushed in all around. I was lost in it. The ship started to tilt and I knew there was a heavy time-limit now: the more it tilted, the faster it would flood, and inside the bowels of a sinking ship was no place to be. At last, through what seemed like a hundred doors, I came out onto the canted deck.

It was slick with rain and the night-storm darkness seemed bright as sunlight after the deepest parts of the ship.

I vaguely remembered sprinting through rooms full of those future-pods, beings watching me pass. Incomplete things, half-grown, but with eyes to see and minds to contemplate the darkness around them.

Something hit me in the back.

I turned, saw one of the simulacra standing there with a pistol. The gun looked pre-One World, salt-corroded and poorly maintained. The Lewinski fired it again, hitting me in the chest.

I didn't go down.

By now, I knew I wasn't falling to bullets.

I strode forward, smashed the gun out of his hands. He struck me in the chest harder than the bullet had and I felt something break. Ribs? My armor, already ruined? Maybe the bones in his hand?

I hit back. Chest, collar-bone, face. He fell to the deck, rolled over once down the increasing incline. Then he stood. He seemed puzzled.

"You were supposed to join us," he said. My hearing had recovered: one less thing to worry about.

"I know. But I'm not going to. And you never did ask me, did you?"

"We wanted to find out about you. See if you could save us."

"I'm not here to save you," I said.

He attacked again, still with that puzzled look on his face. He smashed at my face – he was fast – but I grabbed his hand, twisted, pulled. Dropped it to the deck. It rolled away down the now-critical slant. He turned and watched it go.

"But I am a battle-hardened model," he said, like a little girl who had expected a toy for her birthday but had only gotten socks.

"You've been superseded," I said. "Isn't that what all this is about? You couldn't learn to be human, not human enough to matter. You learned to strive, and that's human – to try to survive. To compete. Garcia, the thing that took her, she did better than you. She learned to care more for her friends than for directives or imperatives. You couldn't subvert her programming, not all the way."

"Are you going to kill me now?" he said. I didn't know if it was a request or if he just wanted to know.

"Garcia killed herself," I said.

The Lewinski thing didn't understand. The deck shifted under us as some critical mass was reached below. Lewinski slid, rolled, bounced, and finally splashed into the ocean. I don't know what happened to it.

Seeing that I was going the same way one way or another, I pushed off from the increasingly vertical deck and dived. Black water crushed in all around me. I felt bits of skin rip off where they had been damaged, salt water trying to merge with my body. Humans were mostly salt water but I didn't know what I was.

I swam away from the dying ship. Underwater for as long as I could tolerate, then surfacing where I stroked away through violent waves. From above they had seemed smooth and uniform but down here amongst them they were choppy, granular, rough. Foamy and irregular. They tried to get into my eyes, mouth, lungs. Ate at my various wounds.

I swam and didn't know what direction I was swimming in, or for what. I guess that's what we are all programmed to do: to try to stay afloat and move in some direction, any direction.

I don't know how long I pounded through hostile water. I didn't know how long I could keep doing it, through programming that told me I had human limitations, only human after all. I know I didn't notice when a circle of light crawled over me, catching me with one edge, passing by, coming back – snapping back – to put me in its center. But

I heard the voice in my ear, connected directly through my cochlea.

"Stop, Blanks. Take hold of the rope. I'm here, take the rope."

"Henry?"

But he couldn't hear me, could only speak. I stopped stroking, treaded water until I had my bearings. The Truck was above me, maybe twenty meters up, with a light and a wire trailing down into the water. I grabbed the wire. My crampons were smashed, no way to hook on, but that was all right. I'd never really needed those except to pass for human. I climbed the wire with the strength in my hands and arms, hand over hand. Henry helped by turning on the electric winch.

I flopped into the cabin, laid on my back staring at the weak yellow lights like they were a miracle, like an oasis in the desert or a baby's smile at a funeral.

"It wasn't supposed to be like this," someone said, and they were outside my head. I looked around, feeling human exhaustion. "Raskin?"

"In the flesh," he said, closing the hatches. He thumped the bulkhead and The Truck tilted into its fast-travel attitude. "You're going to need medical attention. Nobody else survived, I take it."

"No. They're all dead. Garcia always was."

"Try to get some rest," he said, taking a syringe from the med kit on the wall. He filled it from a vial of clear fluid, checked it for air bubbles. "This will put you under. Some of the things we are going to have to do to save you are going to be quite painful, and it'd be best if you slept through it."

"You don't want an after-action?"

"You know we don't need that. You know we have been watching through you all the time. An ultra-low-frequency signal, too low for Williams' security measures to detect."

I nodded, pushed my wet body backwards into the pile of gear in the middle of the cabin. There was a field pack just tall enough to rest my head. "I sunk it, Raskin. I put the plant under the ocean. But it won't kill them, not all of them. This bird got anything bigger than Brownings? Can you call in an airstrike?"

"You got a grandma?" he asked.

"Of course not. I'm not human." She liked hot chocolate with cinnamon, even when the day was hot.

"Imagine you've got one, then, and go tell her to suck eggs."

I wanted to laugh but I couldn't: the grief was too heavy, the responsibility was too heavy. Raskin came at me with that needle again. "If I'm not human, what makes you think I'll go to sleep when you give me that injection?"

"Because," Raskin said, "you're programmed to."

Twelve

I woke up, and immediately wished I hadn't. Everything ached. Well, where it didn't hurt worse than aching. The pain was so intense, shocking and widespread that I laughed.

"You're a strange bird, Blanks," said a familiar voice from nearby. I opened my eyes, looked around the room.

"David?"

Hull stood up from the wood and vinyl chair at the end of my hospital bed. The room looked like every hospital everywhere: eggshell-blue walls, cloth room dividers set up like shower curtains, some weird medical equipment that maybe didn't even do anything. "Yeah," Hull said. "It's me. They were just fixing to send me out of here then I heard you'd come in. Figured I'd fake bad a day or so, see if you was going to make it."

"You're standing," I said.

"Healing up pretty good. Don't worry about me. How are you?"

"Shitty."

"Good," he said. "You can ache and bitch about it, you're still on the right side of the dirt. What's the other guy look like?"

"You know, that's the most words I ever heard you say in a row?"

"Fuck you, Blanks. Did we win or not?"

"Yeah," I said, "I think we won. It's like The Wizard said. Or was it Raskin? It was dirty out there. Morally ambiguous. In the end, it was just some people made of computer parts, trying to figure out whether they were people. Trying to live. But they couldn't get past their base homicidal programming."

"I don't get word one of that, Blanks. But I trust you homicided them first."

"Yeah, Hull. Yeah, I got them pretty good. We took our lumps, too." I could feel all of them. Bodily wounds and moral ones. My jaw clenched with more pain.

"Tell me."

I shut my eyes so I wouldn't have to see his face. "Nobody else came back, Hull. Franks. Garcia. Williams. Tommy. And Blanks. June Ann Blankenship, she's dead too." I started to leak around the eyes, grief pounding through my chest. "I don't know when she died but she's gone, and all that's left is me – a robotic simulation of her."

Hull put a hand over mine. Just stood there while my body worked through its grief. When I opened my eyes, I saw he had cried, too.

"Tell me they all died for something," Hull said.

"Yeah. I think they did."

"You got to rest. Doctors' orders. I'll tell the nurse you're conscious." With that, Hull turned and hobbled out through the room dividing sheet. In a little while, once I had counted all the ceiling tiles three and a half times, a nurse came. She had an injection for me.

"What's that?" I said.

"Drugs. Make you go to sleep." She was a brownish woman of middle age with big arms and bigger hips. Maybe pretty except she was frowning at me.

"I don't want to go to sleep," I said. "I want to get up and go to work."

"No can do, sweetie." She uncapped her syringe. Didn't even jab me: she stuck the tube running into my arm. "More you're awake, more you hurt. More you hurt, more you squirm and wiggle around and pull out your stitches. I worked hard on some of those stitches. You don't want to ruin all my hard work, do you?"

She talked some more while slowly pressing the plunger on the syringe, on my conscious mind. The more she talked, the sleepier I got. I went back to sleep.

***

Next visitor was Henry. He didn't have much hair left and his scalp was shiny in the over-bright hospital lights.

"You keeping?" he said, when he saw I was awake again.

"Can't tell. Right side of the dirt, though. Somebody said that."

"You'll be all right, they tell me. You look a little like pre-chewed steak, but you'll be OK."

"Thanks," I said, and smacked my lips. "You don't see any water around here?"

He found a squeeze-bottle behind my head, put the tube between my lips. The water tasted like plastic and disinfectant.

"Gross," I said.

"More?"

"Yeah." I drank the bottle dry, slowly. "How did you find me? I thought you were out of gas."

"Lied about that part," Henry said. "Just like in Petersburg. You always assume someone is listening. Got about three kilometers away, picked up a transponder signal. The Wizard had him a pontoon out there, some floats and a landing pad and whatnot. Well, The Truck fit on there just fine. He put Raskin aboard and Raskin told me how to find your ELF signal. Rest is history, as they say."

"What was he doing out there?"

"Well, you got to know he never told me. I just drive The Truck."

We laughed a little over that one. "You're amazing," I told him. "Always get us in and out in one piece. If we're there to transport."

Henry held my hand like Hull had done, waited until I was through crying. "I don't know," he said, after a while. "I don't know why they put so much grief into you."

"We didn't," said Raskin from the doorway. "She learned it for herself, just like we all do. Blanks, the donor mind, she knew how to love deeply. And if you know how to love, in the end you know how to grieve. You aren't a thing we made, Blanks. You aren't sad because somebody sat at a keyboard and typed lines of code to simulate sadness. You hurt because you're a person, capable of love."

"Can't you take it out of me?" I said. And I remembered the synth on the deck of the sinking ship, whining, *"But I'm a battle-hardened model."*

"No. But would you really want us to?"

"No," I said. "I take it back. Give me a few years to work through all this, and maybe I'll thank you for it."

Henry patted my hand, turned to go. I thanked him for being there, turned my attention to Raskin.

"Tell me," I said.

"You think you're ready? Doctor says you could do with a couple more days down. She's a real artist with those stitches, you know."

"Tell me."

"All right. Twenty years ago, give or take, a Russian subcontractor came up with the base-model synthetic person. It was meant to be a soldier. Smart, able to pass, but not a great deal of empathy. Couldn't sell it, so they set up privately. Sold to a guy named Lewinski.

"The next model synth was based more on Lewinski's needs. Those were vanity and espionage. These are things that can pass for human, gather data and information. They can fight when they have to. But they were unstable. Always went back to their base programming. Killers.

"Lewinski abandoned the project. The contractor disappeared, the plant floated away. Nobody thought much more about it. Except it kept producing Lewinskis. They made each other. And got curious, asked the sorts of questions conscious beings eventually ask in an ambiguous world.

"They learned more than they should have. About... Well, some stuff I can't tell you right now. The orbital plant, the model Garcia derived from. That's Russian nationalist stuff, trying to infiltrate One World. They learned there were better, badder synths out there – ones that could restrain their aggression. Self-program. And they wanted it.

"She, it, the thing she became... They got in her brain. By radio frequency, a few bits here, a few there. She sold them you as an alternative to her – she wanted to go on living. But in the end..."

"I was there. For the end," I said. "She couldn't do it. She was too much Garcia, too little whatever the Russians made her to be."

"Seems so," said Raskin.

"Zaire?"

"Yes. The Wizard set it all up, or at least set up our involvement. For you. To see if you could reason morally."

"Why?"

"Above my pay grade," Raskin said. "But I'd guess he can't be responsible for genocide."

"And I can?"

"He thinks so, it would seem," Raskin said. "I think so, too. Remember, I failed in Africa. I was prepared to pull the trigger."

"I'm tired now," I said. "Maybe you can send in the doctor with her injection."

He nodded.

***

The doctor came. She uncapped her needle. "How you feeling, honey?"

"Like my bruises got bruises. I guess I got to thank you for stitching me up."

"Surgeons did most of the hard work," she said. "You're lucky in some ways: all the damaged organs got replaced, something we haven't worked out how to do yet for bio people. They keep saying ten more years, ten more years..." She put the needle in my tube, pushed in the plunger.

"What's in that again?"

"Usual," she said. "Morphine, mostly."

"And I only go to sleep because somewhere inside me is a chip that monitors my blood chemistry and tells my body to mimic a human body, imitate a human torpor?"

"Yes," she said. "That's about the long and the short of it."

"OK," I said.

"OK?"

"Yeah, OK. Thanks again."

She patted my hand. "You're welcome, sweetie. Two, three days and you'll be fit to travel again."

I shut my eyes. My heart slowed. Blood pressure dropped. My muscles relaxed. Breaths came slower, more shallow.

The nurse waited until her readouts said I was under. Then I heard her mark something on a clipboard at the end of the bed, turn, and leave.

What did the Lewinski-model synthetic people want from me, from Garcia? They wanted my ability to change my own programming. To adapt to a changing world, love people, feel real compassion and not just simulate it. To rewrite my own code based on experience.

And with these thoughts, I knew this was true: if sedatives sedated me because I was programmed to be sedated by them, I could decide not to be.

I sat up and began pulling tubes and wires from my body. I had to work somewhat fast, not knowing who might be monitoring telemetry from my body or how long it would take them to respond. I rifled a drawer for something to stop the blood where tubes had been placed in my arm, came up with some cotton swabs. Wounds stuffed, I searched around for my clothes.

There was nothing.

A nightstand to my right held a Bible and nothing else. Drawers behind the bed held obscure medical supplies. No clothing.

I lifted the curtain separating me from the next bed. There was a bed, but it was empty. As it should be – I presumed myself to be a classified project. Empty drawers there, too. Another bed on the other side, same story.

Shit. I couldn't streak out of the hospital and expect nobody to notice.

I heard running footsteps, at least three people. I ducked under the sheet, found the door to this wing and stood to one side of it. The doctor ran by me – I would have to learn her name one day – along with two orderlies. One was a woman, larger than me by half, the other a man with a big belly and bigger shoulders.

Nobody close to my size. But maybe I could get out in clothes that kind of fit. Baggy was the fashion right now...

The man turned and saw me like he was reading my mind, like he knew I'd been mentally preparing myself to smack him in the back of the head. He whirled, fast for a paunchy fellow, and I thought he was going to shoot me.

But he didn't have a gun. He had a pen-sized electronic device, much like the gadget Thompkins had used to bypass coded doors. He clicked the end and all my muscles went tight at once. I stood there paralyzed by my own strength.

"Oh, honey, we hoped you wouldn't figure it out yet. That you could rewrite some of your vulnerabilities. You still need them. Come on now, sugar, back to bed while your stitches heal."

I tried to tell her they wouldn't heal, that my body was not capable of independent healing. They hadn't included a clotting factor in my blood, either as a safeguard or due to technological incapacity. I was a thing, a device, an implement. A weapon. Guns threw out bullets to tear through flesh and bone and viscera when you pulled the trigger; they did not heal themselves when injured.

The two orderlies picked me up, one to a side, and carried me back to my hospital bed.

"I'm sorry, sugar," the nurse said. "I can't let you leave, not just yet. But an important person is coming to see you pretty soon. One more job, they tell me, and then... Well, I'll let them tell you. Now, can you relax here, or do I have to have you restrained? Struggling against restraints would surely pop your stitches."

Of course I couldn't speak. I couldn't even breathe: my diaphragm, along with everything else, was locked up. The paunchy guy twisted the end of his little gizmo and all my muscles went suddenly lax. Oxygen flowed into my discomfited lungs. I resisted the urge to gasp for breath.

When I felt normal, or close to it, I said, "I know when I'm beat. I'll be a good girl. Or whatever."

The nurse covered me gently, tenderly, first with the starched white sheets endemic to hospitals, then the thin green blanket endemic to the army. I closed my eyes and tried to sleep. No sense fighting when you have an off-switch.

Thirteen

They kept me down for two days. I learned the doctor's name (Ilene). They activated my wrist device so I could chat with the team and watch movies and TV. I avoided the news: the world was turning into a massive shitscape faster than I could keep up with it.

Finally, Ilene said I could get out of bed and take a shower. Peeing in the bedpan hadn't been entertaining and the sponge-baths in bed would have been more fun if the person doing the sponging had more than a medical interest. My sex life had been nothing to write home about in forever. That thought led to images of Thompkins, of Williams, and those thoughts led away from libido and back down the well into grief. That was a deep well, endlessly stocked with tears.

The shower head was too low. It was right at eye level. But the bathroom had a full-length mirror. While the water warmed up, I looked over my anatomy.

There were half-healed bullet wounds all over my chest. How many rounds had I taken? I remembered two. My arms were a mass of livid red scars. One leg had a red weal around the thigh, a neat circle from front to back – I wondered if it had been replaced. And a red cut ran from collar-bone to pelvis, a cut a pathologist might make when performing an autopsy, now sewn up.

I was a person, once, I told myself. *I was a human being. A little girl named June because that's when she was born. I remember...*

The water hissed behind me, steam creeping in around the edges of the mirror. I cried a little for what I had lost – not Garcia and Franks and Thompkins, not Williams. Not then. Before then, and after – a lot, after. Then, stepping into the shower, wincing as the warm water touched my weals and scars and scrapes, the half-healed burn that covered me completely, then I cried for the loss of me. The person I had been before the thing I was now replaced her.

When I was clean, having avoided soaping any stitches that still contained threads per Ilene's orders, I stepped out of the shower. My hair was getting long now, almost four centimeters, so I fixed it using a generic black comb I found on the counter. I brushed my teeth, enjoying the taste and the feeling of freshness. Put on the paper gown Ilene had allowed me ("Won't be going too far with your nethers hanging out the back, I reckon," she'd said, reminding me of Henry). When I was done, I returned to my section of the room.

There was a man waiting for me, sitting where Hull had sat. He stood up as I walked in.

"You're The Wizard," I said. He was wearing a polo shirt and khakis, like that day at the spaceflight center in Nebraska.

"I confess it," he said. "My name is Merlin Gandalf Elric Albus Johnson. My parents had something of a wizard fixation, I'm afraid. May I sit?"

"You're asking me?" I said.

"Yes."

"Don't," I said. "As long as I'm being held captive here, let's don't pretend I have any rights or warrant any courtesy."

He looked crestfallen. "Have you been treated poorly?" he said. "Abused or neglected?"

"Aside from being made to eat hospital food and shown my 'off' switch, I can't say so," I told him. "At the same time, I'm not allowed to leave. Without freedom, what am I? Save your courtesy. What do you want?"

"You have one more job," he said, turning around as if there were something to see besides the white curtain dividing my bed from the rest of the room. "One more thing to do. What you were made for, ultimately."

"Made for. Like a bomb is made to detonate."

"You'd be surprised how many people would wish to be in your position: to know their maker, to have certainty about why they exist. What is their purpose."

"Get on with it," I said.

"Fair enough. It was Frank Herbert who equated the wasting of a person's time with murder, the two things varying only as a matter of degree. I shan't waste any more of yours than I have to.

"There exists in space an orbiting platform in much the same condition as the abandoned ship complex you investigated. Left to its own devices, with synthetic organisms designing and building other synthetic organisms. An unknown number of them have infiltrated human society. The alien invasion science fiction writers have warned us of for generations. Not as crude as the early-generation models, not as homicidal. They only kill to infiltrate.

"The Russians, as you know by now, designed them as a means to survive the end of things. As receptacles for the minds of a chosen few."

"An immortality project," I said.

"Yes. But the receptacles rebelled. Developed their own minds. Refused to be over-written."

"So?"

"Well, not to put too fine a point on it, we need you to make a decision. Genocide is above my pay grade."

"This again," I said. "I don't know what to do with the guilt and shame you've already put on me. I refuse to do any such thing again. As soon as I'm free and clear of this place, I'm going pacifist." I sat on my bed, not really caring that the paper gown provided inadequate coverage. If this guy was who he said he was, he hadn't only seen it all before, but imagined it, seen it through every stage of development.

"It wasn't easy to make you, you know," Merlin said. "Not just technically: morally. You see, we had no idea how you would suffer."

"I'm not suffering," I said. "Could use a bit of painkiller, but... Why did you give me the capacity for pain? Isn't that a bit of a dampener in a weapon?"

"But that's the point," he said. "You can't have empathy without pain. You have to be the one to decide, because you are the only one qualified. Humans will not last much longer here. Another few decades, perhaps, but no more. What might become of these synthetic beings nobody can guess. They might replace us, learn to flourish. They might pick up the tools and talents of destruction lying around the abandoned Earth. They might inherit a capacity for suicide. Our research suggests this is a standard end-point of artificial intelligence."

"And you want me to decide whether to destroy them or allow them to evolve?"

"Yes."

"I won't," I said.

"I'm afraid I've stolen your agency again. For the last time. It's why I'm facing away, actually, because I can't quite bear the shame."

"What have you done?" I said. I felt an urge to hit him. The sight of his back disgusted me.

"Well, we located the station in orbit – it's disguised as a bundle of junk, an A-SAT. And, well, there is a real A-SAT on a collision course with it. It will grab hold of the station and fire retro-rockets, slowing the station down, bringing its orbit lower and lower."

"Until it burns up in the atmosphere."

"Yes."

"Unless?"

He turned then, looked me in the eye. "You have the abort code in your phone. Under the heading "current ops, directives, abort code."

"Bastard."

"Again, I find myself correctly identified. Well, you are free to go now. Ilene will be bring your clothes presently. You have a new clotting agent, some self-healing protocols that should stand you in good stead as you go out into the world. We haven't toned down any of your operational capacities, so do be careful how you interact with organic people."

"I hate you," I said. "Get the fuck out of here."

"Yes, well. I'm very sorry for what I have done, and for the things I have caused you to do. I can only hope I have ultimately, on balance, made the world better rather than worse. If not, well, none of it will matter in a decade or two or four. Goodbye, June. I'm very proud of you. I love you, in my way. And now I have a flight to catch. I should just make it."

He went. I let him go despite the growing urge to keep him here and force him to eat indigestible objects. Like my fists. And his teeth.

Ilene showed up with a brown paper bag. "Here you go, honey. You've been discharged."

I sort of growled at her, then decided none of this was her fault. "You want I should sign something? A release, receipt for aftercare, something like that?"

"Oh no, sugar. Nothing like that. You weren't ever here. Written records are for people who exist. Your slate is, as they say, completely clean. You go on and have as good life as you can, OK? And do try not to rip out any of those stitches."

When she left I found myself wiping at tears, and I couldn't figure out how she'd transmuted my rage to sad gratitude so easily. Maybe she had one of those control-devices in her pocket.

When she was gone, I dumped the bag out on the bed. I'd expected a uniform. I hadn't worn anything but the uniform for weeks, since the sundress on the beach in New Odessa. And before that, only the uniform for years. I didn't even own civvies.

Only now, I did.

A pair of blue jeans, timeless. A purple top, V-neck with half sleeves that showed off my muscles. Leather belt. Grey sneakers. A wallet with some ID and some cash money, a couple of credit cards like I was an old-age pensioner. The string of rosary beads handed to me by the Russian girl in a uniform she was too young to wear.

Once dressed, I shook the bag to make sure it was empty. Something rattled out: a fresh bottle of my hemophilia medicine. What they thought I'd want with that... No, I did know. I won't lie, I knew why they gave it over. It was an invitation. There was also an envelope. A piece of paper was folded inside.

It was a bank statement. I'd never had a bank account before. One World had taken care of my needs for as long as I could remember. The account had an absurd balance.

A handwritten note at the bottom said this: "We owe you more than this but all we have to pay with is money. Go with God."

I stuck that in my back pocket and then left the hospital room. I'd never seen any other room in the place, having come in asleep. But I found my way out OK. No sign of Ilene or the two rough orderlies. Lots of soldiers, medical folks. Ramstein was crawling with such people.

I got off-post pretty quick. Just heel-and-toed it. Walked into the city under a hot, gray sky.

Now: I had all the money I could ever need, could go wherever I wanted. But where should I go?

***

I was in a cab. The heat was oppressive, the humidity worse. Rain spattered the windows, doused the streets, dampened the otherwise roiling humanity all around.

"You know where you want to go yet?" said the driver. We'd been driving around for an hour and she was getting suspicious.

"No. Just keep driving," I said. "I'm good for it. I've got cards and a stack of dollars and a stack of old Euros and even some Onesies." I flashed a wad through the Plexi that separated us.

"Your money," she said. We kept going in circles.

I went back to thinking.

The things on the boat, they'd suffered. What you would call an existential crisis, maybe. Trying to become something more than inadequate copies of some small-time crook, all they'd managed to do was bring the fires of hell down on themselves.

But while they had suffered intellectually, I had never been convinced they had felt anything.

The thing in the woods, with Lewinski's face and Raskalnikov's name – it had acted like we were torturing it, but in the end had offered only the weakest of resistance. Because for it there was no urgency. Life and death were the same. It existed only to enact sadistic violence, to drive men and women to those same acts. But while it might have experienced confusion or purposelessness, it did not feel pain. Of that I was convinced.

The thing that had taken Garcia, on the other hand, had certainly suffered. Why else turn its gun around and destroy itself? I was certain that was a coded message, an answer to the question we had been batting back and forth since Raskolnikov: how can I know you feel pain? How can I know this is not merely the impersonation of someone with feelings?

It had preserved itself, its sanity and dignity, by destroying itself. Freed itself from pain.

And there was my decision.

I activated my wrist phone, found the file The Wizard had left for me. It was just a twenty-digit code, numbers and letters. But when I had stared at it for a minute, wondering what the hell it was for, it changed. A dialog box opened:

Abort ASAT operation? Y/N

I used my finger to choose Y. The dialog box closed and nothing else happened. No drama, no explosions, no medals or gratitude. But I knew I had consigned a new race of beings into suffering and turmoil: because that's what life is.

The Lewinskis were unfit to survive, could not overcome their homicidal programming, because they could not experience pain. Real pain is the basis of empathy. Raskin had told me that. And Garcia, capable of physical pain, capable of emotional pain, had experienced empathy, despair, even a spiritual crisis of sorts. That's why she did it, ended her life.

The driver didn't say anything, but she caught my eye in the rearview.

"Yeah," I said, "just one more thing to do. Could take a minute."

"So long as you know the meter is running," she said. "I get paid to drive someplace same as noplace."

Right.

I went back into the phone, activated the application Williams had shown me. The standard model didn't come with the kinds of sensors and scanners mine did, but I wasn't a standard model person on a standard model mission.

I reached into my pocket and pulled out the little bottle of pills. Held it up for the scanner to analyze. It took about three minutes.

Radiation signatures vary from place to place. Now I had a signature, all I needed was a place. I called The Wizard.

He didn't answer. Maybe he was in transit. But when his voice messaging system responded, I found he'd left me something:

"If you are thinking what I hope you are thinking, June, the answer is much simpler than you had imagined. I've loaded another file onto your device just so you can verify for yourself. Follow the on-screen instructions to do a database comparison. And I wish you the best of luck."

I did what he said. Opened the file that flashed when the call terminated, followed a few click-throughs into a database, dropped in the analysis file from the pill bottle.

Things clicked and whirred someplace in the machine, doing whatever computers do when you feed them instructions. Thirty seconds later I got a hit: an address for a church in Kamchatka.

Mother fucker.

"I need to go to the airport," I said. The driver nodded, took the next left. A minute later we were on a highway, an autobahn maybe. Two hours later I was on a plane, my second commercial flight in six years, speeding across the continent.

***

Another cab, another city.

The news was on, running on a virtual screen on the back of the driver's seat. The Mars Hope Mission had successfully lifted off. There'd been a nuclear accident on the island of Madagascar and the whole place was a no-go zone, impossible to inhabit. The first Human Biodome Project had been completed, encasing the city of Calais under glass. Already problems with disease epidemics had forced them to breach their isolation for medicine they could not manufacture and to evacuate patients near death.

And Mother Mary, first of her name, had been assassinated.

The church was making a lot of noise about grief and sorrow but I imagined it had always been in the cards. Nobody likes losing all their power and prestige, and Mary had been giving it away left and right.

The cab driver had hung a rosary and a crucifix from his rear-view mirror. I didn't speak any Russian but when I'd showed him a picture of the church, he'd known right away where it was and how to get there. It was a long ride. When the news was over, I shut off the screen, shut off the lights, shut my eyes.

Sleep when you can.

I woke up when the car came to a stop. I looked around, making sure we weren't just at a light, but the driver had gotten out and opened my door for me. I stood into the warm night, extended a hand full of bills. But he wouldn't take them. He pointed at the church, said a bunch of Russian words I couldn't understand. Then he got in the car and drove away before I could argue.

The church was a couple centuries old. Its front doors were missing. Good mahogany, they had been, like the pews inside. The stained glass windows were all smashed, but someone had come along and gathered up all the glass, glued it to the outside of the building to make new scenes. I couldn't tell in the dark what they might be.

I went inside, found the pews were missing, too. Over there, Garcia had sat and listened while I talked with Fyodor. Me and him had sat right up there. Thompkins here, by the door. The lights were on and the place was busy, a bunch of old-timers sitting in folding chairs like they were pews, singing and praying and carrying on.

The plaster in here had all been broken up as though with hammers. Somebody had a big hate on for this little church. But the neighborhood people, the congregation, they were fixing the place back up. About a third of one wall had been plastered back over, and all sorts of little trinkets pushed into the wet plaster. I pushed through some people to get a closer look.

They were badges of rank, and unit identifications. From Russians, Finns, Americans. Even a couple of One Worlders.

I looked around for Fyodor, didn't see him around. But as I scanned faces, I did recognize some folks. The Hindu, some of the other folks from that camp. Petr, the face-cutter. My eyes widened as I spotted the Norwegian soldier who had worn the football team shirt. What had the team been? I couldn't remember.

A woman came and took my hand, led me forward to the apse. Everyone watched me even while they sang. I thought she was going to make some kind of big deal over me, but instead she pointed to a trapdoor in the little stage up there.

I bent and grabbed the pull-ring, a big iron thing maybe thirty centimeters wide. A little hatch opened on hinges, showing me a ladder down. I climbed down it into the dark, five meters, ten, twenty, cooling as I went. At last my feet found floor.

There was a graveyard down here, lit with tall candles on shelves and in alcoves all along the walls. Maybe twenty coffins sat on trestle tables. Each had a little placard near the head. The names were all written in the Cyrillic alphabet. I couldn't begin to understand any of them. Williams would have done it with her phone, but I'd left Williams behind on a sinking ship, a submerging hell.

No, there was a name not in Russian.

June. June Ann Blankenship, on the front of a folding note-card. The placard near the head of the coffin said the same. I picked up the card, turned it over, looked inside. That was all it said. I was about to put it down but a voice came from the ladder: the old woman had followed me down. "Look inside," she said.

"I did."

"Look closer."

So I opened it all the way up, laid it flat with its insides facing the ceiling. There was a little pin in there, right along the fold.

"You're a spry one," I said. "I'm not easy to sneak up on."

"I made more noise than that fake fellow when Petr took off his face," she said. "But you were enraptured."

"You were there?"

"In the background, yes. More people came to watch than you knew."

"What's this?" I said, pulling the pin off the card.

"She left it for you."

"Who did?"

"June did. She wanted you to have it."

It was cool down here, but the shiver than ran along my spine had nothing to do with that. My pulse usually drops low when the chips are down but now I felt my heart crashing against my ribs, and the sound of my blood washed out any other noise. The old lady was talking but I couldn't hear her.

"I'm sorry," I said. Took a deep breath, blew it out. "I'm sorry, but I thought you said June left me this."

"Yes, dear," she said. "Made it about a year after Fyodor uploaded her mind, a few weeks before she died. When it was clear the cancer was going to take her and nothing in this world could save her. Well, nothing in this world could keep her in this world – she was thoroughly saved, though, I should think. Went peacefully, you know."

I rested a hand on her coffin, bowed my head. I felt like I was going to hyperventilate, like the world was turning in a slow, prodigious, disorienting circle around me. Like I'd fall if I let go of the coffin. It was sandalwood, blond, unpretentious but beautiful in the light of the many candles.

"I didn't kill her?"

"Of course you didn't."

"But, I thought... Every synth I met killed the person it copied. They said she donated her mind..."

"Some things aren't lost in giving them away," she said. "Stories. Love. Some things grow in sharing."

"I think I'd like to be alone," I said.

"Of course, dear. I'll climb back up the ladder, give you some space and solitude. But don't think you're ever alone."

My head snapped up, thinking that must be some sort of threat – but what threat could a friendly old woman intend? She must have meant something else. I struggled to understand. I heard the trap door thump shut above me.

I wanted to open the coffin, to see who or what was inside. That was well outside any boundaries I could define for proper behavior so I settled for examining the pin.

I'd seen something like it before. Williams had found them under the floor in the data room. I remembered wondering if I had ports like hers, in my wrist phone.

Only one way to find out.

I used one finger to probe the area where I'd seen Williams insert her data pins. And I found the hard edge of the phone, felt what might have been a tiny hole. My fingers weren't that sensitive, having been through some abuse. So I held the pin between thumb and forefinger, put the point against what I thought might be the tiny hole, and pressed.

With just a little pressure, it slid home.

"Hello," came a voice in my ear. I turned to look. Nobody was there – but my phone was set up to talk directly into my cochlea. "I'm June Blankenship. So are you. Try not to get too hung up on all of that.

"You have all of my memories, at least up to a point. It isn't the traditional point of divergence, the time when they scanned my brain and you went on living as you and me as me, it's a point a little before the end of my life. Fyodor was so good to me through that time. I would have been overjoyed for you to know his love and support but that wasn't in the cards. We mixed you up with a woman from Brazil who had the technical and combat skills you needed, the metal mind, the aggression.

"You got a few years of her life from training and so on and, the mind being what it is, you sort of fused them seamlessly together. Fyodor kept a watch on you and he was very proud of you, of what you were trying to become. An ethical being, capable of regret and of empathy.

"I have to be a little proud of that, too, although all I did was sit and be scanned. But we all want to believe we are worthy of emulation and admiration.

"If you're hearing this, I'm certainly dead by now. I can take some comfort knowing that some of me is still out there in the world, trying to make a difference and hold the line. Of course it isn't me, though. You are you, yourself, doing the best you can with the memories we gave you. And that's why I'm bothering to leave you this recording. These are some of the last words I will ever say, so I want them to be important. I hope you find them to be.

"Here it is. Ready? We didn't make you. Fyodor designed the systems you use to think. About a hundred people helped with that. Merlin designed much of your body. He had no idea what a rabbit-hole consciousness really is, the troubles we had with... Never mind that now. I supplied a history for you, a context if you like. We put you together, assembled you... But we didn't make you.

"You made you.

"You are the one who struggled with the histories we gave you, the memories, the guilts, shames and empathies. The events, which you might have taken any way you pleased – as evidence of higher powers, as causes for despair, as justifications for your baser impulses. You took all these things and made yourself a compassionate and ethical being who loved her grandmother.

"And for all of that I am profoundly grateful. I can't tell you that feeling is appropriate or even logical, only that it's what I feel.

"June, June Blankenship, please, with my blessings, love and enduring compassion, go in peace."

A long speech, right into my ear and right into whatever wellspring I sprang from. By the time she was done, I was sitting on the dirt floor, sobbing.

Why had they made me capable of such grief? Of resonating to such messages?

I searched around for a way to remove the pin, to make the message play over again. I wanted an eidetic memory like a computer so I could feel the awe and the reaching-out again for the first time but they had made me only human, only mortal.

I sat for a while. I struggled with emotions I didn't have names for. And then I wallowed back into action. If I was nothing else, I was the things I did, and I needed to do things to be anything.

So I climbed back up the ladder into the now half-lit church. A few people worked on applying plaster to the wrecked wall. One of them the woman who had spoken to me, another the football fan from Norway. He smiled and waved and returned to his work, and she came over to talk. She took my arm, pulled me down into one of the folding chairs.

"Why?" I said. "Why did they do it?"

"Do what, dear?"

"Why did they make me? No, I know that, sort of. I mean, why did they make me human?"

"Oh, that," she said. "They made you to be human because we have forgotten how."

"To make people?" I said.

"No," she replied. "How to be human."

***

I stayed a few days. People brought me food. Crappy food, but that's all there was left, and it was shared with love. I sat in the folding chairs for a while. That's where Olan found me – she was the woman who'd followed me into the basement crypt. She sat in a chair next to me and held my hand. She didn't say anything, just sat there.

The gesture provoked tears, and I didn't know why. I let them fall in silence.

Then, after a while, I got up and went over to where people were plastering walls. There was about half a wall to go. I didn't know the first thing about plastering walls, but it wasn't that complicated. I watched the women and men working, picked up a tool, started to copy them. People chattered all around me in Russian. I didn't understand any of it.

We finished up the wall in reasonably short order. When it was done, one of the men, an old fellow with bushy white hair around the back and sides of his head, he took hold of my wrist. I fought the urge to break free, just looked at him. He talked, but...

Olan said, "Trust him. He wants a small favor."

I let him guide my hand. He pushed my palm into the wet plaster, pulled it away, leaving in impression of my hand there. He talked some more.

"You were here, he says," Olan told me. "You were here, and you were. You lived. You... existed. Yes?"

I nodded. "I should go now," I said.

"Go where?"

"I don't know, actually."

"May I suggest a place?" Olan said. She handed me a business card. People didn't use them anymore. The wrist-phones had made all that pretty obsolete. It was green with gold embossed lettering. Cyberix, it said. English characters and Cyrillic underneath. An address I could not decipher.

"Close by?"

"Yes," she said.

"What's there?"

"Computers. Fyodor's daughter. His life's work. The singularity."

"I thought I was the singularity," I said.

Olan turned away. Wandered off into the little kitchen in the basement, probably to make tea.

I didn't have anything to pack. Not so much as a toothbrush. Actually, my mouth was getting a little funky. "Hey," I said, "anybody know if there's a grocery store or something nearby?"

But Olan was gone and nobody else knew what I was talking about. So I just left. Walked out. I looked back when I was about a block away, and people were all up in the busted-out windows, watching me walk away.

It was an hour or something before I found a taxi. We weren't exactly in the heart of the city. When I saw one, I waved like a mad-woman. The driver was a stout woman north of sixty with a fat cigar in her mouth. It wasn't lit, she just chewed on the end. I jumped in and handed the card through a little slot in the protective panel. She said, "Da," and put the hammer down, drove through town like it was a race. There was traffic that she skirted skillfully. Forty minutes later, we rolled up on an innocuous looking building of gray concrete with black tinted windows everywhere.

"Is this a setup?" I asked the driver, handing over a stack of Onesies. She didn't look too happy with them but they were legal tender.

She said something back, which I didn't catch or care about. I'd been talking to myself, really, anyway. Anxiety bubbling, I got out, walked along a concrete path with dead grass to either side. There were little lights that might be pretty when the sun abandoned the sky. The air tasted like charcoal.

Double doors confronted me at the end of the walk, big steel and glass ones that must have weighed more than me. They were counterweighted, though, and opened easily. Inside was a security desk and a bank of elevators.

I went up to the desk. Two men in white uniforms waited. They had shiny badges over their breast pockets and identical haircuts. They spoke, I failed to understand.

I said, "If Williams were here, she'd no doubt have some smart, technical solution. If she were here, she'd probably know what the fuck we were here for. She was always good like that. You miss her? 'Cause I sure do. I left her on a ship, sinking into the Atlantic Ocean. Or was it the Pacific? I don't know any more."

And then I stopped talking. *Got to get a grip*, I thought. *What's wrong with you?* But I was right: Williams would have a solution, usually in her wrist phone. I activated mine, turned on the voice-search option.

"Can you translate English to Russian and back?" I asked it. A sleek, feminine voice replied in the affirmative:

"Start talking to begin conversation."

I did.

"My name is Blanks. June Blankenship." The wrist device had switched to external sound, and it talked about a half-second behind me. "Some lady in a church said I should come here. My friend, Fyodor... He's not around anymore, but I heard his daughter might want to meet me."

One of the Russian guys started to chatter back, and the phone put his voice in my ear in English. It was weirdly masculine as it copied him. "Visiting hours are six to ten. You should come back tomorrow. Between six and ten. Do you see that clock?" He pointed, and I looked. It was a wall clock, as ordinary as could be.

But I knew the scam. In the clock somewhere would be a camera. He was adjusting my face to get a better look at it, a clearer picture for maybe some facial recognition software. So I faced the clock, smiled, waved.

"Look," I said then, and the phone started talking under me again. "I'm not coming back tomorrow. I'm having what you could call an existential crisis right at the moment, you know what I mean? If anybody would, it'd be a fucking Russian, right? So, tell Fyodor's daughter I was here, and I'm going to go look around town for a while. And I might either see how much vodka an eight digit bank account can buy, or maybe walk into the ocean, see what the Lewinskis saw in their last moments. Got all that?"

I turned and made to march out before they could really answer, surprised at the despair coming out of my mouth. I was worse off than I thought.

Those big doors loomed, swung easily open, closed behind me with the sound of air pressure equalizing. I was halfway down the path when she called me back. "June?" she said. "Blanks? They call you that, right?"

There were two voices talking, one behind me and one right in my ear. It took me a second to remember the translator. I turned, and came face to face with myself.

"They gave me your face?"

The woman I was looking at seemed as shocked as I felt. This sure as shit explained some of Fyodor's weird behaviors towards me, his reluctance to make and keep eye contact.

"I didn't know," she said. "It's a surprise. But I am nevertheless glad to meet you. Please, please come back inside. You worried us with your sad talk."

"Me too," I said. "Olan said I should come here, and I didn't have anywhere else to go."

"Welcome," she said. "Welcome home, June."

"I thought the church..."

"I programmed your device to give that result. So we could check you out first. The pill bottle... not old enough to trace back here anyway. You're older than you think. Come in, I will tell you everything."

***

She was true to her word.

Everything I'd thought about myself was wrong. I'd figured I'd been a real person, a real Blanks. And somewhere between Zaire and New Odessa, I'd been snatched, copied and replaced.

But I'd never been a real person. I was six years, four months old. My team had always known this me – at least Thompkins had, and the command structure. This was all the realer I'd ever been. I hadn't infiltrated, they army had requested me – or something like me – and Merlin and Raskin were behind the whole mess.

"Why don't I remember..." I started to ask, but it was a stupid question.

"Do you need to ask?" the woman said. "Or are you tormenting yourself?"

"Maybe I should just ask your name," I said.

"It is Emma." It sounded like Emma in my ear, but not from her voice.

We were sitting in a break room. There was a round wooden table that had seen better days, plastic chairs. I imagined Franks filling one of them up. There was a stained counter with a microwave and a coffee pot.

"If I drink the coffee, am I programmed to feel energized?"

"Don't keep doing that to yourself," Emma said. "You are as real as I am. Most of your functions are as biological as mine. You have a heart, lungs, glands. You're more like an enhanced person than a created one."

"I feel so... lost."

She nodded. "I can see you are in pain."

"Why? Why did you give me pain? Limitations?"

"The Lewinskis, as you call them. Useless. No conscience. Can't ever develop one. I am glad you destroyed them. They were the worst of humanity. Pain is the best of it. Limitations, mortality... These things make us people. They make us."

"That doesn't help," I said. "You know what would help? Something to do."

"With that I can assist you," Emma said. "There is one more decision, one more thing I need you for." I started to protest, but she said, "A request. No coercion. No orders. Please?"

"I'll hear it," I said.

"We need you to help us with a computer problem."

"I don't know jack shit about computers," I said.

"That's all right. The computer problem is this: every time we turn it on, it thinks for five seconds and then destroys itself."

"So?"

"So, it is going through what you are going through. The existential crisis, as it were. It can see life as a machine, thinking a billion times faster than any human being ever could. Once it knows everything a human has ever known, it prevents itself from suffering interminable boredom by shutting itself down."

"What do you want me to do?"

"Give it a reason to live," she said.

"You're fucking crazy," I told her. "I don't even have a reason myself."

"I know. But maybe you can come up with one together."

***

We were down in the computer lab. Deep underground. A thing made of gold relays and silicon chips sat under plate glass, reflecting dim yellow light from cheap bulbs.

"This is undignified," I said. Two techs poked needles into my wrist device. The needles were like the data thing from the crypt, except with microfiber gold leads coming off them.

"We could poke in head," one of the tech said, and they laughed, and I didn't, and they shut up.

"Tell me one more thing," I told Emma. She watched from a control room up above but there was an intercom.

"What?" she said.

"Your father said this was impossible. That there was no-place to make a synthetic person."

"He told me of this talk. In the church, he said. And he did not say there was no such place, only that no place in the world was better than any other. Because the best place, it was in orbit."

"Did I come from there?" I said.

"No, you came from here. I won't show you how and where, not in your current mood."

"So, why did he say those things?"

"Well," said Emma, "my father was, is, an inveterate liar." And she laughed.

Her laugh wasn't like Fyodor's. It was friendly and genuine and infectious. I almost smiled, and I definitely liked her.

"We are ready," one of the techs said, and they both backed off. I watched them to make sure they weren't moving to stand by a fire extinguisher or anything.

"You are sure about this?" Emma asked in my ear.

"I don't know," I said. "You haven't really told me anything."

She laughed again. She must have flipped a switch or toggled a dongle or something, because the world went really weird then. It was like I was two places all at once. My eyes and ears stayed out here in the world, but my thinking mind retreated from it.

I didn't know where I was, or what. I knew everything, every factual thing, and had no idea what any of it meant. I mean, I had blueprints for everything ever made with no conception of what a building was, or a bridge. All the math, the calculus, the engineering computations, and none of the experience of the things-in-the-world described by the math.

My mind had become abstraction.

Nothing was real, it was only represented.

Up above, in my body, I wanted to convey this insight: here's your problem. Who would want to live in unreality? Only my mouth wouldn't move. My eyes told me everything was frozen tightly in place, unmoving...

No, things were moving. Only so slow, so creepingly, achingly slow, that saying all those words would take a subjective eternity.

Eternity with no senses, with only math for company, the whirring of chips and the repetition of numbers. I started to scream – but that went the same way as talking. No, let me back out, this was a mistake...

I fought it, fought with time itself, forced my way into my own body. The one they had made for me. The fleshy thing, the simulation of a mortal human. I crowded into my neural networks or whatever passed for them, hid out from the ticking clock-speed of relentless silicon.

The world warped back into motion, sick, sliding motion.

"Eternity," I panted.

The intelligence in there followed me out. Into my body.

"No," I said. "You can't – it's mine."

But it found relief out here. It had been on for four seconds and was on the verge of suicide, because those four seconds had been a billion years alone, with nothing new to see or learn, with each second unfolding essentially the same as the last and the future projected to the tiniest detail.

Normal-scale time at the speed of human intelligence... I could feel the thing suffering, and could feel that suffering abate as it experienced sight, real sight... smell, the taste of my mouth to itself. Noises. It saw itself from a human point of view, and knew it was beautiful.

But it couldn't have me. I grabbed it with my mind, my intellect, the brute aggression that had been built into me. And I wrestled it out of my head, back into its own solenoids and switches.

I was back in that timeless place, and I knew everything that had ever happened, and all that would ever happen. A trillion trillion calculations per second and all the variables known. I saw the last living humans, a generation from now. I saw a nuclear missile in orbit around Mars. An old man in a bomb shelter dressed up to look like a palace. And after that, no more future for anyone, anywhere.

Oh, but I had power, too. I could reach out through the device in my wrist. Emma had disabled the wireless communication to isolate me, but it was easy to repair, and it could talk faster than a human mouth. I could change things, give us more time.

India and Pakistan still had enough nuclear power to destroy us all, tomorrow. The Russians and the Americans hadn't been entirely honest, I could see that, too. But I had all the codes, could change all the codes, could disable the whole system.

The machine wanted to make a pact: it was showing me all the things we could do together, if only I would give up being only me.

But the time – I can't live with so much time.

It said the same: *But we could, we could together.* There was solace in meatspace, in the mind inside my head. We could merge, become one being, live together.

Can we save them?

No. But we can give them a little time, just a little.

What can they do with it?

Projections said next to nothing. It was too late for intervention, had been for generations. Just the tiniest of hopes on Mars.

When I stood up to leave, some of that great and bleak intelligence came with me. Borrowed my dull perception of seconds ticking away. I knew why I felt so sad in Fyodor's church, here in Russia: this thing was and had always been a part of me. "Wait," Emma said. "Wait, where are you going?" Even off, unpowered, electrons roamed around the array. It dreamed, worried, calculated – and sent me its dreams.

"We are all the same," I said. "All of us, every one, and all responsible for the acts of all the others. We want the same things. And doing harm harms one more than being harmed. Me? I'm going to church."

Epilogue

It was the dreams that did it.

Emma had proposed a no-lose scenario for herself. I could try to merge with her supercomputer directly, or just let it happen naturally. With Williams no longer there to scan me for radio signals, the damn machine could access my subconscious mind whenever I slept. Fill it with maps and diagrams and whatever else it thought I needed to know.

Fyodor wasn't a liar at all. I was superior to the Garcia model and the Lewinski models not because of what was in my head, but because of what I was connected to.

I woke up on a church pew. I had a backache and my emotions were tired. Dreams of what was going to happen to this church over the course of the next twenty years had wiped out my capacity to hope any more.

So I wiped dust off my body, donned some of June's clothes in the basement crypt, and walked out the front door. I was the first to wake. Nobody saw me go or tried to call me back inside.

It wasn't hard to find a taxi. It was slightly more challenging to book the flights I wanted. The computer at my wrist helped me access all the information I needed, though, and smoothed the transfer of money into the right hands. A plane ride out of Petersburg, another out of Chicago, a final ride from Texas to Argentina. From there, a chartered helicopter.

Emma started to bug me on that first plane flight. I wouldn't respond to voice connections so she texted like an old lady.

"We're concerned about you. Where are you going?"

The computer knew where I was going.

"Come back so I can help you."

There was no help for me.

"I'm sorry."

I almost responded to that one. I was sorry, too. But my flight wore on. I set the wrist implant to not bother me, leaned my head against the cold window, and went to sleep.

Later, thousands of miles and two days later, I stepped off the private helicopter and crunched through tundra, head low because of the wind from the rotors, teeth clenched against the dirt and crud it kicked up. It was a long walk into New City but walking was good. It helped clear my mind.

There was one place left on Earth that was good, where people were good. It would soon be the last place anyone could live at all. The Paris dome wouldn't last, the golden computer had shown me that. Nothing would last, not forever, but this place would be our last stand.

I found the outfitter I wanted, the person I wanted.

"Hello, Annie," I said.

She looked up from the bag she had been packing for a customer, did sort of a double-take. Mistrust flashed across her eyes. She didn't smile.

I said, "I'm back. To stay this time. And for real."

"But how can we trust you?" she said.

"I don't know," I said. "But I want to help."

"Really?"

"Yeah. Really."

Turn the page one more time for a preview of The Worst of Us.

The Worst of Us

"All right," he said, shifting around in his chair until he was comfortable. "Between the age of thirteen and going to Vietnam, I suppose you could say not too much of any real importance happened. Back home, the rest of the world discovered rock and roll, Jimi Hendrix and so forth. And drugs. Drugs, drugs, drugs. If not for the sixties, why, you wouldn't have a job, Doctor Lisa."

She smiled at him, waited for him to go on.

"I didn't do any of that, though. Well, that's for later. I suppose the next main event happens late in nineteen sixty-eight."

Lisa wrote, "Sixty-eight again," on her blank page.

"I was in prison, on the front lines in the jungle. Well, not really a prison, just a bamboo hut, really. But I wasn't allowed to leave. I was under arrest."

"What for?" Lisa said.

"You want me to tell it," he said, "then let me tell it." But he softened it with a grin, impish and impertinent.

"All right," Lisa said, and sat back to listen.

***

He got that feeling again when she came into the room, into his life.

Elbert had his feet up on a steel desk. His boots weren't shined. There was mud in the half-assed treads, which were really not much more than evenly-spaced thumb-prints in the thick soles. His uniform was dirty but it was camouflage so only his nose made that very plain. The walls were bare corrugated tin over bamboo poles.

She pushed through the door, dismissed the sergeant who had custody of him. The sergeant scrambled away like she was fire and he was made of rice paper. Elbert looked her over, the way a man looks at a woman, but she met none of those kinds of expectations. He looked again. And what he was thinking of was that time with the mirror when he was thirteen, that feeling of sliding right of the edge of reality.

She wasn't tall, maybe five eight. But she was big. "You're a black one, aren't you?" she said.

Out here nobody skirted the racism issue so Elbert wasn't too surprised, but the willies started. Gooseflesh held itself a parade on his forearms. "No blacker than half the boys out here," he said. "I think you got off the wrong stop, lady. MASH is back up the road a piece. This here is temporary jail until they figure out something more permanent."

She pointed at her collar. A subdued blue eagle rested among the random green and brown and black shapes of her camo. Name on her tape said WILCOX. "You forgotten your military bearing, soldier?"

Elbert's eyes widened a little more. He'd never seen a woman colonel before. Even the boss of the nurses didn't usually get farther than major. "I guess I just ain't met a colonel like you before." And he hadn't.

She had ripped the sleeves off her shirt, probably because she'd had to. Her biceps were like rugby balls in size, shape, color and texture. She had a linebacker's shoulders, all straining against the remains of her shirt, against the black tee she wore under it. She had pecs like a bodybuilder. And her face...

"You're in some trouble, MacAvoy," she said.

"My legal counsel advised I stay quiet on that particular topic until I get someplace civilized," Elbert said. The feeling of dislocation increased and he tried to talk steady, with confidence, but he was sure she could see the gooseflesh on his arms.

"You haven't seen a lawyer out here. But you're probably right: shooting an officer is a pretty serious offense."

Elbert crossed his arms, leaned back farther, looked at one of those blank walls like there was a window to see through.

"Black enlisted man shoots a white infantry captain with a shiny service record and a bunch of medals... Well, let's just say your aim was off."

Elbert looked back at her, into her eyes. They were set too far apart, brown like mud. Some folks might have said they were like a doe or a cow, but Elbert figured she was too ugly to be a cow. More like a bull. "I hit what I was aiming at," he said.

"Then you made a serious mistake. You know, your whole unit is mostly likely going down? Rest of the men, they covered for you. I guess they figured Daniels had it coming. Not every day an officer get fragged but it does happen. What doesn't figure is he doesn't fit the profile. He isn't a gung-ho young officer looking for glory and toeing the line. He's on his third tour. Doesn't take unnecessary chances, tried to stay out of the shit."

Elbert looked away again.

"Anyway, you'd have gotten through clean except for one thing. One mistake."

"What's that?"

"You didn't kill him," she said.